ONE HUNDRED

AN ASPEN COVE ROMANCE

KELLY COLLINS

BOOK NOOK PRESS

To Jim, Nik, Alec, and Gabby. You are my reasons for everything.

CHAPTER ONE

There were three things Sage Nichols knew with absolute certainty:

Death couldn't be escaped.

Mr. Right Now was never Mr. Right.

Hell wasn't fire and brimstone; it was a cold April day in Denver.

In the dark, dank basement of her sister's house, she held up two sets of scrubs and looked at her dog, Otis, who was sprawled across the bed. This was the time of night his poor body gave out. Missing a hind leg took a lot out of the golden retriever.

He lifted his head, and his amber eyes looked between the two uniforms. He touched the blue one with his wet snout.

"Blue it is."

She ruffled the fur around his neck, and Otis rolled to his back while she gave him his final belly rub of the night. He pulled back his lips to show his teeth in what she could only describe as a smile.

If she didn't hurry, she'd be late to work. She yanked at her unruly curls and forced them into hair tie submission. Dressed, she took the stairs two at a time up to the main level. The exertion got her blood pumping so she'd be ready to take on the triple-shot latte her sister Lydia would pass off at the front door. After two years of working the night shift, Sage should be used to the schedule, but she needed that surge of adrenaline that came from three hundred milligrams of caffeine.

Keys jingled in the front door lock, and she greeted her sister with a, "Hey, Doc. How was your day?"

Lydia handed over the coffee. "Too long. One gunshot wound. A car accident. And can you believe a little boy broke his arm and leg playing Superman? He tied a tablecloth around his neck like it was a cape and jumped off the roof." Lydia shook her head and wrapped her Sage in a bear hug and squeezed tightly. "Have a good night. Don't kill anyone."

"That's always the goal." She laughed at their conversation. Anyone unaware that Lydia was an ER doctor at Denver General and she was a nurse in the geriatric ward of the same hospital might find the comment shocking. Sadly, despite the gang fights, shootings, and average number of car accidents for the city, she saw more death than her sister.

The door closed behind her, and she walked into the thick layer of fog, normal for the spring when winter battled for its final breath. It was as if the cold had wrapped its fingers around the city and refused to let go.

Hopping into her RAV4, she started the engine and pulled out of the driveway to cut through the arctic chill one mile at a time. Usually, the trip to work took twenty minutes, but with poor visibility, she'd be lucky to make it in thirty.

She sipped her latte, grateful that she'd have enough time to wake up before she had to make her rounds and fill out patient charts.

On the seat beside her was a stack of pink paper and envelopes for her favorite patient, Bea Bennett, the third such delivery in as many weeks. It was a good trade. She supplied paper, and Bea brought sunshine into Sage's otherwise gloomy life. Hospitalized for pericarditis, Bea spent her days writing letters that seemed to disappear as quickly as she received the supplies.

Fluorescent lighting blinded her as she pulled into the parking spot reserved for night-shift employees. There was no name on a placard for her. That benefit was reserved for important people like Lydia's boyfriend, Dr. Adam McKay, the hottie who ran the ER.

She grabbed her things and headed inside.

"How's your day going?" she asked her colleague Tina as she arrived on the ninth-floor ward. After tucking her purse into the desk drawer and setting the stationery down for later delivery, she took the clipboard, so Tina could leave.

Tina tucked the hair that had fallen from her ponytail behind her ears. "It's been a busy day."

That wasn't the answer Sage wanted, but it was typical because talking about patients would keep Tina there a few more minutes, and she gave no one extra time.

The halls of the ward were quiet except for the beeping of heart monitors and the whir of oxygen tanks. All seemed in order.

Five minutes later, Sage started her rounds, checking vitals and stats as she moved down the hallway of the nearly full ward. She pulled a chart from a once-empty room to find it was now occupied with a new patient. "Clive Russell." Saying the name out loud helped reinforce the fact that these were real, living, breathing people, not just medical notes and numbers on a page.

She skimmed through his records and understood that Clive's life clock wouldn't tick much longer. He had stage four pancreatic cancer. A shiver raced down her spine. Of all the cancers she'd seen eat up her patients, pancreatic cancer seemed to be the one with the sharpest teeth and biggest appetite. It weighed on her that she couldn't save these people. She cared for them and did her best to bring them joy in their final days, but it wasn't enough.

She pasted on a brilliant smile and walked into his room.

Monitors beeped, and the air was filled with a scent that seemed to be synonymous with the elderly. The closest thing she could come up with was Bengay mixed with contraband candy.

At ten o'clock at night, her patients were often fast asleep, but not this one. He sat up in bed with his thick gray mane shooting in every direction; a roadmap of lines etched deep into his smiling face. At eighty years old, he still had all his teeth, which surprised her. His hand gripped the remote control. The glow of the television lit up his jaundiced skin.

"Hello, Mr. Russell," she said in a quick, caffeine-induced rush.

"I told them not to send in my date until after the news." His eyes shifted between her and the television.

While he watched his show, she moved through her checklist, which started with vitals and ended with fluids.

She wrapped his arm with the blood pressure cuff and pumped the inflation bulb. The bladder filled and released as she counted the ebb and flow to his arteries. "I couldn't wait to see you," she said as she swiped the thermometer across his forehead and recorded his numbers. "They told me there was a handsome new man in town, but they didn't do you justice." She checked his IV fluid levels and the output from the bag collecting his urine.

The old man grinned. "Call me, Clive. I mean, since we're on our first date and all." His blue eyes shone behind the veil of ill health.

"You're a charmer, just the way I like my men—with a bit of mischief and a lot of sweetness." The fact that Clive Russell, a man fifty years her senior, was as close to being her boyfriend as any anybody with an X and Y chromosome spoke to the sad state of her love life.

"A beauty like you must have a boyfriend." He adjusted his pillow and flopped back.

"Oh, I do. His name is Otis, and he has a thing for kibble and Milk-Bones."

Clive laughed, then winced.

She filled his water and pulled a spare blanket from the cupboard in case he got chilled during the night. "Well, Clive, everything looks great." *Great* being a relative term, its scale ran the gamut from "great for almost dead" to "great, you'll make it out of here alive." Clive ranked closer to the former. Even though the pallor of impending death dulled his skin, she was buoyed because Clive clutched on to every moment of life he had left. Or at least he gripped the remote control as if it contained magic elixir, and to Clive, it might because he wasn't watching the news like he said. No, Clive was watching *Game of Thrones*, which included a weekly naked dose of a blonde beauty named Khaleesi.

"Let me know when you get to the weather report." Sage patted the old man's hand.

She left him to his "news" with a promise to check in on him later, then continued her patient rounds. Mr. Dumont needed pain meds. Mrs. Young, who had celebrated her ninety-first birthday yesterday, needed a new IV bag. Nora Croxley needed a hug. Mr. Nolan should be slapped upside the head for flashing his old man parts for the second time this week.

In her second-favorite patient's room, she found David Lark sneaking a Snickers bar. "No junk food for you." She confiscated the candy and reminded him that a man with diabetes shouldn't feed his disease.

"Come on! I gave up women. I gave up alcohol. I gave up swearing. I'm dying." He watched her tuck the candy bar into her pocket.

"Not on my shift." There was no dying allowed on Sage's shift. That was one of her silly rules. One she could never enforce because she understood dying was a part of life. The minute a human was born, they started to die, but somewhere deep inside, she believed if she cared enough, worked hard enough, and brought enough joy to those around her, it would keep them tethered to this world.

As she passed the nurses' station, she picked up the packet of pink stationery from the desk. She shouldn't have favorites, but she did, and Bea was hers. Just walking into the older woman's room lifted Sage's spirits. Despite Bea's failing health, she was full of life. It didn't hurt that she also reminded Sage of Grandma Nichols —"Grandma Dotty"—with her head of white hair and a voice sweeter than honey.

Her mind skated around distant memories of her grandma, who had stepped up to love and care for her and Lydia when their parents died. Had they really been gone for fifteen years? Grandma Dotty for two? She couldn't believe how quickly time evaporated.

Sage stopped at the lounge to get two cups of coffee—sweet and creamy for Bea, black and bitter for herself. She tucked the writing paper under her arm and hurried toward Bea's room, ready for a hug and another story.

Bea entertained her with tales about her hometown of Aspen Cove. A town straight out of a television series. A place where everyone had enough, and no one went without. All residents, though not related, were considered kin. Sage knew the stories were told from the perspective of a woman looking back on her life, where the memory was sweeter than the reality, but Bea said it in a way that made it sound possible.

Coffee in hand, she turned her back on the closed door, pressed the handle down with her elbow, and shoved her tail end into the room. It was alarmingly silent and almost black, except for the outline of an empty bed.

Bea was gone.

The pink stationery fell from her arm and fluttered to the floor, spreading out like a carpet to soak up the coffee that fell next.

Sage stumbled back to the wall and slid down to the cold industrial floor—the lifeless white tile that filled the hallways of so many institutions. As the pink stationery sopped up the spilled coffee, she came to terms with the reality that Bea had passed.

There was no way she'd been released. Just yesterday, she'd had a cardiac MRI, and no changes were noted in her condition. Nothing was better, but nothing was worse. Pericarditis didn't cure itself overnight. No, her Bea had left, and with her went one of the final sparks of light that shone in Sage's eyes.

Pulling herself into a tight little ball, Sage buried her face against her knees. She released a wail that sounded foreign but vibrated deep within her soul. She needed to get on her feet and resume her shift, but her arms wouldn't move from the hug she wrapped around herself. Her eyes remained shut, trying to stanch the impending flood of tears. Her heart beat with a sluggish rhythm that negated the effects of her latte.

Why did Bea's life mean so much more than the others? Why did her death create a cavernous hole inside? It was one more loss in a life full of them. One more soul she'd tried to hold on to without success. Another person who abandoned her before she could say goodbye.

CHAPTER TWO

The heavy door opened, and Sage stopped crying. A sliver of light cut through the shadows, but not the darkness that invaded her soul. She looked up to see the outline of a man, but the blinding light behind him made it impossible to see his face.

"Sage?" She recognized the baritone voice as her supervisor, Mr. Michael Cross. He slipped into the quiet room and loomed over her. "I need to see you in my office." He didn't wait for a reply. The door opened, the light seeped back in for a brief second, and he walked out, leaving her cloaked in blackness once more.

Hands fisted, she wiped at her tearstained cheeks and struggled to stand on legs too numb to feel. She pulled herself from the floor and straightened her uniform. Blood rushed from her head to her cold feet, and the room spun, forcing her to lean against the gray walls for support.

After a quick splash of water on her face at the nearby sink, she returned to the nurses' station to find someone she didn't recognize looking through the charts.

"Who are you filling in for?" Sage asked. With two nurses on the night shift, it was a reasonable question when the one in front of her wasn't a regular.

The woman whose nametag read "Terri" said, "You. I came up from pediatrics. We were overstaffed."

Sage's stomach twisted and sank. "Oh . . . okay." Mr. Cross called for a replacement, so this couldn't be good. "I should go because he's expecting me." It was time to face her fears.

When a boss summoned, there wasn't a choice between staying or going, so she went.

She wound down the corridor and approached Mr. Cross's door. Standing there, she let the apprehension overwhelm her. She'd never abandoned her post before, but since he had to come and find her, it meant he noticed her absence.

She glanced at her watch and groaned. Thirty minutes of her shift passed while she sat on the floor, mourning the woman she'd come to love like family.

It was bad enough she was filled with sorrow, but now she had to deal with the regret of her poor choices.

It took her two more minutes to build up the courage to knock. Her knuckles thunked on the solid wood door.

A muted voice told her to enter.

Her scrubs felt tight, and the stethoscope around her neck choked her like a noose. After a deep breath, she turned the handle and walked in the door.

The last time she was in this office was after her grandmother passed. Surely, having two meltdowns in as many years wasn't that bad—two that were public knowledge. Internally, she suffered each time a patient left, but she'd always done her job—until tonight.

No matter how much Sage tried to convince herself she was allowed to mourn, emotions weren't revered in her field. Grief got in the way of good decision-making.

Mr. Cross didn't stand. He settled back in his big leather throne. "Have a seat." He pointed to the chair in front of his desk, its sleek design more about looks than comfort. When she sat, the fabric's rough texture poked through the thin cotton of her scrubs while the wooden arms offered no sense of softness or warmth.

"Mr. Cross," she began. "I'm so sorry."

He leaned forward and placed his elbows on the dark wood surface of his desk; his steepled fingers pressed to his lips. After what felt like a lifetime, he broke the silence. "I'm sorry about Bea. I know how much you cared for her."

A lump stuck in her throat, forcing her to swallow hard. Tears pooled in her eyes, but she refused to allow them to drop. She looked at the ceiling, hoping they'd go back to where they came from, but her attempt was futile, and she felt one escape and run down her cheek.

Mr. Cross slid a box of tissues across his desk.

She fought the urge to break down. Instead, she pulled a few tissues from the box and patted her eyes dry. "When did she pass?"

He picked up a clipboard and scanned it for the information. "She was pronounced dead just after noon." His voice had a sincere, empathetic quality to it, surprising to Sage because Mr. Cross was always factual, not emotional. "We need to talk about your future here." His monotone snapped back into place.

"I understand how this must look, but I'm only affected because I care." Most people would believe a sensitive person makes the best nurse, but that might not be the case. It is too hard to remain neutral when the heart is involved. Too hard to jab that needle into flesh when it hurts. Too hard to be honest when the truth is so brutal.

"Why did you transfer to this ward?" He pulled a manila folder from his drawer. The tab across the top read "Sage Nichols" in bold black letters. He flipped it open. "You used to work in labor and delivery, where life outnumbers death. What happened?"

Her eyes drifted to her employee file. "I worked there for four years before I transferred to this ward a little over two years ago."

"Why the transfer? Most people don't go from birth to death in their career choices." Mr. Cross scribbled notes on a blank page.

Her heart rate thumped in her chest like the footfalls of a doctor racing to the ER.

Would this be her first negative report? When her grandmother died, no one questioned her tears because Dotty Nichols was a relative.

"I transferred so I could care for my grandmother, who was in this ward. It gave me more time to spend with her." It was a hard sell to Mr. Cross's predecessor. Mrs. Stankowski had denied her initial request, saying it wasn't recommended, but eventually, she gave in to Sage's endless pleading. She had worn her down with numerous calls and visits and notes.

Disapproval etched in the lines on his forehead. "And you stayed because?"

She fidgeted in the chair. "I wanted to make a difference in the last minutes of a person's life."

He lifted the edge of her file and let it fall closed. His dour expression remained stiff as his hand rubbed across his stubbly jaw. Thin lips drew thinner with his frown. "I don't think you're a good fit for my ward." If disappointment had a soundtrack, it would be Mr. Cross's sinking tone—every word an octave lower until only a vibration remained.

The floor felt like it opened up and sucked Sage into a dark pit below. "You don't want people who care on your ward?" She gripped the arms of the chair so hard, she was certain she'd dent the wood.

Mr. Cross twisted his wedding ring in circles and stared at his wife's picture as if to seek her counsel. "Caring is not the problem. You're a good nurse, but not everyone is wired for death. In this ward, it happens with regularity. You have to be able to turn off your emotions like a switch." He moved his index finger up and down, mimicking the motion. "I've talked to some of your coworkers, and they say every patient's death affects you similarly. You can't save them, Sage."

A muscle twitched at the corner of her eye. "Obviously, because Bea died." An unintended edge tinged her voice. In her mind, she listed several dozen patients whose passings had pulled at her heartstrings, and her shoulders drooped. This situation didn't look good.

Mr. Cross opened his drawer and pulled out a familiar piece of pink stationery. "I had the privilege of talking to Bea yesterday morning. I can see why you liked her."

"She was an amazing woman." She bowed her head for a second and pictured Bea Bennett's white hair and wise brown eyes.

"Do you know what the last thing she said was before I left her room?" He turned the pink envelope in his hands.

Sage shook her head. She reluctantly lifted her eyes and let go of her vision of a smiling Bea. "I don't have a clue."

He stood and turned his back to her, looking out the window into the night where the fog moved past, slow and thick. "She told me to fire you."

"What?" His statement was like a dagger to her gut. Sage felt a strong connection to Bea and couldn't believe the woman would suggest such a thing. "She did not." Her voice filled with indignant denial before she grabbed more Kleenex to absorb the new torrent of tears.

"She did. In fact, she begged me to let you go." He turned around and leaned on the desk, dropping the pink envelope to the wooden surface. "Not because you're a bad nurse. She thought you were skilled and wonderful."

"I'm confused."

"She told me this job would kill you. That your heart was big but couldn't hold all the sorrow and pain that came with a job that ended in death."

"That's not true. I love my job." The lie tasted bitter on her tongue. She didn't love her job. She loved the people. Maybe she loved them too much because every death took something from her. Little pieces of herself that she gave only to her patients died when they did. "Are you firing me?"

Mr. Cross shook his head. "On what grounds? Caring too much? It's not a crime, and it's not against your contract." He looked down at the pink envelope where "Sage" was written in perfect penmanship. "However, I will honor a part of Bea's last request." He slid the letter across the desktop. "She asked that I give this to you after her passing. You can't hope to save everyone. All you can do is pray that, at the end of the day, you make a difference. You obviously made a difference in her life."

She pulled the envelope to her chest. "Still feels like you're letting me go."

He pursed his lips and shifted them back and forth. "You abandoned your job today. You were missing in action. You can't do that. Every minute is a minute where anything can happen." He sank back into the soft leather chair that folded around him in a hug that Sage envied. "That's not who you are as a professional and not who I need as a caregiver. Rather than mete out disciplinary action, I'm giving you a professional courtesy and request that you transfer from my department. You're on unpaid administrative leave until another position opens."

The wind left her lungs. He may have given her a break, but it still left her without a job and a paycheck. She wanted to stomp her feet and cry and argue and beg. Instead, she nodded and whispered, "Thank you." Logic told her he was right to let her go, but it stung to know she'd failed the one group of people she wanted to help the most—her patients.

"You have vacation days, so use them. Search your soul for the truth. Is this where you want to be in ten, twenty, thirty years?"

She rose from the chair and turned to leave.

"Bea said your life was wasted on the dying. That a girl like you should focus on living. I don't disagree."

She left Mr. Cross's office feeling worse than she had when she arrived. She approached the empty nurses' station, empty because Terri was doing the job Sage had failed to complete.

Once she gathered her belongings, but before heading home, she peeked in on Clive, hoping to say goodbye, but his light was out. Except for the beep of monitors, his room was silent. He would be another regret.

She looked around the ward for the last time before she walked into the elevator and worked her way back to her car. Sitting behind the steering wheel for endless minutes, she wondered what in the hell she would do. After she tucked the pink envelope into the side pocket of her purse, she drove into the night. In her rearview mirror, the hospital that had been the largest part of her life became smaller and smaller until it finally disappeared.

CHAPTER THREE

Cannon Bishop wiped down the counter of his bar. He fisted the damp rag when Melanie Saunders, a woman he'd shared a few fun times with, put another coin in the jukebox. He didn't have to wait to hear the song; it would be B-13, "Strip It Down." She'd played it three times tonight as if he didn't get the hint she wanted to be naked on the cot in the storage room after the first two times she played it. The truth was, she wanted to be naked anywhere he'd have her. He regretted the few times he indulged his need and gave in to her desire.

Mel waggled her ass. She was a nice woman but always looking for something different from what he offered, which was little.

She wanted long-term, heart-pounding love. Love he wasn't capable of giving since he barricaded his heart behind a wall of steel years ago.

Dalton Black, the cook from Maisey's Diner, slammed an empty pitcher on the counter. "Fill 'er up." He grabbed the bowl of nuts from the worn wooden bar and returned to the pool table. He and his buddies were determined to close the place down, drinking beer and playing billiards.

Sunday nights were slow at Bishop's Brewhouse unless Dalton's friends rode through town. They'd crowd around the pool table for hours, drinking pitchers of beer, and talking about crossing the country on their Harleys. Cannon listened to their stories and remembered a time when his life was different. A stint in jail had changed Dalton's life. A death changed Cannon's.

He skimmed the foam off the top of the pitcher and delivered it to the four men. "Last round." Under the collection of neon beer signs, the men laughed and jeered at each other while Dalton fleeced his friends by running the table.

Cannon returned to the bar and looked at Mel, who'd gone back to her regular stool at the end. She'd been there all night, following his every move like a cat tracked a laser light. "You want me to get someone to walk you to your car?" He took her empty mug and put it in the sink. It floated on a blanket of suds for a few seconds before settling to the bottom with a clunk.

"Nah." Doc Parker, the town's resident physician, sat two stools down from her and answered him when Mel didn't. "I can walk myself." He slid his glass forward and held up a finger. Doc Parker had a two-beer limit. He said it was enough to take the edge off his day, but not enough to hinder his ability to provide care.

Cannon drew another lager and set it in front of his long-time friend and mentor. "I was talking to Mel. She's got a long drive ahead of her."

"She new in town?" he asked.

"You blind, old man? That's Mel from Copper Creek, she comes in a few times a month."

"I'm not blind, but you may be, son." He motioned for Cannon to come closer, and when he did, the old man whispered, "She's looking for a different type of long ride than the one going back home. I may be old, but I'm not stupid." Doc cuffed him upside the head and laughed.

Cannon walked around the bar and offered Mel his hand. A

tentative smile graced her lips when she threaded her fingers through his.

"Come with me." The second he spoke the wrong words, he wanted to rip out his own tongue.

"That was the aim." She turned toward the back room while Cannon headed for the front door. Divergent paths separated their hands.

Mel took a few seconds to figure out he wasn't following and marched after him into the cold, cloudless night.

"Dammit, Cannon, why are you avoiding me?" She stomped her foot and let her hands slide from her breasts to her hips like she was showcasing her goods. "What the hell is wrong with me?" She leaned against her rusted red truck.

"Look, Mel." He stopped in front of her. "I've been up-front with you from the beginning. I'm not that guy—your guy."

"I know." She lowered her head. "I know." The fringe of her too-long bangs covered her eyes. "You're not interested in a relationship, just the benefits."

He brushed her blonde hair aside. The moonlight reflected off the tears glistening in the corners of her expressive brown eyes.

"Did I ever offer you more?" God, he hoped she said no because he thought he'd been clear with her about the non-future of their relationship.

"No. You were straightforward."

The breath he held burst past his lips. A silent *Thank God* filled his thoughts. "Did I ever take more than I gave?"

She smiled, and maybe even blushed, but it was hard to tell. The only lights on Main Street came from the bar's neon "Open" sign, the stars, and the sliver of a moon that hung overhead.

"You know you didn't. That's why this is so hard. I want more."

He knew what wanting more felt like. He'd wanted more for a long time. The building behind Mel was his future. The bar was his life now that he'd come back to Aspen Cove. More wasn't in the cards for him.

"You deserve more, but it will never come from me." He pressed his lips to her cheek and stepped back. "You should go."

She reached out to touch his face. "I could have been good for you."

He opened her truck door and helped her inside. "You're *too* good for me."

Once she drove away, he walked back inside and found Doc halfway through his last beer.

"I hope you let her down easy." He pulled the mug to his lips and took a long, slow drink.

"She'll be all right."

Doc shook his head. "Puppy brains."

"Thirty-two's long past puppy status."

"You're not an island, Cannon. A man needs a mate. She had all the right parts." Doc Parker took a pen from his pocket and drew a grid of nine on his cocktail napkin. It was how he left the bar every night. If Doc beat Cannon at tic-tac-toe, the beer was on the house. If Cannon won, the beer was on Doc.

Cannon grabbed a pen for himself. He was happy to play for a beer with the man who had been more of a father than his own these past years.

Doc marked an X in the center. "Can't believe that Bea is gone." His voice was low. Not in tone, but in a volume that reflected loss. Doc hadn't been sweet on Bea Bennett, but they had been friends since grade school.

"The town won't be the same." Cannon turned the napkin around as if seeing it from a different angle would make a difference.

"She made sure of that," Doc said.

Cannon marked an O in the top right corner, and Doc marked an X beneath him. "You're talking in code."

Doc always talked in circles. It was his way. He'd never tell a patient they were overweight; he'd tell them the trail around the lake was a nice walk this time of year, or he'd say Maisey's Diner served the best oatmeal in town. They served the only oatmeal in town, and it happened to lower cholesterol.

"She had me mail a letter before she passed."

Cannon didn't want to talk about Bea. He didn't understand how God could take away the best people in his life and leave his father. "Drink up, Doc. I'm getting tired." He put an O on the left-center row, and Doc followed with an X on the lower right. Every night, it ended the same. Tied, and a tie went to the patron.

"You tire too easily. That's why that pretty little blonde number is heading back to Copper Creek alone. It's why you curl up by yourself in that lake house each night."

He hated when Doc got all preachy and philosophical. Not because Doc was wrong, but because he always managed to hit Cannon's issue on the head. He was lonely. That was a fact, but there was no easy cure for loneliness.

Doc finished his beer and slammed the mug upside down on the scarred wooden bar.

Cannon marked an O in the bottom left-hand corner. Doc marked his X in the top left-hand column and actually won the game.

"You just gave up, and that's why I won." The old man pulled a few ones out of his wallet and set them on the table. He always left a tip, regardless of the outcome.

"I told you, I'm tired."

Doc looked around the bar. Dalton and his friends were hanging up the pool cues and pulling out cash.

"Where's your old man?"

"I'm not my father's keeper." Cannon assumed the role years ago when his mother died, his brother left, and his father drowned his sorrows in a bottle of vodka. He failed miserably when it came to his dad. "You can't save a man determined to kill himself."

"I've been telling you that for years." He reached out his hand for a friendly shake, but it never ended there. He always pulled Cannon in for a hug, a task made more difficult across the expanse of a wide wooden bar, but not impossible.

19

Dalton and his friends paid up and walked out. Doc followed behind them but stopped and straddled the threshold of the door. "Change is coming, Cannon. You best prepare for it."

When he walked out the door, Cannon locked up behind him. "'Change is coming,'" he mocked. He set the chairs on top of the tables and started his nightly cleaning. "It's hard enough to keep up with the status quo." There was no way he'd be able to deal with change, so he went about his routine, hoping life in Aspen Cove would remain constant. Thirty minutes later, with the bar tidy and locked up, he walked down the street to B's Bakery. In the crease of the door was the business card of a land developer who'd been nosing around since Bea died. He plucked it free and tore it to pieces, like the dozens he'd found there before.

Doc was right. Change would come to Aspen Cove. It was only a matter of time before the cabins around the lake became hotels, and the stores along Main Street became boutiques. He didn't have to like it, and he certainly didn't have to support it, but he would do everything he could to fight it.

CHAPTER FOUR

When Sage walked into the house after two in the morning, she found Otis in the basement, lying in the center of her bed. He hopped down and stood in front of her. His tail wagged so fiercely, it moved his entire hind end. How he stayed standing considering he was a lopsided tripod surprised her.

Despite the tears that threatened to spill, she couldn't help but smile and laugh a little when he rolled onto his back for another belly rub.

"I wish my life was as simple as yours, buddy." She scratched his stomach, and he groaned. "How about some tea?"

Otis bolted up and took off for the top of the stairs, where he'd wait. The word *tea* to a dog must have sounded like *treat*, and that was a word he recognized.

She changed into sweats and an oversized T-shirt. She slipped the pink envelope out of the side pocket of her purse and brought it upstairs with her.

At the top of the stairs, Otis danced with excitement. They entered the kitchen with wants, or maybe it was needs. She wanted a cup of calming chamomile tea, while Otis needed a treat. Once both of their desires were satisfied, they met up on the couch, where she stared at the envelope she weighed in her palm. More than a few pages for sure.

"Why do you think she wrote me a letter?" She wrapped the brute of a dog in a hug, but he was already out. His deep breaths turned into a soft snore. While two in the morning was the beginning of the day for Sage, it was right in the middle of Otis's twenty-three-hour nap.

Fear mixed with vulnerability made her stomach clench and twist. She pressed the envelope to her chest and curled up like a baby next to her dog. His fur lent the warmth her body needed, and his presence made her feel less alone.

She thought about the woman who had made a difference in her life. A big difference, if she counted the fact that she'd lost her job.

"Sage?" Lydia called from the top of the second story staircase. "Is that you?"

Sage wiped at her sore, swollen eyes and croaked out, "Sorry I woke you."

With her words barely out, Lydia raced down the stairs and edged Otis off the couch. He curled up in front of the fireplace that hadn't seen a flame in years.

"Who died?"

Sage pulled herself up. "Am I really that bad?"

Lydia tilted her head.

The lack of response told Sage everything. She let out a ragged exhale. "Bea Bennett."

"Let me get some tea, and we'll talk." Lydia disappeared into the kitchen. The cupboards opened and closed, and the microwave beeped.

All the while, Sage looked at the envelope in her hand.

The couch dipped under Lydia's weight. She faced her, pulled her knees to her chest, and sipped at her tea. "Was that the nice old lady with the bad heart?"

"Yes." Sage gripped the hem of her T-shirt and dabbed at her tender eyes. At what point would she run out of tears? For those she cared about, there seemed to be an endless supply.

"I'm sorry, I know you were fond of her."

She had told Lydia little about Bea since they rarely had time to sit down and chat. Lydia worked around the clock, and Sage worked four ten-hour shifts a week. They were literally bodies that handed off Starbucks and hugs as they passed in the night, but she had mentioned her once or twice because Bea touched her heart.

"It's more than just her. Of course, I'm sad she passed. I feel it nearly as deep as Grandma's death. She reminded me of her. There was a little vinegar and a lot of honey in her personality." She set the papers down and reached for her lukewarm tea. Mimicking her sister's body language, she curled into a tight ball and faced her. "As if that's not enough, I've been put on unpaid administrative leave until they find me a new position." She spent the next few minutes explaining the events of the evening.

Her sister stared at her like she was determining the correct diagnosis or dosage for meds. Lydia set her mug down and leaned forward, putting her chin on her knees.

"I can't say I disagree with Mr. Cross. Having you work in the geriatric ward was a bad idea from the beginning."

The grumble Sage let loose came from the most wounded part of her heart. "I wanted to be there when Grandma died."

Her sister shook her head. "The problem is you think you can save everyone, but you can't."

A louder growl ripped from Sage's throat. "You sound like Mr. Cross. I don't have a savior complex."

Lydia laughed and reached out to pat her sister on the head. "No? What about that time you gave our belly-up goldfish CPR? Then there was that butterfly with a broken wing that you patched together with Scotch tape." She looked at Otis, who was back to snoring in front of the cold fireplace. "Should I continue?"

"Okay, okay. I'll confess to wanting to save Otis." She closed her eyes to picture the fish she called Flip, and the nameless, broken-winged butterfly. "I gave CPR to the fish and tried to save a butterfly, but I'm not on a crusade to save everyone and everything. I just want to make a difference."

"Ah, sis, you do. You make a difference in so many lives. I wish you could see how special you are." Lydia cupped her sister's cheek the same way their mother did when they were little. It was a touch of affection Sage missed.

"Mom, Dad, Grandma, and Bea were special, and they left without a goodbye."

"They didn't have a choice." Lydia pointed at the envelope. "Are you going to open this?"

Sage nodded and picked up the envelope, slipping her finger under the flap, and tearing it open. She unfolded a few pink pages to find several sheets of white paper stapled together. On the first page, right under the bank name, were the words "Property Deed." The next line gave the address of 1 Lake Circle, Aspen Cove, Colorado. The next showed Sage Nichols as the owner. Bea Bennett had left her something.

"Oh. My. God. She left me a property." The deed fell to her lap. Why?

She had only known her for a brief four weeks. A month was not enough. Not enough for Sage, and not enough for Bea to leave her something like this.

She pulled the pink pages forward to read the letter.

My dearest Sage,

The time has come where I must leave. I always thought being left behind would be harder, but when I look around and see the people I have to let go, it breaks my already broken heart again.

I'm sure you're wondering why I'd leave you with B's Bed and Breakfast. It's because you need it, and Aspen Cove needs you.

I approached this gift as I do with everything else in my life. I jotted down all the reasons it was right. And this is right, Sage. I know in my heart you will come to love the little town of Aspen Cove as much as I do.

With love and hope,
Bea

She went to the next page, where Bea's fine script had written *One Hundred Reasons*. Beneath it was a list that started with *1. You need to live a little* and ended with *100. Aspen Cove needs you*.

Sage dropped the pages to her lap and cried.

"What is it?" Lydia scooted closer.

Curved fingernails left crescent moons in the palm of Sage's hands. "All I did was my job with Bea, and look what she gave me." She arranged the pages in order and handed them to her sister.

Lydia looked through them one by one. Her eyes grew big. She glanced up, grinned, then laughed. Not a smile or small giggle more appropriate for a somber moment, but a full-on belly laugh. When she finished, she said, "She left you a house, and you don't think you made a difference?" Lydia put the pages down and moved to curl into Sage's side. She pulled one of their grandma's crocheted throws from the back of the sofa and covered them both. "I massaged a man's heart for over an hour yesterday, and I didn't even get a thank you, nonetheless a house. Today, I went to check on him, and he told me I should have been more gentle because I bruised him."

An unexpected giggle burst from Sage's lips. "Did you tell him he could have been dead and to stop complaining?"

"Oh yeah, I screamed at him silently inside my head and gave him the imaginary finger while I smiled at his wife and upped his pain meds."

Sage tugged the throw to her chin. "Do you ever get tired of being a doctor?"

Lydia leaned her head on Sage's shoulder. "I still love it, although it's not all it's pumped up to be." Her shoulders shook with another bout of laughter. "I expected it to be glamorous. I was told I'd be rich. All lies." She untucked her arms from the blanket and gave the room a wide sweep of her hands. "Look at me. I live in a two-story tract home with my rich but super frugal boyfriend and my sister, who would be happy to live with her handicapped dog in my basement for the rest of her life."

Sage pulled back and frowned. "That's not true."

"Which part?"

She looked at Otis, then whispered, "Hush, he doesn't know he's handicapped."

"You're deflecting."

"I'm not." Indignation colored Sage's voice, but it was a welcome change from the sound of sadness. "You act like I'm that guy from *Failure to Launch*. She loved the movie where the man lives with his parents and doesn't want to leave the comfort and convenience of living at home. Let me remind you that *you* asked *me* to come live here after Todd and I broke up." Sage yanked on the blanket and wrapped the lion's share around her body.

"Really? You want to go there? You didn't leave your bed for weeks except to pull your shift at the hospital."

"I was tired." She knew Lydia was right. When Todd told her he'd taken a job out of state, she was stunned. She didn't even know he'd been looking. When she asked him about their relationship, he laughed and told her it was fun while it lasted. "Okay." She relented. "I was broken up, but I gave him everything for three years and ended up with nothing." He abandoned her.

"And therein lies the problem. You give everyone everything, and you have nothing left for yourself. Isn't it time you did something for just you? You're thirty years old. Staying in my basement isn't really living." She pointed to the papers. "Maybe this is the opportunity you need. What do you have to lose? Go see the place."

"I don't even know where it is."

"Does it really matter? Bea gave you a gift. The least you can do is check it out. It might be everything you want. If not, you can sell it and come home. Just go. It might make you happy."

Leaving Lydia terrified Sage, but maybe she was right. She was always the voice of reason.

"Are you happy, Lydia?" Sage wrapped her arms around her big sister and squeezed.

"Oh . . . you know . . . I'm as happy as a girl who works herself to near death can be."

Leaving would be hard. Then again, she couldn't depend on her sister for her own happiness. One look around, and she had to admit, if only to herself, that she had overstayed her welcome.

"I'll go, but don't rent out my room just yet. I might be back."

"Okay, but if Matthew McConaughey wants to move in, I'm letting him."

"Never gonna happen, but what will you do once I'm gone?"

Lydia maintained a neutral expression. "I'll do what Terry Bradshaw did. I'll get a big fish tank and turn your space into a naked room." Lydia couldn't contain her stoicism any longer and let out the laughter Sage was sure to miss.

"Do nothing with my space until I'm settled somewhere." She was certain she'd get to Aspen Cove and turn right around, but she owed it to Bea and herself to take a look.

CHAPTER FIVE

On Tuesday, Sage packed her car with what little she had. Bea would be buried tomorrow, and she intended to get to Aspen Cove in time to say goodbye.

All her worldly possessions fit into the rear compartment of her silver SUV. As she shut the hatch, she reflected on how sad it was that her life could be contained in a couple of duffel bags and a few boxes.

Lydia stood in the doorway, sipping coffee, while Otis sat at her feet with a have-you-lost-your-mind expression. The truth was, she wasn't positive she *hadn't* lost her marbles. She lost everything else. Her job. Her focus. Why not her mind?

"Come on, Otis," she called. "It's time for an adventure." The dog teetered back and forth on his hind leg and looked up at Lydia with pleading puppy-dog eyes.

Her sister lifted her chin toward the car as if to say, *Go on.*

Otis lumbered down the front steps and over to the SUV, where Sage helped him climb into the passenger seat. He curled up, and she tucked his stuffed bunny into the curve of his body. Otis might be her comfort, but that bunny with its soft fur and floppy ears was his. He'd had it since she'd adopted him from the shelter.

A quick goodbye hug with Lydia turned into one she never wanted to end. Sage reluctantly pushed away. It wasn't like she was leaving forever, just a few days at most. Something about that thought comforted and depressed her equally. Her status quo was anything but exciting. She had few friends and no lovers. It was a sad day to admit that her best buddy was a three-legged golden retriever in love with a stuffed rabbit named Phineas.

"Call me as soon as you get there." Lydia gave her a final squeeze. "It will be different. Don't decide if you love it or hate it on the first day."

"Right," Sage said with little conviction. "Bea loved it. How bad could it be?"

Lydia raised her coffee cup. "You need to look at things from a glass-half-full perspective."

Sage snatched the cup and drank the remaining coffee. "Fine, but *your* glass is now empty." She pressed the "I'm a physician not a magician" mug back into her sister's hand and gave her a weak smile before she walked down the steps, climbed inside her SUV, and backed out of the driveway.

Too bad Lydia wasn't a magician. She could use a little magic in her life right now.

As the flats of Denver grew distant in her rearview mirror, she focused on the landscape in front of her. A stray pine tree or two turned into a forest. Small rocky outcroppings turned into mountains. She wound through the pass and broke through the thick cloud cover that had blanketed the city and her life for days. Her first glimpse of the sun appeared. Did its arrival after days of gray mean something? Was the darkness behind her? Were brighter days ahead? She hoped so and drove toward the light.

Almost three hours later, she arrived at her destination. Tucked between Longs Peak and Mount Meeker was the tiny town of Aspen

Cove. She pulled onto Main Street and took a deep breath, hoping the air filled her lungs enough to keep her sinking heart in place.

The metropolis of Aspen Cove wasn't even the length of a full city block. Trade the few visible cars for horses, and it would have been the perfect backdrop for an old spaghetti western.

She pulled her car into an empty slot at the end of the street, intent on exploring. Before she offered her personal diagnosis, she wanted to give Bea's town a chance. With the way some of the windows were whitewashed and others boarded up, she feared the town had flatlined years ago. The deserted block confirmed that Aspen Cove had less life pumping through its veins than the patients in the geriatric ward.

With Otis sound asleep, she rolled down the window and went to check out the neighborhood Bea had once called home. The air was crisp and clear, and the scent of pine hung in the breeze like perfume.

There was no one in sight. She crossed the street to stand in front of the Corner Store, aptly named for its location. It was the kind of place she'd stop to get a soda but never produce. Next in line, a tailor, a hairdresser, and a dry goods store sat clustered together, but sadly alone in their abandonment. Just past the dry goods store was Maisey's Diner. It still had life, but not today because it was after two o'clock on a Tuesday, which was closing time for the diner whose door sign said it opened two days a week.

Across the street sat a building with the word *Sheriff* etched into the frosted glass window. The only thing missing was a man in a cowboy hat with a star pinned to his chest.

She'd made it halfway through the town's meager offerings. There was nothing to write home about, and no way she could stay. Aspen Cove had no Starbucks. No Safeway. No Target. No Sephora. There wasn't even a McDonald's, a Taco Bell, or a Dunkin' Donuts. Nothing here offered the comforts of the life she had in Denver.

There was a small pharmacy, not the kind where she'd get a prescription refilled, but the kind she imagined was stocked with expired cough syrup and last month's *Penthouse Forum*. In the window, "The Doctor Is In" blinked in bright neon red.

She moved quickly past.

Beside the tiny pharmacy sat a storefront with crystal clear windows and a big wooden sign that read "Bishop's Brewhouse." Despite the town's rundown look, this place appeared cared for from its neatly lined liquor bottles to the jukebox glowing in the corner. How could a town support a bar but not a full-time diner?

She hurried past the closed Bishop Bait and Tackle store and ended her tour standing in front of a bakery called B's. It couldn't be a coincidence. She pressed her nose against the glass to see inside. Black and white checkered floor tiles supported white café tables. Pinstriped wallpaper was the backdrop for the cross-stitched pictures that hung on the wall. A glass display case stood empty next to an old-fashioned black cash register. On the other side of the bakery, a woman slumped over a café table. Her hands cradled her face, and her shoulders shook.

Could she be a relative of Bea? A recipient of the pink stationery Sage had replenished for Bea with regularity.

She rapped against the cool glass several times before the young blonde lifted her head.

"The bakery is closed." Although muffled by the door, her voice nearly broke with each word, and Sage could practically feel her grief.

"Can you let me in for a moment? I just want to talk to you."

"I have nothing to offer you." The woman looked behind her at the empty display case. "Can't you see there's zip, nada, zilch here?"

"You're here, and I'm not asking for anything except that you open the door. I'd like to talk to you about Bea."

At the mention of Bea's name, the woman's features softened. She rose from her chair and walked to the door, unlatched the lock, and pulled it open.

Sage wasted no time in pulling the woman in for a hug. "I'm so sorry for your loss." With each death she'd experienced, those words had comforted others.

The woman cried while Sage lent her shoulder for tears and a hug for support. When the racking sobs transitioned to a warbling whimper, she led the woman back to the table, where they each took a seat.

"I'm Sage Nichols." She reached across the table and offered a touch of comfort.

The young woman, with deep ocean-blue eyes, took a breath and shook Sage's hand. "I'm Katie Middleton." A smile lifted the corners of her lips. "Not that Katie Middleton."

Sage giggled. "No? And I was excited to finally meet a royal."

Katie let go and pulled the sleeve of her sweater over her hand before brushing the tears from her eyes. "Well, I'm a royal pain in the butt." Her voice drawled with a twang. "If I were that Katie, I'd be knee-deep in crown jewels and philanthropy. Not to mention her rather dreamy husband. Dreamy if you like designer suits and polo ponies." She bobbed her pageant-worthy hair. Sage thought Katie might be a southern girl, but she couldn't quite place the accent. Texas? Louisiana? She looked past the voice to the woman.

"Some girls have all the luck," Sage said.

"I've got luck, but it's mostly bad." Katie ran her fingers through blonde hair streaked with a caramel-strawberry that could only come from nature. "I'm so sorry. I don't even know you, and here I am blub-berin' like an idiot and talking about Prince Charming. You must think I'm crazy." She sat back in the chair. "I'd offer you some sweet tea or somethin' else if I had it, but I was being honest when I said I have nothing to offer."

Sage didn't want Katie to start a flood of tears again, but she wanted to offer her condolences. "I don't need anything. I only wanted to make sure you were okay."

Katie waved away her comment. "Just having a moment. I'm okay, really."

"It's such an enormous loss."

Katie sat up taller—taller than Sage could ever sit, being just five foot two. "Did you know her?"

"Yes. I got to know her pretty well." Should she tell Katie that Bea was sweeter than the coffee she drank? That she watched game shows for hours and ate cheese puffs by the bagful? That she smelled like maple syrup and cinnamon? Sage was pretty sure Katie would know those things. Instead, she told of their association. "I was one of her nurses."

"Oh." Her voice came out a whisper. "Did she suffer?"

Suffering was such a broad term. There were many ways a person could suffer, but not once did Bea succumb to pain, anguish, or fear. "No," she said. "She was one tough lady." She was the light of every shift Sage pulled. "Bea spent hours talking about Aspen Cove." She looked out the window at the ghost of a town. Never once did Bea mention the whitewashed windows or closed-down shops. This town had died long before Bea. "She shared a lot. And yet, I'm not sure she told me much of anything. All I know is this town and its people were her life."

Katie sighed as if Sage had finished reciting a love story. "I'm glad she had a good life."

"What about you? How does Bea fit into yours?"

Katie's expression turned flat. "I have no idea. I never met her."

CHAPTER SIX

For a split second, Sage's breath halted. "What do you mean, you've never met her?" Had she assumed wrong? It was possible the bakery belonged to another person whose name started with a *B*, but it seemed highly unlikely in a town so small. "I'm talking about Bea Bennett. I assumed this bakery belonged to her."

"It did." Katie reached for her purse and pulled out a pink envelope and a packet of stapled pages. "I got this in the mail a few days ago."

"She left you her bakery?" It was a statement with a hint of a question. What was their connection? The scientist in Sage knew there was a logical answer, but then again, Bea had left Sage the bed and breakfast, and she couldn't find the reasoning for that either.

"Yes, but why?" Katie smoothed the papers out on the table.

Sage reached into her own bag and pulled out a matching envelope. "I don't know, but she left me her property." She opened the papers and pointed to the top where it said B's Bed and Breakfast. "I imagine she saw something she liked in us."

"That's great for you, you met her. I've never been to Colorado. In fact, I've never left the state of Texas until this letter arrived."

Sage was no detective, but at least she'd pegged the southern accent; now it was confirmed to be Texan, but a new mystery was surrounding the gifts. Would more people be showing up in Aspen Cove with pink stationery tucked inside their bags?

"Are you sure you never met her?"

"Positive. Unless she lived in Dallas at one time or another."

"No, I know for a fact her family homesteaded here, and this town had been a part of Bea's life since she was born." Sage reached for the packet of papers in front of Katie. "Do you mind if I look at this?"

Katie slid the pages forward.

She rustled through them and found what she expected. *One Hundred Reasons.* She anticipated the letter would read the same as her own, starting with, *1. You need to live a little* and ending with *100. Aspen Cove needs you,* but Katie's was different. She had her own set of reasons Bea felt she belonged in the tiny town.

Her page started with, *1. You have a good heart. 2. You are generous with your time and talents* and ended with *100. Aspen Cove will care for you.*

"Not sure what's crazier." Katie looked at the pages. "That I got this letter, or that I packed up my stuff and left Dallas?"

"I know what you mean. Although my situation is different, it's eerily similar."

She tossed Sage a questioning look. "How did you end up here?"

Sage began her story at the same time as Katie's hobo bag rang. She pulled her phone from the pouch on the side of her purse and rolled her eyes before lifting a finger. "Hold that thought. I'm sorry, but I have to take this." She rose from the chair and walked behind the bakery counter.

"Hey, Mama." Seconds of silence followed. "I'm okay. I need this." Her voice teetered between pleading and exasperation.

Though several feet away, she could clearly hear an argument that had too many rounds and no solution. There was no murmur of patrons to drown out the call. No hum of an oven. No whir of a mixer. The bakery was like the rest of the town—silenced. She went to the window to avoid eavesdropping.

Across the street, a very pregnant woman walked into the Corner Store with six kids in tow. In Denver, everyone working in the labor and delivery ward would have called her a breeder, but here, in this small town, Sage imagined the woman was bored. She laughed at that ludicrous thought. With six kids and one on the way, she would never be bored.

By the sound of Katie's, "I'm twenty-eight years old, and for once I will live by my rules," she expected that Katie's mom wasn't bored, but rather concerned.

Sage remembered her last fight with her mother. Did they really argue over whether Sage should go to the dance? Her mom didn't hold her back but pushed her forward to take risks and live a little. It sounded reminiscent of Bea's reasons for giving her the property.

"I'm not telling you where I'm at." Katie's voice rose. "I'll call you soon." She ended the call with an exaggerated exhale, and when it rang again, she silenced the caller by powering down the phone.

"I'm sorry about that." Katie flopped so heavily into the chair that the red plastic cushion wheezed as the air beneath her escaped.

"Moms can be tough."

Katie rolled her eyes. "Mine treats me like I'm seven. What about yours? Does your mom respect boundaries?"

"My mom was protective, but she made us push boundaries. My sister Lydia and I didn't get away with much, but we could do a lot, so there wasn't much need to break out of parental confines." Sage took in a big breath. She was over the pain of losing her mother, but she would never stop missing her. "I lost my parents when I was a teenager."

"Oh. My. God, I'm so sorry." What little pink was left in Katie's cheeks blanched to white. "That was so insensitive of me."

"Not at all. You didn't know, and honestly, it's nice to hear that I'm not the only person who was driven crazy by their mother's meddling. Of course, I was fifteen, so she had a right and responsibility to meddle when she did."

Katie laid her cool hand on top of Sage's in what could only be considered a loving gesture. She knew immediately that Bea was right. Katie had a good heart.

"My mother is why they coined the term *helicopter parent*. I can't remember a time when she didn't hover over me. It only got worse when ..." Katie paused. "I shouldn't complain. She just wants what she thinks is best for me."

"Yes, but at twenty-eight, I'd say you get to choose."

Katie lifted her hand in a dismissive wave. "Enough about me, what about you?"

Sage told her the whole story. She started from the day Bea entered her ward asking for stationery and ended it with the night she found out Bea died.

"I wish I could have met her because she sounds amazing." Katie glanced around the bakery. "The last thing I want to do is abandon her gift, but honestly, I used what money I had on hand to get here thinking I'd just take over the place. I thought there would be employees and supplies." Her shoulders rounded. "Look at this place. Maybe my mama is right, and I am completely naïve."

What Katie undoubtedly saw was the peeling wallpaper. The chipped floor tiles. The oven without a handle. The yellowing cross-stitch pictures hanging askew. Half the chairs were torn, with golden-colored foam seeped through the cracks in the red vinyl. A quarter of the tables were turned black where years of use had worn off the white paint.

What she didn't see was the charm, the warmth, and the love that had lived and passed through this little sugary delight.

"I can help." The words were out of Sage's mouth before she tested the logic in them. Offering to help meant she'd have to stick around for more than a day. After seeing the town, she wasn't sure she wanted to stay the night. But the words were out, and she believed words had value. "Let me get settled at the bed and breakfast tonight. We'll figure out a schedule tomorrow. All this place needs is a little love, and maybe some cleaning. Bea said you have a good heart, so you have the love part covered. I'll provide the elbow grease."

Katie flung herself forward and wrapped her arms around Sage. "You may be my favorite person in town." She pulled back and gave her a blue ribbon, tiara-winning grin.

Sage laughed. "By the look of things, I may be the only person in town." Except, of course, the mother with the kids. There were nine confirmed residents, counting Katie and her, and by her size of the pregnant woman, almost ten.

"Do you think I can make a go of it? I don't even know how to bake."

"I'm going to give you some Sage advice. It doesn't mean the advice is good. It's only Sage because it's coming from me." She shrugged her shoulders in a take-it-or-leave-it fashion.

"I'm open to any suggestions at this point."

"Take it one minute and one problem at a time. Sometimes even a minute can seem overwhelming, and that's when you take life a second at a time." She would do well to follow her own counsel.

"*Overwhelmed* seems tame for what I feel inside."

"Let's start small. Cleaning is the easy part, and learning to bake isn't rocket science. Don't get me wrong, it is science, especially when you add high altitude to the mix, but there are a thousand chefs who have simplified the process. I'm sure there are a ton of recipes online. Have you looked around the bakery? Maybe Bea left recipes behind."

Katie nodded her head. "She did." She dug back into her purse and pulled out several recipe cards like she was yanking a rabbit out of a hat. There was a flourish of excitement as she waved them through the air. "Muffins. She left muffin recipes."

"Perfect. Then you start with muffins."

Katie gazed out the window. "Once I bake 'em, who will buy them?"

"That's a problem for another day." She rose from her chair and looked to where she'd parked her SUV. Otis sat up in the front seat with his head bobbing back and forth like he was taking in the scenery. "Tomorrow is Bea's funeral. I imagine it will be a good opportunity to meet people. Will you be going?"

"Yes, I'd like to hear more about her from the people who knew her best."

Sage bent over to give her new friend a hug. "I'll see you tomorrow." She walked out of the bakery, filled with a purpose that was sure to keep her in town a few days.

She caught movement to her left and turned. Coming at her like a panther running the plains was the most gorgeous man she'd seen in her lifetime. Despite his size, he moved with the speed and grace of a hawk. Everything about him screamed to her. As he neared, her breath hitched. He might have been handsome with his thick brown hair, sexy scruff, and hazel eyes, but the man moved with the determination of a predator, and he targeted her like she was his next kill?

CHAPTER SEVEN

Cannon woke at noon when a call from Sheriff Cooper asked him to pick his father up from the jail. Ben Bishop had been found on Dalton's mother, Maisey's front porch. She'd tripped on him when she stepped outside to head to work at the diner.

He slid into the last parking spot on Main Street, his body working on autopilot. Next to him was an SUV he didn't recognize. Maybe it was a preseason tourist or the land developer he'd never met but already despised.

If Bea were here, he would have stopped to say hello and pick up a muffin or a couple of cookies. In the weeks since she'd left Aspen Cove, he still hadn't gotten used to the fact that she was gone for good. Part of him had been expecting her to return and open up the shop again.

He'd have to alter his routine, and he hated change.

He almost made it past the bakery when the door opened, and a woman walked outside. Doc said there would be change, but he didn't expect it to be packaged in a slip of a woman with red hair.

He blazed toward the stranger like a man on fire. His skin prickling with irritation. "Who the hell are you?" Even he didn't recognize the roar that erupted like lava spewing from an active volcano.

He towered over the slight little thing, but she didn't cower.

Instead, she stepped back and tilted her head to look at him. "Who are you?"

He ignored the question and tried to remember if Bea had any living relatives, but he couldn't recall a single person visiting over the years. It was only her husband and the townsfolk around when she lost her daughter Brandy, and only the residents of Aspen Cove were present when her husband Bill passed a few years later. Cannon launched into another tirade. "The poor woman isn't even buried, and you're hovering over her assets like they belong to you."

The woman's eyes grew big. "The bakery doesn't belong to me, and I wasn't hovering." She pointed to the window where a slim blonde looked out. "The bakery belongs to her, and since her day has been rough already, I suggest you be nice."

"Or what?" The woman standing fearlessly in front of him had the greenest eyes he'd ever seen. They reminded him of the first leaves to bloom on the Aspen trees for which the town was named.

"Or nothing. It's not an ultimatum, just a suggestion. Being surly isn't the best way to make friends."

He stepped back and shoved his hands into his pockets. "I'm not interested in making friends, especially with money-grubbing opportunists. The least you could do is wait until Bea is buried."

"We're not opportunists." Her voice stuttered. "We're fulfilling Bea's final wishes."

An imaginary hand reached inside Cannon's chest and squeezed. "I hardly think you being here to change things is what Bea had in mind. She loved this town the way it is."

"I'm not here to change things." She looked down the street before turning those mesmerizing eyes back on him.

Doc's warning about change warred within him. "Your very presence means change. We don't need you to come here and save us from ourselves."

She laughed. "I've been accused of having a savior complex most of my life, but even I don't have the desire to save this place."

"Everything okay out here, Sage?" The blonde stepped out of the bakery to stand beside the redhead she called Sage.

"Everything is fine, Katie." Sage's smile didn't reach her eyes. "Aspen Cove sent over their friendliest resident to welcome you to the neighborhood."

"I wouldn't call me the welcome wagon." He bit his tongue. Arguing with a woman was not only unwise, but it was also deadly. "My advice to you is to not waste your time or money." He turned in a circle as if to say, *Look around you.* "You'll be bankrupt within a week."

The prideful woman pulled herself up to all five-foot-few inches of her frame. "You're wrong."

He was a foot taller than her, but somehow she made him feel small. Maybe it was because, in the face of an obstacle, namely him, she didn't back down. He hated her presence, but he respected her courage. He gave the duo one last shake of his head before he turned and headed for the sheriff's office.

"He's cute." Katie laughed behind his back.

"Sure is, if you like a man that's half donkey and half snake."

AT THE SHERIFF'S OFFICE, Cannon tried to forget the two women he left on the sidewalk. He focused on his father sleeping off another drunken night. No doubt, he was tucked up on the small built-in slab of concrete at the back of the cell.

"He's still in a mood." With keys in hand, Sheriff Cooper headed for the cell.

"Do I owe anyone money?" Cannon reached for his near-empty wallet.

"Not that I know of, but I imagine if you do, they'll stop by the bar."

42

It was the same shit, different day, with his dad. "Can he walk?"

"Couldn't when Dalton carried him inside, but it's been hours. There's always hope."

Cannon leaned against the brick wall. "I lost hope after I sold my second cabin to finance his second stint in rehab." He kicked at the wall behind him. "He stayed sober for all of ten days."

"They say third time's a charm."

Cannon ran his hands through his hair. "I have nothing else to sell. If I sell the bar, I don't have the money to pay his debts. If I sell the house, we have no place to sleep. The bait-and-tackle shop belongs to my brother, and I refuse to sell what I've got left to a developer." He pushed off the wall and walked with the sheriff to the door, where he'd wait for his father. "Hell, I didn't want to sell the last cabin. The buyer still hasn't shown up to claim it, and it's been months."

A few minutes later, the sheriff led his father out of the cell and into the front office, where a big desk took up one half of the room and a row of chairs took up the other part. Cannon's father, Ben, stumbled forward, cussing up a storm.

He would welcome a change where his father was concerned, but it was always the same old story. His dad staggered out the front door onto Main Street and ambled to the end of the block, where Ben opened Cannon's truck and fell into the front seat.

Once the old man was in the truck, the sheriff buckled his seat belt and shut the door. He returned where Cannon stood on the curb, facing B's Bakery. Inside, the blonde sat at a table, shuffling through papers, but the redhead was gone.

"Someone new owns the bakery—a stranger."

"They're only a stranger until you introduce yourself," the sheriff said.

Cannon nodded. He'd introduced himself all right, but it wasn't friendly. "That one is Katie." He looked around to see that the silver SUV once parked next to him was gone. "There's a redhead named Sage somewhere around town."

"Two of them? Both women?" Sheriff Cooper smiled.

"They aren't staying. You'll see."

"Let's hope they do." The sheriff patted Cannon on the back and walked with him to the driver's side of the truck. "We need a little change in this town."

"I like things fine the way they are."

Sheriff Cooper leaned to the side to take a look at Cannon's father, who was slumped against the passenger-side door. "You sure about that?"

He wasn't in the mood to have his life rubbed in his face. "What I've got wrong won't be fixed by a couple of strangers, high-rise condos, or gift shops."

The sheriff rubbed at the whiskers emerging on his chin. "Doesn't mean we shouldn't welcome them. It would be the neighborly thing to do."

"You be neighborly. I've got nothing left to give." He climbed into his truck and started the engine. "See you tomorrow, Coop." It was unlikely, but the sheriff could be right. He'd moved up from Colorado Springs a stranger and was now a friend.

The stench of alcohol and body odor filled the cab of his truck. For the life of him, he couldn't figure out where his dad was getting his booze. He'd cut off his supply in town, but then again, Copper Creek wasn't too far away. Sometimes he wished his dad would leave and never come back, and then the guilt of those thoughts would eat at him. Change might come, but in his experience, it was always painful.

CHAPTER EIGHT

Too angry to face more, Sage took Otis on a drive up and down the streets of Aspen Cove. There were close to a hundred houses lining streets with names like Hyacinth and Rose and Iris.

Aspen Cove was laid out like an old-fashioned key. The town itself started on the straight edge with a few cuts here and there where side streets intersected with Main Street.

A charming mix of homes in styles ranging from Victorian to rustic homestead cabins dotted the landscape. She made her way back to the town center and then drove toward the bed and breakfast. She followed the road until she came to the rounded end of the key that circled around the lake.

Off to the left was 1 Lake Circle, the property Bea had left her. It was so much more than she expected, but then again, she had no idea what awaited.

Her tires crunched on the pine-needle covered driveway. As soon as she came to a stop in front of the lodge-like cabin, she hopped out and rounded the SUV to free her dog. He lumbered out of the front seat and found a tree to the side of the house, where he marked his territory. "Don't get too comfortable," she told him. "This is temporary." She planned to stay a day or two since she opened her big mouth and volunteered to clean.

At the top of the steps, next to the front door, stood a stump of wood carved into a bear that held a welcome sign. A wooden placard with "B's Bed and Breakfast" painted in white swung from a rusted chain in the light breeze. She halfway expected Bea to open the door and welcome her inside.

Next door, tires kicked up dust and gravel. Like Bea's, the house was wooden and well cared for, maybe even loved.

Raised male voices carried on the breeze. Bits and pieces of an argument floated on the wind. She refused to be an audience to a private battle, so she turned toward the door Bea said would be unlocked.

An unsecured door was unheard of in Denver. That was as good as asking someone to come in and rob or rape or murder you. Then again, this was Aspen Cove, with a population bordering on extinction.

She sucked in a big breath and gripped the door handle, and just before she turned the knob, she heard the unmistakable sound of a fist hitting flesh. She swung toward the fight taking place next door.

The angry guy from downtown straddled an older man who struggled, wiggled, and bucked, but the younger one pinned him to the unrelenting ground.

Sage marched over to where the two men fought for dominance.

"You're an asshole, Cannon!" The old man screamed. A spray of spittle rushed from his mouth with each word.

Sage had to agree, the man he called Cannon was an asshole. He'd barely met her and snapped judgment. Now he beat on a frail old man.

There was one thing she couldn't ignore, and that was elder abuse.

"Get off him." With her hands on her hips, she stomped to the edge of the porch next door.

"You're a waste of space, Dad." Cannon pushed off the ground and swiped at the blood running from his nose. "I don't know why I still care."

The old man rolled onto his stomach and struggled to get to his feet.

Sage rushed to his aid.

"Don't touch him," Cannon yelled. "Leave him alone."

"I will not. He needs help." She laid a hand on the old man's shoulder, and he spun around and punched her in the nose.

Pain splintered through her skull and branched out like an explosion full of debris. She fell to the ground. "Holy hell." She covered her nose, but the blood poured through her fingers and dribbled onto her T-shirt.

Cannon rushed from his truck and waved a white towel in front of her like a flag of surrender. "Let me help you." He knelt in front of her and pressed the cloth toward her nose. "Give the bridge a good pinch. The bleeding will slow down soon."

Sitting on the cold ground didn't make her more cooperative. She snapped the towel from his hand. "I know how to stop a bloody nose, you oaf." She pressed it to her injury. "Just leave me alone. I don't want your help."

He backed away. "Fine, but your best bet is to stay away from him. He's bad news." The old man was on his feet, stumbling toward the house.

"And you're not?" She tried to rise but fell back down. She pulled the cloth back to her nose to stanch the ongoing flow of blood.

Cannon dabbed another towel at his bloody nose before hopping inside his truck and driving away.

The old man stopped at the front door of his cabin and ran a hand through his silver hair, leaving tufts of it pointing skyward. "You got in the way." He disappeared inside, leaving her sitting alone on the cold, hard ground.

Otis lumbered over, laid down next to her, and put his head in her lap. "Where were you when I needed a wingman?"

Between the cabins, the view of a calm lake gave the impression that Aspen Cove was a quiet, pleasing community, but she knew better. By tomorrow, she'd have a black eye or two to confirm its unpleasantness.

Aspen Cove wasn't *Mayberry R.F.D.* In fact, she'd liken it to a nightmare where at any minute, a killer would rush out of Cove Lake and chase her out of town.

She rose to her feet and walked Otis back to the car. The bed and breakfast would wait for its introduction, but her nose couldn't. She looked into the rearview mirror and gasped. It was already swelling, and a shadow of purple bloomed below her eyes. Perfect. Just perfect.

Sage put her car into reverse and headed back to town, in hopes the flashing red sign that read "The Doctor Is In" wasn't a lie.

CHAPTER NINE

Cannon drove to the Aspen Cove cemetery that sat on a quiet plateau overlooking the town. It was the one place he could go to be alone with his thoughts. At least no one there had advice or an opinion to give. And if the residents talked to him, it was through fond memories he kept tucked deep inside.

He walked past the graves of people he never met until he reached his mother's tombstone. It read "Carly Bishop, Loving Wife and Mother."

He could almost hear her tell him she missed him. "I miss you, too, Mom."

He plucked at the weeds that sprouted around her plot. Spring was here, and with it came the only kind of change he liked. Soon, Mom's favorite flowers—tulips he'd planted years ago—would break through the ground and bring new life to the barren landscape. The yellow flowers were there to remind him that she had lived.

Cannon sat at the silent grave and told his mother about his father. Ben Bishop hadn't been a drunk or an asshole when she was alive. Back then, he'd been wonderful.

He knew his mother would be disappointed if she could see her husband now. Even if he had been a drunk back then, she wouldn't have given up on him. She would have done what was right. That was why Cannon stayed in Aspen Cove. Not because it was what he wanted, but because it was the right thing to do. He didn't do it for Ben. He didn't do it for his brother Bowie, who had left to join the army. He did it because his mother would have wanted someone to care for his father. He did it because there was no one but him to step up to take responsibility. Cannon's shoulders sagged under the weight of that burden.

About a hundred yards to his right, a backhoe dug into the thawing ground. Tomorrow, he'd stand there and say goodbye to Bea.

In the whisper on the breeze, he could hear her voice telling him life was a give-and-take. That a heart once emptied could be filled. That a life hollowed out by despair could be renewed, given a thread of hope.

Years ago, when he arrived back in Aspen Cove after two deaths rocked this community, she comforted his loss of his mother, despite her own grief over the horrible death of her daughter. Bea told him there were a hundred reasons he belonged here, but today, it was hard to come up with a single one.

He thought about Sage and why she was at Bea's. Was she a recipient of Bea's love, or an opportunist? The woman was probably still sitting in his front yard, bleeding. Guilt ate at him for leaving her alone and not fighting harder to help her. He should have offered her more than a towel.

CHAPTER TEN

The bell above the door rang as Sage entered the tiny pharmacy. Despite the swelling in her nose, the smell of rubbing alcohol and burned coffee was in the air.

Florescent lights bathed the stocked shelves in unnatural light. She'd been wrong. Not only did the store have the necessary cures for the common cold, athlete's foot, and normal aches and pains, there was a candy selection that could rival her favorite Target at Halloween.

"Can I help you?" The voice arrived before the man, who looked like he'd just stepped out of a scene from *Back to the Future*. With white hair and eyebrows that appeared ready for flight, she half expected to see a white dog named Einstein sitting behind him.

He set his cup of coffee on the counter, leaned in to inspect her nose, then squinted. After a shake of his head, he said, "I'm Doc Parker, come on back." Seconds later, he led her past a swinging door and down a hallway to an examination room that could have been in the hospital where she had worked. He patted the table covered in white paper. "Hop on up and let me take a look at that."

She balanced herself on the edge of the table. The doc pulled out tape and cotton rolls along with a plastic basin he filled with water. He washed his hands and donned a pair of gloves.

While he cleaned up the wound, she spoke.

"I took a direct hit to my nasal bridge. I think it's broken. My septum is extremely sore, and my sinuses are swollen." She scooted to the center of the table and swung her legs back and forth like a kid. It had been a long time since she'd been the patient. "I'm pretty sure I'm going to need a rhinoplasty."

Doc chuckled. "Most people in town would say they broke their nose, and you sit here and tell me you need a rhinoplasty. Who are you, and what are you?"

"I'm Sage Nichols, and I'm a registered nurse."

He pressed his gloved thumbs to each side of her nose. "Take a deep breath, because I'm about to give you a nose job." Before she could inhale, he popped the cartilage into place.

"Holy hell!" She cried out. "That was worse than the break."

Doc shoved two cotton rolls up her nostrils. "Breathe through your mouth."

His image blurred behind her tears. Breathe through her mouth? Like she had a choice. "How long do I have to leave these in my nose?" Her words came out lispy and muted.

The old man smiled. "A month or two should do," he teased. "Give them an hour or so to stop the residual bleeding."

When she opened her mouth, the man popped a Life Saver from its wrapper straight into it. The cherry flavor coated her tongue. She wasn't sure if it was supposed to ease the pain or shut her up. It did both.

"I hope you like the color purple because you will have a doozy of a shiner." He stabilized her nose with strips of tape. "You want to tell me how you came about it?"

She thought a moment about her answer. "I walked into something." It wasn't a lie. She walked into the old man's fist.

He pulled off his gloves and washed his hands. "Are you the girl who took care of Bea in Denver?"

"Yep, that's me." The thought of Bea filled her equally with happiness and sadness.

Doc looked her over like she was a specimen on a glass slide. "I visited her a few times. You took fine care of her."

She sighed heavily. "I still lost her."

"Not really, we never completely lose anyone." He tapped his fingers above his heart. "Those we love are always right here. It's where I keep Bea."

"Were you two close?" She wondered if they had been a couple. His age seemed about right.

Doc moved around the examination room, straightening up. "We'd shared most of our lives together. She was my wife's maid of honor. I was her husband's best man. I delivered her daughter. We supported each other when our spouses died."

Sage heard everything he said, but she was glued to the mention of Bea's daughter. "Bea has a daughter?"

The old doctor sunk into the chair in the corner of the room. He kicked out his legs and picked a speck of lint off his white lab coat.

"Bea had a daughter. She said you reminded her of Brandy. I don't see the resemblance myself. You're no taller than a fourth-grader, and Brandy stood nearly five feet eight. Her hair and eyes were brown, whereas yours are ... well ... different. She obviously wasn't being literal and must have meant your personalities were similar."

"Where is Brandy?"

The doc lifted his bushy brows. "She's buried up at the cemetery, waiting for her mother to join her."

Sage's hand came up to her mouth. "Oh my God, that's awful. No mother should have to bury their child."

Doc lifted from his chair and offered her a helping hand down from the table. "No mother should, but it happens all too often."

"Was her daughter's death recent?" Sage wondered if the strain could have pushed Bea's body too hard, or the grief she experienced had affected her health. Many people gave up when they lost something or someone dear to them. Given the losses Sage had experienced, she understood how a person could want to give up.

"No, she died almost a decade ago in a car accident. It was a bad year for Aspen Cove."

He walked her to the front counter, where Sage waited for him to ring her up.

"What do I owe you?"

The old man smiled. His brows lifted to his hairline. "I'll take it in trade. You can work a few hours at the clinic next Monday. Not everything in Aspen Cove requires money. The gift of time has more value, but I imagine you already know that, don't you?"

She pulled her wallet from her purse. "I have to pay you because I don't plan on staying in town."

The way Doc shook his head reminded Sage of her father when he was disappointed. "That surprises me since Bea was always a good judge of character. I'd never guess she'd pick a quitter."

"I'm not a quitter," she said, but it sounded more like "I'm not a *quither*" with her stuffed, broken nose.

She snagged a few of her favorite candy bars from the vast selection. If she couldn't drown her woes in Starbucks, she'd eat them away with lots of chocolate and corn syrup.

Doc rang up the candies and took her money. "Anything else?"

"No. Thank you." She turned toward the door and got about two steps before she whipped back around. "Who owns the property next to B's Bed and Breakfast?"

A sly smile enhanced the crinkles around his eyes. "That handsome young lad is Cannon. He's a good man in a tough situation."

"He's a man with a bad attitude who should be enrolled in anger management courses."

The doc's eyes grew wide. "Did he hit you?" The look on his face was nothing short of shock. "Don't tell me it was his fist you ran into."

Sage touched her nose and winced. "Is that a common thing

around here? Do you get a lot of patients who meet Cannon's knuckles, face-first?"

"Not a one. If you're claiming he hit you, I'd suggest when you leave here, you march your little self down to the sheriff's office and file a complaint. Violence is way out of character for that boy, no matter what his issues are."

"It wasn't Cannon. In fact, he offered assistance." Sage was being very generous in her description of aid. He gave her a towel and a few choice words, but that was all she would take. She pointed to her injury. "I got this from some old man. They were fighting, and I thought I should help."

"Looks like you got in the way." He walked her to the door and opened it. "That would have been Ben. He's Cannon's father and the town drunk. Every town has one, and he's ours."

She had the urge to give the doctor a hug. He'd been kind to her. Instead, she gripped her bag of candy and walked toward her car, where Otis sat at attention.

"Sage?" Doc Parker called from the door.

She gripped the handle but didn't open the door. "Yes?"

"You should stick around for a while. It's not fair to judge a town or its people by your first-day experience."

She lowered her head in shame. That wasn't who she was or who she wanted to be. "I'll try."

He lifted his chin to the right, to where none other than Cannon exited his truck. "He's a good man. Give him a chance to prove it."

Doc disappeared into the pharmacy, while she climbed into her SUV and watched as Cannon pulled a few boxes from the bed of his black pickup truck before he walked into the bar.

Like father, like son? Doc Parker was right. She didn't know Cannon, and she didn't know his father. She had no connection to anyone in Aspen Cove but Bea, and she was gone. The problem was that Sage wasn't sure if she wanted to put forth the effort, and that was out of character too. Bea wasn't wrong about her. Sage Nichols was no quitter.

She chastised herself all the way up Main Street until she'd reached 1 Lake Circle again. She looked around for Ben but saw no one. "Are you ready, boy?"

Otis tilted his head and rose excitedly in his seat.

"Let's see if we can make it past the front door this time."

CHAPTER ELEVEN

The redwood porch creaked under Sage's feet as she approached the front door of the bed and breakfast for the second time in what had already been a very long day. She looked down at Otis and smiled at the dog, who was happy to be anywhere she was.

"No matter what happens around us, we're ignoring it and plowing straight forward." Otis sat and waited. "Drumroll, please." She rapped on the door with both hands before she gripped the handle.

Would it be like removing a Band-Aid? Pull it off slowly, and it caused more pain, or strip it free in one swift motion, and it only stung for a second?

She had enough pain today to last a lifetime, so she twisted the handle and threw open the door. She shielded her face with her arm in case it swung back to hit her, but it didn't.

Otis led the way, and she followed him into the great room, where years of traffic scarred the hardwood floor. The room appeared to be carved from the center of a tree—a huge tree with tongue-in-groove paneling and an exposed-beam ceiling.

Light from the wall of windows showed particles of dust hanging in the air.

The room smelled like lemon oil and damp wood; its scent heavy and musty.

Otis traversed the open space and stopped at every piece of furniture to sniff and investigate. He passed the worn leather sofa, then stuck his head into the fireplace and looked around. He came back to the first plaid upholstered chair, climbed up, and curled his body into a ball. Within seconds, he was asleep.

She was on her own for the rest of the tour. At first glance, it was a charming house. The oversized sofa faced a wall of windows that looked out at Cove Lake. Two plaid chairs sat side by side, facing the floor-to-ceiling stone fireplace. Everything was old but sturdy. Well-worn and well-loved but in need of a good cleaning.

She traced her fingertips across the thick, dusty beam that jutted from the fireplace to create the mantel. It held no pictures, only a collection of treasures Bea had kept.

There was a family of pinecones, with two much larger than the third that sat in the middle. She wondered if they were simply pinecones or symbolic of the family who had lived here. Next was a collection of whittled wood animals. Sitting in the center of the mantel was a rack of antlers whose prongs reached toward the ceiling.

She looked back at a sleeping Otis and laughed. If he had any idea those were up here, the dog would never have taken a nap. Oh, the money she'd spent buying him antlers to gnaw on.

Sage's stomach growled, and she reached into her purse for a candy bar. It was the closest she'd come to a meal today.

Walking back to the front door, she closed it, blocking out the beam of light that blended into the picture window on the other side of the room. Tucked behind the front door on the floor was an overflowing basket that caught the mail shoved through the wall slot. She would have to wade through that later.

Past the entry was a table where a guest log sat open and waiting for its next signature. She devoured her less-than-healthy meal while she scrolled through the pages. It appeared the bed and breakfast stayed busy during the spring and summer months. The rest of the year was quiet, with a sprinkling of visitors here and there.

A big red star jumped off the calendar next to the log. "Mr. and Mrs. Morello" was written in Bea's precise handwriting. They were due to arrive Friday. Surely, there wouldn't be guests arriving so soon.

She knew nothing about running a business that served home-cooked meals. She ate Pop-Tarts for breakfast. *Homemade* meant it was heated in the microwave. How was she supposed to provide a meal for Bea's guests when she didn't know how to cook?

She mentally corrected herself. They were once Bea's guests, but now they were hers. What in the hell was she going to do?

No. Guests would never work.

Under their names was a phone number. She lifted the old rotary handset and listened for a dial tone that was miraculously still present. She dialed the number one digit at a time. On the third ring, a woman answered with a sweet-sounding hello.

"Hi, this is Sage Nichols, from B's Bed and Breakfast."

"Oh, please don't tell me something is wrong with our reservation." A voice reminiscent of Katie's before her breakdown ramped up in volume.

"Umm," Sage started.

"No, no, no, no," the woman cried. "You can't cancel the reservation. Everything has gone wrong. The minister got the chicken pox, and the restaurant where we were holding our reception burned down. I've eaten my weight in Little Debbie snacks, and my dress doesn't fit."

Sage considered the woman's luck. It was like Katie's—if not for bad, she'd have none at all. Not wanting to be another black moment in the woman's life, she made an impulse decision. How bad could one couple be?

"No, your reservation is fine. Just calling to confirm your arrival." Sage lifted her head from the calendar on the desk to see her reflection in the mirror that hung above the table. Her eyes were a nice shade of purple. Maybe the couple would arrive, take one look at her, and run in the opposite direction.

"Oh, thank God. We'll see you Friday."

Sage wasn't sure she'd made the right choice, but she'd made a choice.

Guests meant they needed a room, so she continued her tour of the home. Her path offered two options: the hallway to the left, and the one to the right. She chose right because something had to go right today, even if it was only a direction.

She poked her head into each room as she made her way to the end. All the rooms had en suite bathrooms. The décor was mountain lodge, with quilt covered, four-poster log beds. Crocheted throws hung over chairs in the corners of each room. Cozy. Warm. Inviting.

All the closets were empty, which meant these had to be the guest rooms. Each opened to a deck that overlooked Cove Lake. As the sun set, lights flickered to life around the glasslike surface, and smoke plumes rose from distant chimneys.

It was barely spring, which meant thawing ice and crocuses bursting through the ground, but the chill in the air still screamed winter.

Back in the great room, she took in the fireplace, where logs and tinder were piled neatly inside a crate. Out the window to her left, patches of ice floated like bergs across the calm surface of the water.

She moved left down a hallway that appeared to have been Bea's private quarters. There was something about walking into her rooms that felt like she was trespassing, but she reminded herself that this was what Bea wanted.

The first door opened into a bedroom, where a monstrous bed made of tree limbs was the centerpiece. It was a true work of art. Embedded into the wood were treasures like shells and fossils and shiny stones. Like the other rooms, a handmade quilt sat folded neatly on the end of the bed. Although Sage knew little about quilts, she appreciated the work that went into them.

Behind the next door, an overstuffed chair sat tucked into the corner where bookshelves full of cozy mysteries lined the walls. On a table in the opposite corner was a small television. The kind with tubes and a knob to change the station. It was obvious Bea loved books more than blockbusters.

Next to the chair was a collection of photos—five in all. An eight by ten of Bea and her husband on their wedding day. Her blonde hair spilled onto her shoulders to rest against the lace of her sweetheart neckline. Her husband looked debonair dressed in a tuxedo with his hair slicked to the side. He gazed at Bea like a man in love. She supposed that look was expected on a wedding day.

Would a man ever look at her that way?

Surrounding the larger picture were four smaller photos. The first was a toddler with pink, pudgy cheeks, brown hair, and brown eyes. The second was a little girl sitting in front of a birthday cake with six lit candles. Bea and her husband stood behind the little one with puckered lips to help her blow them out. Sage looked at the child and her parents, realizing that Bea was an older mother—maybe in her forties when she gave birth.

The third looked like a high school prom photo with the same girl, only older, leaning against her date. He was a tall, young man who looked at the girl like she was the last person on earth. The final picture had the same girl, who was now a young woman. She sat with a quilt on her lap, and on closer inspection, Bea's daughter wasn't enjoying the warmth of the quilt but sewing it. It was the one that lay at the bottom of Bea's bed. Obviously, it was a gift of love.

Her heart ached knowing this was Bea's daughter. The pain she must have endured to survive the loss had to be unbearable. The ache Sage felt over the people she loved and lost never left her.

This was Bea's private space, her sanctuary, and it felt like it wasn't her place to intrude. She backed out of the room and closed the door to return to Otis. A doorway near the wall of windows led her to the country kitchen. On the counter sat an old-fashioned percolator like her grandmother used. She rustled through the cabinets to find coffee. No Starbucks for Bea. It was Folgers all the way.

She started the pot to brew and went outside to grab some of her things from the car.

She wasn't staying, she reminded herself. She'd be here long enough to help Katie get the bakery in shape and get the newlyweds through their romantic weekend. After that, she was gone.

Her biggest decision tonight would be where to sleep. She chose the first room down the guest corridor for its easy access. Why cart her stuff any farther when she'd be packing up and leaving soon anyway?

Back in the kitchen, she poured a bowl of kibble for Otis and a cup of stale Folgers coffee for herself.

She gathered the mail and curled up on the couch to sort through Bea's correspondence. She tossed the junk to the coffee table and put the important stuff that needed closer inspection back into the basket. The last piece of mail in her hand was a postcard addressed to the current resident. It was an ad from a real estate developer interested in the property. Seeing this as a sign, Sage pulled out her phone and left a message. She gave her name and address and asked the agent to swing by and take a look.

Her next call was to Lydia, who answered on the first ring. "I was getting ready to send out a search team. You said you'd call when you got there."

How did she tell her sister her day hadn't gone quite as planned? She approached it like she did a patient file. There would be no embellishments. Only facts.

"I arrived in a ghost town. Made a friend. Made an enemy. Got punched in the face. Saw the town doctor. Called my first paying customer to confirm her stay. Made shit coffee. Inspected the house, and now I'm talking to you."

"That sounds great," she said as if Sage hadn't told her she'd been accosted. "What's the doctor like?"

"Oh, you mean the one that set my broken nose?" Sage kicked her feet up and rested them on the table made from the trunk of a tree. "He's old but capable. He runs a clinic in the back of a drug store, which actually has a good selection of over-the-counter medicine and an excellent assortment of candy. He even sells the new Butterfinger peanut butter cups and Sour Patch Kids."

"It sounds like heaven."

"Oh. My. God. Are you listening? I'm in hell. You thought it was a fiery pit in the center of the earth, but it's not. It's a tiny town in the mountains of Colorado."

"No giving up yet. I've called Matthew McConaughey's agent and told him I have a room for rent."

"This is no joke, Lydia. I'm coming home."

"Not tonight, you're not. I've already texted Adam and told him I'd be waiting in bed naked."

"Is he on his way home?"

"Nope, he's covering a shift." Resignation and irritation spiced her voice. "We'll pass each other in the hallway tomorrow."

"I'm sorry."

"Me too." Lydia's voice sank low. "Call me soon, sis. I'm glad it's working out." She hung up without giving Sage a chance to reply.

She wasn't sure if she should reach through her phone to shake her sister or hug her. Lydia was only trying to bolster her courage to give Aspen Cove an honest try, but what was the point in wasting time? There was nothing here for her: No possibility for a new beginning. No Starbucks. And no chance at love.

She longed to be in love, but maybe love wasn't as good as she thought it should be. Her sister was in love and lonelier than she was. She found her handsome fur baby in the kitchen, finishing his meal. She tapped her leg, and he followed her to their room. Now that was love.

CHAPTER TWELVE

Sage woke up to a paw in the face. On any other day, it was a fine way to greet the morning, but not today.

"Oh holy hell, Otis." Her hand cradled her nose. Afraid it was bleeding again, she rolled out of bed and into her slippers to make a mad dash to the bathroom. Certain she'd be greeted by a murder scene, she pulled her hand away slowly. Both of her eyes were black and blue, the bridge of her nose was the color of her favorite cabernet, but there was no blood.

Otis sat at her feet, looking repentant, or maybe just hungry. "It's okay, boy, I'll live to see another day. You want to go outside?"

Outside got her a response on par with treat. The dog danced and pranced until she opened the door and led him into the great room.

Beyond the windows, the lake reflected a cloudless sky. Only the ripple of feeding fish broke the glasslike surface. She poured a cup of day-old coffee and put it into the microwave before she swung the back door open.

Otis leapt forward and took off like a greyhound chasing a rabbit. Sage took one step and tripped over a prone body.

She stumbled but caught herself on the wooden banister that ran the length of the deck. She looked back at the old man lying like a rug outside. He grunted and rolled toward the door tucking his face against the wood. It was her neighbor, Ben Bishop.

There was no way she'd touch him unless it was with a stick—a long stick. His punch to her nose was too fresh to forget, and she wasn't a glutton for punishment.

Once Otis had done his business and chased a bird along the lake's edge, they both hopped over Ben and back into the safety of the kitchen.

She was torn over what to do about her unexpected guest. Did she make him breakfast? Pretend like he wasn't there and hope he woke up and moved on? Should she bring him a pillow and blanket and let him sleep it off?

After a few seconds of debating, she realized that a passed out drunk wasn't her problem. In Denver, it was a police issue. She gave Ben a last look and picked up the phone, to call the law.

"Sheriff Cooper, is this an emergency?"

She stopped for a second to process his greeting. The sheriff answered his own calls.

"Hello?" The deep voice vibrated through the line.

"Umm, yes. This is Sage Nichols, at 1 Lake Circle. Ben Bishop is passed out on my porch."

"And?" His voice held no concern.

She realized no lives were at risk, except maybe Ben's if he woke up aggressive. "I need you to come and get him off my porch."

"Ms. Nichols. If you know it's Ben Bishop, then you also know he lives next door. Go get Cannon, and he'll come over and get his dad."

"No, I'm not about to get him. He's dangerous."

Sheriff Cooper laughed. "You're accusing Cannon Bishop of being dangerous?"

She stared at the man lying on her deck. "Is that such a crazy notion?"

"Do you know Cannon?"

Grabbing her coffee out of the microwave, she made her way to the great room and settled on the sofa. "Not personally, but I've seen him in action, and I have reason to believe he's violent."

"You think Cannon is violent?" A louder laugh filled her ears.

"Yes, I was witness to him abusing his father yesterday, and I will not call him."

It was a good thing she wasn't staying in town. What good was a sheriff if he ignored valid complaints? It may have been a ghost town, but it was also a lawless one.

The sheriff let out an exhale that vibrated from the back of his throat into a growl. "I'll be over soon. Just leave him alone. Do yourself a favor, and don't touch him."

No worries there.

Thirty minutes later, Sage opened the door to find a clean-cut man dressed in brown from head to toe. On his chest was a gold star.

After he pulled his eyes from her injuries, he reached out to shake her hand. "I'm Sheriff Aiden Cooper. Welcome to Aspen Cove."

She eyed him with suspicion. Could she trust someone who basically told her to do his job? He looked straight out of central casting for *Bonanza* or any other cowboy movie made in the last century, except that Sheriff Cooper bathed and pressed his uniform.

"You got quite a shiner there. How'd you come across that?"

She moved to the side to let the man enter. Otis sniffed at his pants and then retreated to what he'd already claimed as his chair.

"I got this from Ben." She shut the door behind them.

"It was a welcome gift to a new neighbor." She tried to discipline her voice, but it was all snark and sass.

The sheriff regarded her with an unreadable expression. By most standards, he was handsome if you liked tall, dark, and dangerous-looking types. The one thing Aspen Cove had going for it was good-looking men. Even Doc Parker was attractive in his crazy professor sort of way.

"That makes more sense than Cannon being dangerous." His nod kept time with his words.

"I came in on the tail end of a fistfight. I startled Ben, and he took a swing. It wasn't his fault."

She led him through the kitchen and pointed to the door.

"You're not the first to be on the receiving end of Ben's fist. Do you want to press charges?"

She shook her head. "No, he's a sad old man." She opened the door and noticed that he hadn't moved an inch. If it weren't for the rise and fall of his chest, she would have thought him dead. "Look at him. He's a walking corpse. He's underfed, dirty, and his skin is sallow and saggy. Surely, you have programs in place to assist the elderly."

The sheriff looked down at Ben, then closed the door. "I'll take him off your porch and deliver him to his house, but you need to understand a few things about him and this town." He leaned against the counter and crossed one boot in front of the other. He looked comfortable like he'd been in this kitchen in this exact position many times before.

"All I know is what I saw. Cannon had the man pinned down to the ground. He was the aggressor."

The sheriff crossed his arms over his broad chest. "Sometimes things aren't always how they seem."

"Tell me, Sheriff, how are things here in Aspen Cove?" She placed tight fists on her hips. It drove her crazy when people made excuses for others. She was raised to look at the world realistically. She didn't wear rose-colored glasses, unless, of course, it concerned the people she loved, but she felt nothing for the people of this town. This was a black and white, no gray-area situation. Ben's was a classic case of elder abuse. "I've been here less than twenty-four hours, and I've been assaulted. There's a man who needs help on my deck, and when I called you, I was told to get the one man who poses the biggest threat."

"Again, I think your fears are misplaced." He nodded toward the door. "That's your aggressor. If you saw Cannon pinning his father down, it was to protect both of them. That boy is usually on the receiving end of Ben's knuckles, so your concern for him, while nice, is misdirected."

"But he's old and frail."

"He's fifty-six, and he's frail because he drinks his calories. He's meaner than a wet tomcat, and the only reason he's alive is because of Cannon."

Sage knew what she saw, but she refused to argue with a man who could cause her more grief than good.

"Do you need anything else from me?" She'd been up for less than an hour, and all she wanted to do was crawl back into bed and forget the day. "Do I need to sign something?"

The sheriff pushed off the counter and walked toward the door. "Nope. I'll deal with him. This town takes care of its own. We don't ignore need, turn away from danger, or neglect our citizens. But you can't save someone who doesn't want to save himself." He opened the door and let himself out.

She had heard plenty of talk in the last few days about saving people. If Ben was intent on drinking himself to death, there was very little she could do to stop him. Nevertheless, she made a pact to help with whatever she could while she was in town. Maybe he needed a hot meal, or a shower, or strong coffee, or an ear. Those were things she could offer. As for Cannon, she'd try to keep an open mind. Maybe she misjudged him. It was unlikely, but she had to consider the possibility.

She wished Bea had left her a short bio on the townspeople, but then again, what little she knew of Bea led her to believe she would want her to come to her own conclusions. In fact, she was positive Bea would be disappointed that she'd judged them at all.

In truth, she'd barely given it a day, and that was hardly enough time to decide anything. Everyone has bad days. Too bad she seemed to share hers with Cannon.

Out the big window, she watched the sheriff fireman-carry Ben next door. She went back to her coffee and pulled another candy bar from her purse. If she was staying for a few days, she needed to get some real food.

Rummaging through Bea's cabinets, she found nothing more than chicken soup and crackers. If she weren't in such a hurry, she'd sit down and have a bowl, but she had an hour to get ready and drive to the cemetery, and with the shape her face was in, it would take every one of those minutes to camouflage the bruises.

For the next half hour, she proved that her talents definitely didn't lie in makeup or special effects. She'd removed the tape and covered what she could, but when she walked out of the house, she still looked like a prizefighter without the prize.

CHAPTER THIRTEEN

Parked behind a dozen trucks, Sage climbed out of her SUV and took a lint roller to her black pants. Yellow dogs and black clothes were never a good mix. She would have been wise to invest in 3M stock, with all the sticky tape she used, but hindsight was 20-20.

"Wait up," a soft voice called from behind.

When she turned, she found Katie running to catch her and dressed more like a model than an impoverished bakery owner.

"Hey, you made it." She had all but forgotten her injury, but the look of horror on Katie's face put it front and center.

"What the heck happened to you?" Katie lifted her hand to touch Sage's nose.

"Don't touch." Her voice was razor-sharp and made Katie shrink back. "I'm sorry to snap at you, but it's so sore."

"It looks awful." Her eyes opened wide.

"Thanks for that." Sage pulled the flat of her hand to hover over her injury. She had hoped to blend in, but seeing Katie's reaction, she knew she wouldn't.

"Not to offend, but how does the other guy look?"

She thought about Ben. "Nearly dead."

Katie raised her hand in a high five. "That's my girl." She reached into her purse and pulled out a pair of oversized sunglasses—the kind movie stars wore when they didn't want to be recognized, which was stupid because sunglasses that size shouted *look at me*. "Put these on. They'll hide your black eyes."

Sage put them on and gingerly let them rest on the bridge of her nose. "What would Bea say if she saw me now?"

Katie shrugged. "I can't help you there." She took another long look before they started up the dirt road again. "What really happened?"

What should she tell Katie? It was obvious she was going to make a go of things in Aspen Cove, and it wouldn't do any good to tarnish her opinion about the town or its inhabitants. Katie had enough challenges in front of her without worrying about some old man who may or may not be aggressive.

"It was a silly accident. I ran into something."

"I'd say."

They walked up to the graveside service but stood back. Many people were there to pay their respects to Bea. The crowd was so thick, they could hardly see the casket.

Sage did a quick count of bodies and lost track after the first hundred. She'd been wrong about the population of Aspen Cove and she might have been wrong about other things, including Cannon. She scanned the crowd and found him near the front, where family would stand. He had a matching set of bruised eyes—most likely a gift from his father.

She analyzed the positions of the townsfolk and wondered if there was a hierarchy. Was Cannon close to Bea? Next to him stood Doc Parker, who had a long history and a soft spot for the kind woman. On his right was the sheriff.

The pregnant lady she'd seen across the street with her brood of children stood a few rows in front of Sage, but she didn't have her kids in tow. Sage wondered if she was a fan of 3M products as well.

Maybe she had used Velcro or duct tape to babysit while she attended the service.

Katie leaned in and said, "Look at all these people. Where did they come from?"

While Sage had been thinking about tape, another twenty people arrived.

A man stood on a wooden crate so he could be seen above the crowd. Considering he wore a clergy shirt, she assumed he was there to officiate. He started with a prayer, but that was where anything resembling religion stopped.

"Bea Bennett was a stubborn old goat," he said. "She was also a loving neighbor, a good woman, and an amazing friend." He pulled a pink sheet of paper out of his bible and opened it. "These were Bea's final wishes." With a shake of his hand, he opened the tri-folded page. "Not normally short on words, Bea was pretty direct about her last requests." He pulled a pair of glasses from the front pocket of his crisp black shirt. "I don't want you at my grave. Get to Bishop's Brewhouse. Raise a mug in my honor. Don't shed a tear or mourn my death. Instead, laugh and celebrate my life. Share a memory. Bring food. Get going."

Everyone appeared to wait for more. The minister cleared his throat.

"Every person here is a recipient of Bea's generosity. Even though this isn't part of Bea's funeral plans, I'll leave you with this from 1 Timothy 6:18: 'Tell them to use their money to do good. They should be rich in good works and should give generously to those in need, always being ready to share with others whatever God has given them.'"

They lowered Bea into the ground, and handfuls of dirt were lovingly sprinkled on top of her casket. The minister stepped down, and the sheriff stepped up. "Cannon is opening the bar early for Bea's celebration of life. Come over, share a drink, a dish, and a story."

Sage and Katie stayed behind and let the crowd move past them. Once it thinned, they started down the dirt road toward their cars.

A hand settled on Sage's shoulders, and she turned to find Doc Parker. He looked past Sage to Katie. "You must be Katie. How are you feeling?"

It struck Sage as odd that Doc would ask a stranger how she felt, but then again, they were standing in a cemetery, and he was a doctor, so it was probably part of his normal vernacular.

"Good, thank you."

Doc introduced himself, and Katie gave him a warm smile.

"You girls are coming, right?"

They shook their heads.

Sage spoke first. "It's not really my place. I imagine it's a gathering more suited for people who knew her well." She looked toward Katie, who agreed with a nod. "Besides, I have nothing to share."

Doc's eyes narrowed to black beads. "She thought enough of you to leave you everything, so I imagine you can spare a few minutes for her." He hurried ahead. Over his shoulder, he said, "As far as food, the people of Aspen Cove will bring enough food to feed an army. You have no excuse."

CHAPTER FOURTEEN

Cannon pulled several pitchers of beer from the taps while Dalton and some of the younger men in town pushed tables against the wall for the food that would show up, because nothing said "goodbye" like a tuna casserole.

He watched the people funnel into the bar until it was standing room only.

"Your dad hit you again?" Bobby Williams asked.

"Yep. Enough about me. Don't you have cars to fix or babies to make?" It seemed to Cannon that the man in front of him was working on a sports team. Poor Louise hadn't seen her toes in close to eight years.

"Making babies is more fun than watching reruns."

"You haven't had cable in ten years." Cannon passed a pitcher and a mug toward his friend.

A sly smile spread across Bobby's face. "You should find a woman and make babies."

"Pass. Women are trouble, and babies are expensive. I've got my hands full as it is." He pulled a roll of quarters from the register and asked Bobby to put them on top of the jukebox.

With his eyes focused on the entrance, he tried to tell himself he was simply looking to see who came to honor Bea, but that was a lie. His eyes were trained on the door, looking for one little redheaded woman.

Someone put a quarter in the jukebox and chose D-34, "The Dance," by Garth Brooks. Cannon went to the back room to grab a couple of boxes of Kleenex because if that song inspired anything, it was tears.

Sheriff Cooper walked in and headed straight for the bar. Cannon poured him a cup of coffee. Although the man could slam back a few beers, he never drank in excess, and he never drank on duty. In fact, he had never seen Coop drunk.

Mark Bancroft, his deputy, trailed behind him. He was young, about twenty-four or so, and wet behind the ears, but Coop offered him a part-time position when Mark came back to Aspen Cove after a four-year stint in the army. Aspen Cove folk took care of their own.

He turned his back to the crowd and gave his undivided attention to Mike, a one-eyed alley cat that made his home in the corner of the bar. He found the poor thing in a dumpster in Copper Creek outside the discount liquor store where he bought supplies.

Mike wasn't injured; he was born without an eye, but for a one-eyed cat, he was an excellent mouser.

"Hey there, bud. You eat today?" He pulled a box of Mike's favorite treats from the cabinet and placed a few in front of him. The cat looked at him like he'd lost his mind because he liked it when his treats were hidden around the bar. It was a kind of game with them; Mike liked to work for his food. "Sorry, but there are too many people here today." Cannon scratched the top of Mike's head and turned around to see the girl everyone called Sage standing at the end of the bar. Her eyes were covered in ridiculously large glasses, which meant his father had left his mark.

Even though he'd snapped at her yesterday, he felt bad today because, in hindsight, she was only trying to help. It was a thankless job that he'd been saddled with for years.

75

"Can I get a beer?" Her voice was small and uncertain. "Any kind will do."

He pulled a frosted mug from the under the counter freezer. "Do you prefer light or dark?"

She stared at him for a minute. Her gaze focused on his nose and the purple shadow sitting below his eyes.

"I prefer dark." She slid into the empty barstool and pulled off her glasses.

He winced at her injury. "I'm so sorry you got hit yesterday."

She ran her fingertips under her eyes. "Oh, it's okay. It hurts worse than it looks." She gave him a half smile.

"It looks pretty awful."

"I tried to cover it up, but my makeup skills only go so far." She leaned forward to get a better look at his injury. "We could be twins."

He poured a pint of Amber Bock and set it in front of her. "If that's true, I'm the ugly one." He smiled, hoping it conveyed something nice and friendly.

"I think we got off on the wrong foot." She wiped her hand on her pants and offered it to him. "I'm Sage Nichols, and for now, I'm your new neighbor."

He dried his hand on a bar towel and took her tiny one in his. If he closed his palm, hers would have disappeared. "I'm Cannon Bishop. It's nice to meet you."

She looked at Mike, who was sprawled next to the cash register. His orange tail swished lazily back and forth.

"Your cat has one eye."

He brought his finger to his lips. "Shh, he doesn't realize he's different."

When she smiled, his icy heart thawed.

CHAPTER FIFTEEN

Sage wanted so much to dislike Cannon Bishop. It was easier to think of him as an awful person than a kind man who cared for a one-eyed tabby cat. "What's his name?" She sipped her beer and let the cool tickle of carbonation ease down her throat.

"Mike, after *Monsters, Inc.* The cat reminded me of the one-eyed character. Silly, I know, but 'Mike' was a better name than 'Cyclops.'"

She laughed, nearly spitting her beer across the bar. "I totally agree about the name. Besides, I love that movie, even though I'm fonder of Boo than any of the monsters."

Once again, nothing about Cannon made sense to her. He came across as gruff and unfriendly, but that didn't mesh with the guy loving a special-needs cat. She hated that she liked him. "You don't seem like a cartoon kind of guy."

"You've got me all figured out from our limited exposure to one another?" A lift of his brows opened his eyes to show a blend of colors that started as green at the pupil and faded to a slate blue at the edge.

"I'm not trying to judge you, Cannon. I can only work from my experience." Their first meet and greet was anything but pleasant. "How's your dad?"

"Same as every other day. He's either drunk or gone." He wiped at the already clean counter.

"Can I help in some way?"

She watched the wall go up between them at the mention of his father.

"Just because you moved into a saint's house, doesn't mean you get to wear her wings." He walked to the other end and dove into conversation with the sheriff. They looked at her a few times, which convinced her that she was the subject of their discussion.

"Oh my God, have you tasted this?" Katie pulled up a stool next to her. "I just love a good casserole."

Sage looked down at the plate piled high with pasta, green bean bake, and a selection of desserts large enough to feed a village. "Sweet tooth?"

"It's important to know the competition." She picked up a cookie and took a bite. Her eyes rolled to the ceiling. "So good. You should get some food."

Sage knew she was right. All she'd eaten in the last day was candy, so she slipped from the stool and walked to the tables that held at least two dozen casseroles and half a dozen pies. Not the store-bought kind, but the type that used fresh fruit and hand-rolled dough.

In that moment, she missed her grandmother all the more. They had lived in the city because Dotty Nichols wanted her granddaughters to have options, but it was a place like Aspen Cove where her grandmother truly belonged. In her heart, she knew that if Dotty had met Bea, they would have been friends.

Not ready to offend another person in Aspen Cove, Sage placed a spoonful of all offerings onto her plate. On her way back to Katie, she met a few locals—women who were warm and welcoming to a stranger.

A beekeeper named Abby guided her around the room to introduce her to others, and by the time she made it back to Katie, she was overwhelmed with their kindness.

No sooner had she climbed back onto the stool when Doc Parker tapped a glass to gain the crowd's attention.

"If it had been up to Bea, she would have lived a hundred more years because she loved this town and everyone in it." He looked around the room and pointed to an old man who resembled a miner with his long beard and soot-stained skin. "Except you, Ray, she loved you less." The entire room erupted in laughter.

Katie and Sage shrugged. Another old man leaned over and told them that Ray had been caught cutting Bea's roses for a woman he liked.

"How sweet," Katie said. "Kind of romantic."

"Unless they're your roses," Sage replied.

"I suppose, but still." Katie had that warm, fuzzy look that came after watching a Hallmark movie.

Doc continued. "I had the pleasure of visiting Bea during her last days." He held up a stack of pink envelopes. "You all know Bea and the way she insisted on having the last word." He walked around the room, giving out the letters to their intended recipients.

Katie had gone in search of another cookie when Sage saw Doc put a pink envelope in her palm. She hoped it explained Katie's connection to the sweet old woman.

Doc circled the room and ended back at the bar, where he handed her an envelope. It was funny how the pink paper had come full circle. She tucked the envelope into the side pocket of her purse. It was a déjà vu moment. One she hoped wouldn't change her life again.

Doc gave Cannon an envelope that he put in a drawer under the register.

The murmuring of voices silenced when Doc spoke again. "Before I leave you, I want to introduce Katie," he pointed to the dessert table, "and Sage." He lifted his chin to the bar where she sat. "These women were important to Bea, and she wants you to welcome them to Aspen Cove."

Without much forethought, Sage raised her hand like a child at school. All eyes were on her. "If Bea meant so much to you, why was she alone when she died?" It had been the one question that bothered her for days. All these people had amazing memories and anecdotes, but the only person who visited her was Doc Parker.

There wasn't a sound except for another Garth Brooks song playing on the jukebox. It was as if everyone disappeared, and only she remained.

Doc cleared his throat. "Bea requested no visitors. She chose a hospital too far away for a visit on purpose. She only allowed me to come because she needed someone to pick up her letters and hand-deliver them to the people she loved, you included. Distance was what Bea wanted, and we honored her wishes."

Sage sunk back into the stool and tried to make herself smaller. She felt bad for questioning the integrity of a group of people she didn't know. Many assumptions were made since she'd arrived in town, and every time she thought one thing, she was proven wrong.

Despite her outburst and personal attack, the people of Aspen Cove approached her and Katie and welcomed them to town. By the time the bar had emptied, the women had enough donated food to last them weeks.

Cannon walked out of the back room with a few cardboard boxes. "You might need these. Check the bottom of the dish for the name and recipe. That way, you'll know how to recreate it and where to return the dish."

Katie immediately lifted the tray of cookies and fist-pumped the air. "I already love Lorelei Watson."

They hefted their boxes and started for the door when Sage turned to face Cannon. "I'll see you in the neighborhood."

The only confirmation she got from him was a lift of his chin.

"I think he likes you," Katie said.

"The only thing Cannon likes about me is my intention to leave."

"You have to admit that he's cute. Not my type of cute, but I can see you two together." Katie led them to the bakery, where she opened the unlocked door with a push of her hip.

"Are you insane? We're like ice and fire." Sage set her box on the table and followed Katie into the kitchen. "I never asked, but where did you stay last night?" She felt a blanket of guilt wrap around her. There was no room to consider anyone else when she was consumed with her personal pity party. For all she knew, Katie slept on the floor next to the mixer. Her dislike of herself grew with each error she made.

"There's an apartment upstairs."

Relief washed over her. "Oh, thank God. I should have asked because I have empty rooms, and I could have offered you one."

She piled the casserole dishes into the industrial size refrigerator. "Come and look."

They climbed up a back staircase. "Bea really did think it through, didn't she? Living above the bakery is perfect for the woman who has to be up at oh-dark-thirty to bake the muffins."

"She did," Katie said with a sigh. "Too bad I'm going to let her down."

They walked into a small living room, where Katie flopped onto a blue sofa, and Sage fell onto the cushion beside her.

"What do you mean?" She looked around the apartment that was more modern with its newer furniture and bigger television than the bed and breakfast with its antiques.

Off to the right was a galley kitchen and hallway that probably led to a bedroom or two. A large bay window looked out toward a mountain peak.

If she didn't know better, she would have never guessed this apartment sat above the bakery. It was open and airy and felt like a home.

"I have an apartment and a bakery and recipes, but nothing else. I can't make muffins from air." She leaned forward and rested her elbows on her knees. "I can't afford to buy soap to clean, much less ingredients to make a decent muffin."

"There's nothing downstairs?" Sage moved closer to her new friend and wrapped an arm around her shoulder.

"I can't say there's nothing. I found sugar and flour and some butter. There's a gallon of vanilla and a container of salt. I've got the basics. I can probably make a sugar cookie."

"Here comes a little more Sage advice."

Katie sat up. "I'm listening."

"Remember, it's only *Sage* advice because it comes from me, not because it's necessarily wise."

They both laughed.

"Dying to hear."

"I learned this little tidbit from a movie. If you build it, they will come."

Katie rolled her eyes. "I'd have better luck getting Kevin Costner to visit than enough people to keep me in business. I came here to be independent and look at me. Cannon was probably right, and I'll be bankrupt by week's end."

"It sounds like you're there now, so you've got nothing to lose." Sage realized she didn't either. All she had to sacrifice was time, and she had plenty of that. "Worst case scenario, I'll float you some cash."

"I don't want to be a charity case, but I'll still take the free labor."

"Otis and I will be by tomorrow with cleaning supplies. That's something I do have, and as you've heard many times today, here in Aspen Cove, we take care of our own."

"Who's Otis?"

"You'll see."

CHAPTER SIXTEEN

When Sage pulled up in front of the bakery the next morning, she found Katie on the sidewalk out front, bent over with her shoulders shaking. It took her seconds to let Otis free to come to the aid of her friend.

She knelt beside her and expected to find red, puffy eyes and tears. Instead, she found Katie laughing hysterically.

"You told me to build it, and they would come." She pointed to the recessed doorway and laughed some more.

Blocking the entrance were bags of flour, sugar, tubs of butter, and crates of berries. Everything she'd need to bake her first batch of muffins sat right there in the doorway.

Tears reached Katie's eyes, but they weren't the kind shed because of sorrow. They were jumbo drops of happiness.

"You better get that sidewalk cleared off, or I'm going to have to ticket you for something," came a deep voice from behind that Sage recognized as the sheriff's.

They turned together to see he wore a bigger smile than Katie.

Sage rose and faced the man who, despite his smile, looked

dangerous and foreboding. His dark eyes, dark hair, and sheer size could make a gladiator tremble.

"Do you know who dropped this stuff off?" Sage glanced over her shoulder at the timely gift.

The sheriff shrugged. "Hard to tell in this town." He walked forward to inspect the supplies. "Raspberries are my favorite." His thick fingers plucked a red berry from the top basket and popped it into his mouth. "You need some help carrying stuff inside?"

Katie nodded and opened the front door. "I can't afford to turn down help."

It took two trips to bring everything inside the bakery. Katie washed a cupful of berries and handed them to the sheriff. "Once I get the place cleaned up, I'll make you some muffins, Sheriff. You can be my official taste tester."

He tugged on his belt. The man didn't have an ounce of fat. "I have a hole or two left in my belt and would be happy to taste what you bake." He looked at both of them. "You need anything else?"

Katie shook her head. "I've got it from here. Thank you for your help." She went about putting the ingredients away.

"I'll walk Sheriff Cooper out and get the cleaning supplies." When Sage moved from the back room to the café area, she found Otis curled up in the corner. She didn't understand how animals could sleep so much and thought maybe it proved he had a truly good life.

The sheriff gave a single nod to the corner. "Saw him earlier, is he yours?"

Sage nodded. "Yes. That's Otis."

"Nice looking hound."

"He's special." She heard a happy hum come from the back room. "Speaking of special, it would be great to know who left the supplies so Katie could thank them." She gave the sheriff a please-tell-me look.

"The people in this town don't need a thank you, but they obviously need raspberry muffins." He held the door open. "What about you, do you need anything?"

Sage chewed the inside of her cheek. "Um … I need the name of a real estate agent." She walked outside and looked down the street at the abandoned storefronts. "There's nothing here in Aspen Cove for me."

He retained his affability, but there was a distinct hardening of his jaw. "How can you be sure if you've only been here two days?"

She had never been a quitter, but she'd never been stupid either. The best decision would be to cut her losses quickly and return to Denver. She could be miserable here among strangers, or unhappy living with family. She leaned toward returning to the misery she knew. "I'm sure."

"That's disappointing."

If Sheriff Cooper repeated Doc's words about Bea being a good judge of character, she'd scream. She was a good person, but Aspen Cove hadn't been good to her. She'd be feeling that welcome punch for days. "It's disappointing for me, too."

Part of her would regret her decision to leave because she wanted Bea to be proud. Bea's legacy would die because she wasn't the right choice. Her old boss, Mr. Cross, was right. Everything died. People. Hopes. Dreams. Nothing was exempt from death. That was part of her problem. She wanted everyone and everything to live, but maybe the lesson was to find a healthy way to let them die.

"I'll send someone over to the house tonight."

She'd only been at Bea's for two days, but somehow the cabin on the lake had already filled up a tiny hole in her broken heart. It was a connection to a woman who gave more than she took. Sage hoped the person who took over B's Bed and Breakfast would be worthy.

The sheriff walked away while she gathered the cleaning supplies from the back of her SUV. When she entered the front of the bakery, Katie was on her haunches, looking at Otis.

"So, this is the infamous Otis." The dog looked up at her as if to say, "Nice to meet you."

"Yes, ma'am. This is the man in my life." Sage set the supplies on a table and knelt down to scratch Otis's belly. "He's missing a leg, but he makes up for it in heart."

Katie rubbed the dog's stump. "That's a good trade. You can't live without a heart."

The two women started in the kitchen, where the cooking would begin as soon as the equipment was cleaned.

"I'm grateful for your help," Katie filled a bucket with soap and water. "I wish I could pay you."

"I'll work for food. In fact, I have my first and only guest arriving Friday, and since it is a bed and breakfast, and I'm at a bit of a disadvantage because I don't cook, I'll trade my cleaning services for a few muffins to serve my newlyweds."

Katie jumped up and down. The soapy water splashing from the bucket onto the white linoleum floor. "You have paying guests? Of course, I'll make you muffins. No guarantee they'll like them, but I'll bake them. And I bet they won't be your only guests."

Sage didn't want to tell Katie she was leaving, but it wasn't fair to lie. "I'm not staying. I'm only here this long because I like you and wanted to help."

"What do you mean, you're not staying?" Katie pulled a sponge from the bucket and cleaned the stainless steel table. "This place is magical. Yesterday, I was in the same boat as you. In all honesty, I'd packed my bags last night and set them by the door. My plan was to meet you outside and tell you goodbye, but look at what happened? You were right, and I'm going to trust Bea. Even though I never met her, she's given me a chance at a new life, and I'm not turning my back on her generosity, and you shouldn't either."

Sage dipped a dry, lifeless sponge inside the bucket and watched it grow. The same thing had happened to Katie. Just yesterday, she was empty like the sponge, and today she was filled with hope.

"Let's get this place clean because I'm craving a raspberry muffin." Sage wiped down the wire storage racks and tossed the muffin tins into the sink of hot sudsy water.

"Nice try, but I'm not letting you go until you give this place an honest chance. Maybe tomorrow you'll wake up to a porch full of paying guests."

"Bite your tongue. That is my worst nightmare." Sage threw her sponge at Katie, which started a water fight. By the time they were finished, both women were soaked, and there was more water on the floor than in the sink.

"Oh. My. God. Look at us." Katie's once-perfect hair hung damp over her shoulders. Mascara slid down her face in dark streaks, but she still looked radiant. "That was so much fun." She picked up her sponge and flung it at Sage, hitting her smack dab in the center of her face. "I'm so sorry." Katie gasped, running forward to help.

Sage laughed. "Actually, it's fine. Yesterday, it hurt worse than it looked. Today, it's the opposite." She found a mop in the corner and sopped up the water while Katie cleaned the big mixer and pulled out her recipe cards and ingredients.

The mixer whirred while Sage went to work out front. There was nothing a little elbow grease and glass cleaner couldn't take care of.

Behind her, the ovens hummed, and the heat spread throughout the room. The display case sparkled under the overhead lights, waiting to show off Katie's first treats.

Sage found coffee and set the pot to brew while she cleaned the soda machine and flipped the compressor on. The ice machine whined before it settled into a soft vibration.

"Here goes nothing," Katie said as she put the first dozen muffins into the preheated oven.

Sage opened her arms and gave her new friend a hug. When she stood back, she pointed to the two muffin tins baking on the center rack. "That right there is everything."

They grabbed a cup of coffee and sat at one of the tables and waited for the treats like they were waiting for the birth of a child.

"What made you drop everything and come to Aspen Cove?" Sage sipped her coffee and waited for Katie to answer.

"I can't explain it, but it felt right."

"What did you do in Dallas?"

Katie frowned. "Data entry for an insurance company."

"Ugh. That sounds awful. I would have dropped everything as well."

"You did drop everything. Why is that?" Otis lumbered over and laid down by Katie's feet. He groaned and settled his head on her shoes for another nap.

"It's a long story."

Katie looked at the timer she'd set on her phone. "We've got eleven minutes, so get started."

Sage took in the surrounding bakery and was amazed at how fast things could change. Just a few hours ago, this place was a dusty, abandoned business. The air had smelled like despair, and now it smelled like muffins and hope.

"I was put on administrative leave the day Bea died."

Katie's eyes grew large. "Oh my. That sounds serious."

Katie's expression told her she thought she'd done something wrong.

"My only crime was caring too much. If that's wrong, then I'm guilty." By being honest with herself, she'd be honest with Katie. "It's hard for me to let people go."

Katie placed her hand on top of Sage's. "Oh, honey, compassion is never a bad trait."

"I never did get that Nurse Ratched persona down. It's not in my nature."

"Thank the good lord for that, mean nurses are a dime a dozen." Katie said it like she had some experience. "You're a softie like me."

"Speaking of soft-hearted people, did you open your envelope from Bea?"

Katie's smile faltered and then beamed. "Yes, she sent more recipes and a note."

Sage wondered if she got the only letter meant for someone else. Last night before she climbed into bed, she opened Bea's last correspondence, hoping it would give her wise counsel, but inside was another envelope that said, "Give to Katie on her darkest day."

"You got one too, right?"

The buzzer rang, and Katie rose from her chair and walked to the oven to remove the first of what Sage hoped were many muffins.

"Yes, I got a note as well." That was the truth. It wasn't personal to Sage, but personal to Katie. The biggest problem now was trying to figure out how she'd know about Katie's darkest day if she left.

"You ready to be my guinea pig?" Katie asked while they stared at the delicious looking muffins.

"A girl can only eat so much tuna casserole." Sage filled up their coffee cups and waited for Katie to serve the muffins.

They sat across from each other, picked up the colorful treat, and brought them to their mouths. "On three." Katie said. "And if they're awful, just lie and say they're good, okay?"

"One thing I'll never do is lie." Sage readied her muffin and counted. "One. Two. Three." She bit into it and let her eyes drift closed as the flavors danced across her tongue. Sweet. Salty. Sour. A perfect combination.

"It tastes like ..." She didn't want to say perfect, because it was so much more than that. This woman's future rode on a raspberry confection. And in truth, it wasn't the muffin at all, but the love of a town. "It tastes like ... success."

Katie let out a sigh of relief. "It's pretty good, huh?"

Sage finished hers and emptied her coffee cup. "It's more than good, but don't take my word for it. Go ask the sheriff. They're his favorite, and you promised he could be your personal taste tester."

Katie rose from her chair when Sage did. Otis lifted himself up onto his three legs. Katie looked around at the peeling paper and damaged floor. "It will take some time to get this place renewed, but I can do it."

Sage believed she could. Katie had heart, and that beat money or ambition any day.

CHAPTER SEVENTEEN

Cannon walked around the garage, staring at his unfinished dreams. A lifetime ago, he worked in Los Angeles as an intern for a master furniture maker, but that was before his life turned to crap.

He carved and whittled and joined until his fingers bled, and when he mastered the craft, he went in search of his dream.

After graduating from high school, he packed up his truck with his best work and showed up on Sebastian Raine's doorstep. He studied the man's work for years, which meant replicas filled the houses of many Aspen Cove residents.

Against the wall was an unfinished headboard woven from the thin branches of the Aspens made famous in the cove. Embedded in the wood were arrowheads and rocks found from his walks around the lake. It was these items that made the work unique. No two pieces would ever be the same, but the day his mother died was the same day his desire to create took its last breath.

In front of him were remnants of a life not lived. He walked over to the headboard that had been abandoned and ran his fingers along the smooth wood. How many hours had he sanded? How many coats of wax had it taken to get that shine? Even under nearly a decade of dust, the wood was beautiful.

He picked up an awl and carved into the end post. At first, it was a deep line. Nondescript and heavy—an error to the untrained eye, but Cannon had a vision. He followed it up with a spray of finer lines.

He blew off the excess and looked at the beginnings of a pine bow. Pulling up a stool, he continued until several hours passed. Why had he stopped doing the one thing that gave him pleasure?

Leaning back, he admired the pinecone cradled on a bed of needles. He'd stopped because what created so much pleasure for him was a reminder of so much pain.

This would have been Bowie and Brandy's wedding gift, had she not died with his mother.

CHAPTER EIGHTEEN

After Otis ate, he crawled into his chair and stared out the window toward the lake.

Sage picked up her phone and called her sister.

"Lydia's love nest, how can I help you?"

Sage laughed. "Did you finally get laid?"

"Yes," Lydia let out an exasperated sigh, "but it was a quickie on the counter before my shift. You'd think Adam would be up for more than that."

"The counter where we prepare food?"

"I wiped it down. Besides, you don't live here anymore."

"This week." She walked to the window and leaned her head against the cool glass.

"Are you still intent to bail on Bea? I thought you said the house was nice?"

In the background, she heard the Keurig spit and sputter. "Are you making coffee?"

"Yep, Starbucks bold brew."

"I'd kill for a cup of good coffee."

"I'd kill for better sex. We get what we get. How's the nose?"

Sage took a selfie and sent it to her sister.

"Holy shit, you're the poster child for domestic abuse. Don't come home until that's healed because I don't want someone to think I beat you for losing your job."

"Speaking of ... has anyone called the house and left a message for me?" She checked her phone regularly, hoping to find a message from HR, telling her something had opened up.

"Nope, it's a tough market right now, and no one is leaving jobs. It could take some time. Are you okay on money?"

Unlike Katie, money wasn't her issue. She had a decent-sized savings account. Her parents' life insurance policy had paid for college, so neither Sage nor Lydia was saddled with student loans. Since she'd been living with her sister, her expenses were almost zero, and she had piled away a good little nest egg.

"I've got plenty of money, but I don't have Starbucks." Her mouth watered at the thought of a good, strong cup of coffee.

"I'm sure they have a Costco or a Target or something. Go buy a Keurig and some K-cups."

It all seemed so easy for Lydia because she hadn't seen Aspen Cove.

Her belly ached. "Have you listened to anything I've said? I'm in the middle of Timbuktu. Ever heard of it? It's a small town swallowed up by two mountains. I've got the Corner Store, a bar, a diner that's open two days a week, and a bakery that made its first muffin today."

"Oh, I love muffins. Were they good?"

She let out a phlegm-clearing growl. "Yes, they were good, but that's not the point. Living here would be like me asking you to take care of a gunshot wound with a pair of tweezers and a Band-Aid."

There was a moment of silence. "I could probably do it."

The worst part of this conversation was that Lydia could save someone's life with tweezers and a Band-Aid because she was an excellent doctor.

While Lydia talked about her last shift in the ER, Sage walked away from the window and sunk into the soft cushion of the other plaid chair. A noise came from the fireplace. Most likely, it was a breeze drifting down the flue, and she ignored it until Otis lifted his head and growled.

"Hey, I've got to go. Otis hears something. Besides, I've got my first guests coming, and this place needs a good cleaning."

"Are you staying?"

"For a few days."

"That's great. Love ya, and don't kill anyone."

"Whatever." She hung up the phone. What her sister didn't realize was, if she had to cook her guests' breakfast, there was a real possibility of that happening.

When Sage heard the noise again, she went to investigate. On her hands and knees, she crawled into the fireplace opening and looked up. Nothing but black greeted her. With the nights so cold, she knew she'd need to build a fire for her guests, and a debris-packed flue would be dangerous. The last thing she needed to do was burn down the only inn in town.

Otis was all ears and teeth at this point. The low growl was a warning to whatever lurked beyond. "It's okay, boy. It's probably pinecones settling." She patted his head. "Let's get it cleaned out."

She gripped the metal handle for the flue and pulled. A cloud of soot and debris fell to the brick floor, while several black winged creatures flew at her. Her bloodcurdling scream filled the air.

One winged beast got tangled in her hair while another flew down the guest hallway while Otis gave chase. She ran around the great room and swatted at whatever attached itself to her hair. A *thunk* and a *bang* and a *crash* came from a room down the hallway.

Sage slapped at the creature, certain it was a bat. Screaming like a bear was chasing her, she bolted outside in hopes the allure of fresh air and freedom would get the damned thing to let go.

When she raked her hands through her hair, a sharp bite pricked her skin. The animal broke free and flew away. All Sage could think about was rabies and how painful the treatment would be. She inspected her finger and was grateful her skin wasn't broken.

At the slight pressure on her shoulder, she spun around, confident the bat had come back for a real bite, but instead, she found Cannon standing there while she struggled to maintain her balance.

"What the hell is wrong with you?" He gripped her shoulders to stop her from falling over.

"There was a bat." She moved her hands through her hair. "It was in my hair, and it bit me." She pointed her finger at him to show him the indentation.

"Really? A bat?" He lifted his hand to push her wild, mussed-up hair away from her face. "I guess there could have been a bat, but I've never seen one. They generally stay out of populated areas."

She looked down at her finger. "It bit me. You can't tell me all hundred and fifty people living in this town make it a populated area." She pulled her finger to her mouth and sucked on the dent left behind.

"Let me see that." He plucked her finger from her mouth and pulled it close to his face to inspect. "The skin isn't broken."

"It still hurts," she whined.

Cannon did something unexpected. He pulled her finger to his lips and kissed it. "Feel better?"

Somehow, it did. A warm feeling spread through her body. "Yes, thank you."

"As for population, if you count the entire county, we are well over seven hundred and growing, especially if Bobby Williams doesn't leave his wife alone."

"Pregnant woman working on a baseball team?" She tilted her head. "I saw her walking into the Corner Store."

"Good people, but they need to get cable."

Otis walked out of the house, and Cannon knelt down to pet him. "Who's this?"

Sage introduced Otis and told Cannon the dog's history.

"It seems we have something in common," he said. "We collect strays."

He just confirmed it. She had judged Cannon harshly. "I'd invite you in for coffee, but I'm pretty sure there's another bat in the house." Otis barked, as if confirming her story.

"Tell you what, you make coffee, and I'll find the bat."

That was the best offer she'd had in a long time. "Deal." She led him into the house and pointed him down the hallway. "Look for the room with the broken glass."

Moments later, Cannon appeared with his hands cupped. He opened his palms to reveal a wounded sparrow.

"Oh my God, I've killed it."

The warmth of Cannon's smile calmed her racing pulse. "He's not dead, just injured, but he won't fly anytime soon."

The bird flapped its wings in an attempt to take off, but one wing wasn't working right. It lay loose in Cannon's large hand. He folded his palms around the bird and brought it to his mouth, where he whispered in a calming tone, "Shh, it will be okay."

Right then, she knew she could never hate Cannon. He was a bird whisperer. How could she not love that?

"What now?"

"Where did you find the birds?"

She pointed to the fireplace.

"Open your hands."

She did as he said, and he placed the tiny thing in her palms. Closing her hands around it, she brought it to her chest while Cannon dropped to his knees in front of the fireplace. He reached inside and pulled out a nest, and Sage's world crumbled around her. She'd wiped out an entire family in seconds.

"I'm a bird murderer." She hugged the injured sparrow and whispered a litany of *I'm sorrys*.

He held the nest out to show her it was empty. "It's still early. They didn't have time to get it on. No eggs."

Relief washed over her but was short-lived when she realized she still had an injured bird in her hands. "What about this one?"

He looked at her, then looked around the cabin. "You can put it outside and let it die a dignified death, or you can nurse it back to health and hope it will fly again."

"Can you take it and get it healthy?" She could nurse a person back to health if it was doable, but she didn't want to take on a bird.

His laughter rose to the ceiling beams. "No." He shook his head. "The last time I checked, cats and birds aren't compatible roommates. You might as well put it outside and let nature take its course."

The feeling of warmth she had toward Cannon quickly evaporated. She almost blurted out something unpleasant like, *if he abandoned his father, she couldn't expect him to care for a bird,* but a knock at the door saved her from putting her foot into her mouth.

She cradled the tiny thing and opened the door to find Doc Parker standing on her porch. He looked over his shoulder to Cannon and smiled.

"House call?" Cannon asked.

Doc shook his head as he stepped inside. "Nope, I'm putting on a different cap today. Sage asked for a real estate agent, and I'm the only one in town."

She closed the door behind him. "You're the agent Sheriff Cooper sent?"

He leaned over in a mock bow. "Paul Parker, real estate agent and doctor, among other things."

"You're leaving?" Cannon said it like he was surprised. "Give me the bird so I can put it in a bush and hope it dies quickly."

"No, I'm not letting it die." She sheltered the bird against her chest and turned away from Cannon.

"You can't nurse him back to health if you leave, and it would be cruel to take him with you. Its poor mate already flew away, and you can't take it home."

Doc stood to the side and watched as the two argued. A sly smile lifted his lips like he enjoyed the exchange.

"Fine," she yelled. "I'll stay until the bird heals."

Doc turned and walked to the door. "If you're staying, you don't need me."

"Wait," she called. "While you're here, can you look at it?" She held out her hands.

Doc grumbled. "I wear a lot of hats in this town. Veterinarian isn't one of them." Despite his rebuttal, he turned around and walked into the kitchen. "Is that coffee I smell?" He took off his coat and hung it over a chair. "Get me a cup and a towel."

Minutes later, the bird was in the hands of Doc Parker, who examined his patient no differently than he would a human.

The poor bird tried to flap its injured wing. Doc turned to Cannon. "Calm him down, son." As soon as Cannon covered the bird's head, it stilled, which surprised Sage because she found nothing about Cannon calming. His very presence made her heart beat hummingbird fast.

Cannon picked up the cup of coffee Sage poured him and sipped. A visible shudder ran down his body. "This is awful. Do I need to show you how to make a decent cup of coffee?"

She scoffed. "Just drink it. It's not that bad, and it's not like you're drinking Starbucks every day."

Doc took a sip and grimaced. "You're right, it's swill." He walked to the door and disappeared for a few minutes, only to return with a black doctor's bag.

"You really do house calls?" Sage asked.

"Not if I can help it." He pulled out a piece of gauze. Doc flexed the wing and said, "It doesn't look broken, and it's not bleeding. I'd say it's a pulled muscle, but then again, what do I know? I'm not an ornithologist." He stabilized the wing and packed up his bag.

"What do I feed it?"

The doctor lifted his shoulders. "A cheeseburger?" He looked toward Cannon. "You making a liquor run tomorrow?"

He nodded. "You need anything from town?"

"Nope, but you can take Sage with you. Drive by the pet store so she can get some worm meal or seed or whatever they feed birds." Doc started back toward the door. "Keep your feathered friend covered and quiet and give it water." He was almost outside when he turned to her and said, "That's two you owe me. I expect to see you at the clinic on Monday."

Cannon piped in, "If she's still here."

"Oh, she'll be here," Doc said. "You two lovebirds have a good night." He pulled the door shut behind him.

CHAPTER NINETEEN

Cannon led his father from the front seat of his truck, where he'd spent the night, into the house, where he cleaned him up and put him to bed.

Why his father couldn't take the extra twenty steps inside the front door was always a mystery, but at least he landed at home and not on someone else's porch this time.

He picked up two cups, a thermos of coffee, and an empty shoebox, then climbed into the driver's seat of his truck.

Even a spritz of his cologne couldn't cover the smell of stale alcohol, sweat, and urine that filled the cab. He rolled down the windows and drove the hundred yards next door, then exited his truck with his offerings.

Greeting him at the top of the steps was the bear he'd carved when he was fifteen. Above the door swung the sign he'd made for Bea when he was ten. All the members of Bea's family had names that started with a *B*, so it made sense to use one letter to honor everyone. B's Bed and Breakfast.

With no free hands, he tapped the bottom of the door with his boot and waited. Seconds later, it swung open, and there Sage stood. Despite her poor attempt to cover her injury, she was beautiful.

"Good morning." Her sweet voice greeted him.

She had consumed his thoughts since their first meeting on the sidewalk, and he hated it. "I come bearing gifts." He lifted the thermos and cups.

She did a happy dance before she stepped back and let him inside. "Please tell me that's real coffee."

A smile lifted his lips "It's bold brew." In his experience, it took more than a good cup of coffee to please a woman. The simplicity of his gift and exuberance of her reaction made him like her more. She wasn't who he thought she was. Not a land developer, and not an investor, but Bea's nurse, as he found out last night when they hovered around the tiny injured bird.

"You accused me of trying to be a saint, but *you're* wearing the wings today." She took the thermos and coffee cups into the kitchen and made quick work of pouring them each a mug.

He walked to the table, where a large stockpot sat with the lid partially in place. "I brought a more suitable living environment for the bird."

Sage laughed. "You don't think keeping it in a stockpot by the stove is a good idea?"

He opened the lid to expose the tiny thing that sat on a soft towel. "I'll only worry when you add water and spices."

She playfully punched him in the arm, and it felt good to have a moment of lightness in a life covered by clouds.

He opened the ventilated shoebox and transferred the bird to its new home.

Beside him, Sage let out a hum after her first sip. "Oh my God, that's so good."

His mind played with her words, and his imagination had her naked and under his body, saying the same thing for different reasons. He shook the image from his head.

"It's just coffee." He positioned the little dish of water to the side of the box and covered the bird back up. "You ready?"

Cupped like a treasure in her hands was the mug. "It's life's elixir, and yes, I'm ready." She tucked the thermos under her arm and snatched her purse from the table. "Can Otis come? He loves to ride."

Cannon peeked into the great room to find Otis waiting at the door. "No problem."

He rushed ahead and opened the door for Sage and her dog. "Do I need to lift him in?"

Sage leaned close and whispered, "Let's see if he can make it himself. He doesn't know he's different."

That comment hit him in the chest—hard because he had the same thoughts about his cat, and she understood. He didn't coddle Mike because he had one eye. He celebrated his ability to overcome the obstacle. There was something to learn from how animals faced adversity.

He patted the seat and watched as Otis leaped up without help. Sage, on the other hand, needed a little boost, or maybe he simply wanted to touch her.

His hands went around her slender waist, and he lifted her to the seat. Her snug sweater and jeans didn't go unnoticed. She was a tiny package of perfection. Her personality was as fiery as her red hair, but he liked that she had spirit. She was a welcome respite to his mundane life in Aspen Cove. Part of him wanted to ignore her because she wasn't staying. The other part wanted to enjoy spending time with her while she was present. He rounded the front of the truck and climbed in the driver's seat. Otis sat like a chaperone between them.

"I hate to ask, but can we stop at a grocery store? I have guests arriving tonight."

"Friends?" His first thought was *boyfriend*.

Her head shook. "No, they are guests booked by Bea."

He pulled out of the driveway and headed north. "Really? I would have thought you'd cancel."

She twisted to face him. "Oh, I was going to until the woman cried. I didn't have the heart to ruin her weekend. She's a newlywed."

"You're one of those." Otis curled into a ball and laid his head on Cannon's lap.

"One of what?"

"A bleeding heart." She was a softie. It showed in her concern for his father and the way she reacted with the bird. Additional proof sat next to him, drooling on his lap. Most people wouldn't adopt a tripod. Sage was a rescuer.

"Call me what you want, but I couldn't take away the girl's honeymoon weekend when it took so little to provide it."

He couldn't argue with her logic. It was what brought him back to Aspen Cove. He couldn't let his father wither alone, so he came home, not realizing he'd wither alongside him.

"You should have lots of guests on the books. This is the time of year when things pick up. I'll have to open the bait and tackle shop soon for the fishermen."

"You run both the bar and the shop?"

He shrugged. "I have little choice." He left the words unsaid and hoped she didn't bring up his father. "I run the shop during the day, and the bar at night."

"That's a lot of work."

"I've never been afraid of hard work. What about you, tell me more about yourself."

Over the next forty minutes, he learned Sage was an orphan with one sibling who was a doctor.

"It's funny," she said, "but the plan was for us to work together someday. She'd be the general practitioner, and I'd be her nurse."

"Is that possible?" He pulled into the Liquor Warehouse and killed the engine.

"Not really. She got her residency in emergency medicine, and I got hired in a different ward."

Her hand sat on Otis's back, and he laid his palm over hers. "Don't give up your dreams."

"What about you?" She didn't move her hand but stacked her other palm over his. "What are your dreams?"

Her touch created a sense of vulnerability. Did he dare share pieces of himself with a woman destined to leave? "Right now, my dream is to run our errands and grab the best burger within a hundred miles for lunch." He pulled his hand free and exited the truck.

She'd opened her door and hopped out before he could reach her. Cannon lifted his chin toward the dog. "Is he staying or going?"

"He'll stay."

She followed him inside the warehouse.

Just his luck that Melanie was on shift today. She didn't normally work Fridays. Was it a coincidence that she happened to be here on the day he always came for supplies?

Mel approached like a cat burglar slinking toward him. The glow of jealousy lit up her eyes. "Good to see you again, Cannon." She ignored Sage and pushed her body into his.

Sage took a step back, and he didn't like that Mel's presence disrupted his day.

"Mel, this is my new neighbor, Sage."

Mel licked her lips and smiled. "Hey." She leaned in like she was inspecting the competition. "That looks painful. I hope the other guy looks worse." She looked at Cannon. "You're not the other guy, are you?"

Sage lifted her hand to her nose. "He's not, and everyone survived."

Mel ignored Sage and turned her eyes back on him. "I can come to the bar tonight." She tugged on her low-cut T-shirt so hard, Cannon feared she'd expose herself.

"I can't stop you from coming, but all you'll get from me is a beer." He jumped over the flatbed cart to stand next to Sage. He wasn't sure if he was protecting her or seeking refuge.

"Dalton's friends are still around, though, in case you're looking."

Red spread from Mel's neck to her cheeks. "You can be such an asshole." She turned to Sage. "Walk away from this one. He's as slippery as a fish." She pivoted and stomped away.

"Spurned girlfriend?" Sage asked as they moved down the row of whiskey.

"Never a girlfriend." He put a case of Jack Daniels on the cart and moved toward the Jim Beam.

"Just spurned, then."

"Something like that." He wanted to talk about Mel as much as he wanted to discuss his father. "You need something from here? I get a discount."

Her smile was so wide it nearly split her face. "Wine. I could use a few bottles."

Cannon led her to the wine aisle, where she chose two reds and two whites. He moved on to pick up several kegs of beer, and they checked out.

Next stop was the pet store for worm mush and seeds. The final errand was Target. He'd never seen a woman get so excited over a superstore, but as soon as she went to the appliance aisle and put a Keurig into her basket, he understood. A good cup of coffee made the difference in a day.

"Had I known this was here, I wouldn't have suffered through days of drinking sludge." She tossed everything from Milk-Bones to eggs in her cart. When she passed the floral section, she let out a whoop of glee. "Lilacs ... they're my favorite." She touched the pinked petals of the flower.

"They look like pom-poms."

She lowered her nose to the buds and inhaled. "I don't know. They're happy flowers. They look hopeful." She pulled back and stared at the delicate petals. "I look at these, and I see something wonderful. If nature can make something so perfect, then anything is possible." She tucked several bouquets into her basket, and he followed her to the checkout.

They put their purchases into the truck, thankful he had a super cab. "If we buy anything else today, Otis will have to ride in the back." Cannon shut the door to the back seat. "Are you hungry?"

Otis lifted his head while Sage nodded. "Starved. I've been working through the casserole dishes, but a girl can only eat so many noodles."

Copper Creek offered many options for dining, but his favorite place was a little hole-in-the-wall called Chico's that sold the best green chili burgers around.

"How brave are you?"

She laughed. "I packed up my car and came to Aspen Cove."

"Let's go to Chico's then." Cannon drove to the little hidden gem. Once he parked, he looked at Otis. "Can he join us, or do you want to leave him here?"

Sage shook her head. "There's no way he'd stay in the truck when there's a hamburger around." She climbed out with Otis following close behind.

Cannon left them at an outside table. The sun was high in the sky, and its warmth soaking into him. Or maybe that was Sage's presence. As long as she wasn't yelling at him or talking about his father, he liked her. She was easy to be around. Uncomplicated.

When he returned, he had two green chili-drenched burgers and a plain patty for Otis.

"I think you're trying to win my dog's heart." She pulled their meals off the tray and set the table for two.

"I think your dog, like my cat, likes whoever has food."

She nodded. "There's no loyalty these days."

"Maybe you're trusting the wrong people." He picked up his burger and took a bite.

"I trust everyone until I can't."

"I trust no one until I can." He knew a lot about trust. He'd been dealt some shitty hands in life and found out the hard way that trust is not without limits.

"I'll trust this is the best burger I've ever eaten because you said so."

"Not sure I should be trusted." He wanted to be the kind of man a woman like Sage could count on, but he wasn't certain he had anything to offer.

She took a bite, and her eyes grew big. "So good." She waited a few seconds. Her cheeks turned from pink to red, and she grabbed her soda. "So hot."

"Good, though, right?"

"The best." She fanned her face. "I'd say you're trustworthy."

An hour later, they were back in Aspen Cove, unloading her groceries. While she put them away, he cared for the bird who picked at the seed and worms placed inside the box.

"I should go." He rose from the chair and walked toward the front door. He'd spent a thousand lifetimes in this house. Some of his best memories happened in the great room, where both families got together for game nights and dinner.

He turned around to call out a goodbye but found Sage standing next to him. She flung her body into his, wrapping her arms around his waist and settling her head against his chest. Despite being over a foot taller than her, she fit perfectly against him.

He held her for a long minute before they both dropped their arms and separated.

"Sorry," she said. "I just ... Today was nice. Thank you."

When her eyes fixed on his, he realized he was in big trouble. This woman would drive him crazy, but he wasn't sure if it was crazy good or crazy bad.

"It was kind of nice, wasn't it?" He didn't elaborate on what he was referring to, but he liked the day and the hug.

CHAPTER TWENTY

Sage had two hours before her guests would arrive. In that time, she second-guessed everything from the wine she put in their room, to the vase that held the flowers.

She had no idea what was expected, but she didn't want to fall short of success, so she erred on the side of excess. Next to the wine glasses and wine, she placed a tray of snacks that included chocolates and cookies and fresh fruit.

She fluffed pillows and folded towels into pretty little parcels. She wrote a welcome note that included a wish for a happy and long marriage. After she'd dusted for the second time, she left the room.

The fireplace was ready with stacked logs and crumpled papers. All it needed was the strike of a match.

She transferred the bird to her room and closed the door to the guest wing. With a glass of wine and Otis right behind her, she went to the back deck and sat in one of the adirondack chairs.

Otis settled in front of the wood rail to stare through the spindles at the lake. She was happy to have the enclosed deck, even though he would never run off. Otis liked food and Sage's belly rubs too much.

While she waited for her guests to arrive, she phoned Katie.

"Are you psychic?" Katie's voice was buoyant and happy. "I was going to call you because I have so much to tell you."

"I'm all ears."

"Apparently, Saturday is apple-spice-muffin day."

Sage sat up in the chair. "Another delivery?"

"Yes, ma'am. Everything to make Saturday's special muffins."

Aspen Cove was small on amenities but big on heart. They fully embraced Katie—a stranger. "How did the raspberry muffins go today?"

She sipped her wine and settled into her chair because Katie was long-winded. It took five minutes to get to the meat of the story. "I opened with two dozen muffins, thinking I'd have leftovers, and by ten o'clock, I was out and had to mix again."

"Wow. Who bought them?"

"Lots of people came in. Some I recognized. Some I didn't. Sheriff Cooper bought half of them. He told me I wasn't charging enough, but how can I charge for a muffin made with donated materials?"

"I'm giving you more Sage advice. The sheriff is right. Your muffins are made with love. How can you put a fair price on that?"

Sage told Katie about the bird and her trip to Copper Creek.

"How was spending the morning with Cannon?"

How did Sage describe bliss? "He's not who I thought he was. I still don't like the way he treated his father, but I don't think he's as bad as I believed."

"So, you like him?" There was a hint of delight to her voice.

"I wouldn't say I like him, but he's tolerable." She didn't want to give Katie false hope. Liking Cannon would give her another reason to stay in Aspen Cove, and she didn't need the temptation to stay. At first, the town had offered way less than Denver, but now, she found herself conflicted. Aspen Cove had Katie and Cannon and Denver had neither.

Sage heard a noise at the front door. "I think my guests are here. I've got to go."

Katie promised to deliver the muffins by seven thirty in the morning before she hung up.

After the knock on the door, she counted to five so as not to seem too eager. It surprised her that she was excited; then again, Sage never turned down a challenge. How many people got to test their hand at a new career without risk?

She checked her face in the mirror. Her bruising had faded, and the new concealer she bought did a satisfactory job of hiding the worst of the injury. Just days ago, she'd hoped the couple would look at her and run, but today she wished they stayed.

With a smile pasted on her face, she opened the door. Stuck together like Velcro was a young couple not older than midtwenties, and by the look of happiness on their faces, they were in love.

"Welcome." She stepped aside and opened her home to her guests. *Her home? Her guests?* "I'm Sage Nichols, your host."

The couple walked inside. "Where's Bea?" the young woman asked.

Sage smiled and simply said, "Bea couldn't make it." There was no way she'd tell them where Bea really was. Talk about a downer on a honeymoon.

She showed them to the last room at the end of the hallway and prayed the buffer of one room between them would be enough. She didn't want to disturb the newlyweds, but she wasn't prepared to move into Bea's room either.

"There are beverages in the refrigerator, coffee in the pot, and breakfast will be ready at nine, unless you need it earlier."

The Morellos looked at her and laughed. "Even nine sounds too early," the husband said. He leaned in toward his bride and nipped at her lip. "I've got everything I need right here."

That was Sage's cue to leave. She backed out of the room and shut the door. She hadn't even reached the end of the hallway when a loud thud came from the end of the room. It took on a steady rhythm —an incessant banging. She blushed for the couple, who wasted no time making the bed rock and the frame hit the wall.

She exited the hallway and closed the door behind her, trying to gain distance from the noise that mixed with moans and groans and expletives that could make a trucker blush. She poured herself a glass of wine and took Otis to the deck. They inched farther and farther away from the room, trying to escape the passion play going on in the house.

She had to hand it to Mr. Morello, because he had staying power. She thought about his wife and wondered if she'd need an ice pack.

There was a lull and quiet for about thirty minutes before it started again. This time, Sage gave up drinking wine by the glass and took the bottle and a chair down to the water's edge. Even at that distance, she couldn't escape the couple's bliss.

Each time she heard the silence, she snuck into the house to get what she needed. A jacket. Snacks. More wine.

The sun had set, and the air cooled, but the lights that flickered across the still lake mesmerized her. Otis lay on her feet, keeping them warm. Each time an *Oh God* or a *Yes* came from the house, he lifted his head, and she lifted the bottle.

A shadow fell over her. "Bad day?"

She startled and looked over her shoulder to find Cannon. "You have no idea." He flopped on the ground next to her chair.

At the next *Yes! Yes! Yes!*, he laughed. "Oh, I get it."

They both looked back at the last room, where the light seeped out from between the curtains.

She picked up the bottle of wine and emptied it. "They've been at it since they arrived. I don't know if I should be jealous or annoyed. I'm leaning toward annoyed."

He pushed forward and wrapped his arms around his knees. "Why annoyed?"

She faced him. The moonlight caught the blue in his eyes. Maybe it was the wine or the constant soundtrack playing in the background, but he looked damn sexy.

"Seriously? I'm sitting out here in the cold while they're doing ... whatever they're doing that requires a thousand *Oh Gods* and *Yeses*.

I'm fairly certain the wall will have holes in it from the banging headboard." She rocked the empty bottle between her thumb and finger and let it swing like a pendulum. "To make it worse, I'm out of wine, so I can't even drown out the noise with alcohol."

He rose to his feet. "I'll be right back."

He left for a few minutes and returned with a chair, a blanket, a bottle of wine, and two glasses. "Looked like you needed reinforcements." He sat the chair next to hers and cloaked her shoulders with the blanket before offering her a glass of wine.

While she tipped the glass back, Otis climbed under the tent the blanket created and moaned as if his life was perfect. To a dog, life was simple. Eat. Sleep. Eat some more. Sleep again.

"Do you think it's wise to keep alcohol in the house with your father?" She didn't want to create a divide between them, but it wasn't much different from offering a diabetic a candy bar.

He stared at the wine in his glass, twirling it around until the red liquid coated the inside. "There's nothing he can access. I keep my stash in the gun safe, locked up."

"That's good." She needed to give him more credit. "Thanks for the wine."

"Here's to being neighbors." He raised his glass and tapped hers. "For as long as you stay, at least."

She peeked over his shoulder to the cabin where he lived. It was dark and empty. "You should go inside. I'm pretty sure it's warm and quiet in your house."

He sipped his wine and studied her. "Probably, but it wouldn't be neighborly to leave you out here by yourself. Besides, I like your company better than I like my own." His head hung. "I'd invite you in, but Dad is unpredictable."

"Probably wise to stay put, or at least less painful." Too much wine gave Sage the giggles. "You could be out here until sunrise. I swear they have the stamina of Olympians."

"I'll stay with you until they wear themselves out." He topped off both wine glasses and stared at the lake.

"I'm not sure that's possible. Have you ever ...?" Sage shook her head and dropped the sentence. She couldn't believe she almost asked him if he had ever made a girl cry out like that.

"Yes."

She snapped her head in his direction. "You don't even know what I was going to say."

"It's easy to assume. There's a triple-X-rated soundtrack playing in the background, and you have that wistful look about you."

"It's not wistful." She held up her half-empty glass. "I'm drunk. You have no idea what I was about to say."

He moved his chair closer and pulled the corner of the blanket around his shoulders, too. His body touching hers warmed up the part the wine hadn't numbed.

"There are several questions I can deduce from that look. One is, have I ever stayed up having sex all night? Another would be, do I have the skills to make a woman scream in ecstasy? Maybe you were simply thinking, have I ever wanted what they have? And the answer to all three is yes."

The man had the most beautiful lips. She watched them speak every word. Would they be pillow soft? Warm? Wet. She moved her eyes from his lips to his hand. Would the fingers that held the glass so gently be as tender on her body? Caught gawking at him, she turned away embarrassed.

"You're wrong. I was going to ask if you've ever sat outside because the noise inside was too much to take?"

Cannon chuckled. "Sure. *That's* what you were thinking. The answer is also yes. My brother and his girlfriend were active and loud."

"You have a brother?"

"Yep, he doesn't live here anymore." Cannon looked off toward his house as if recalling a memory. "They would lock me out of the house." He picked up the bottle and divided the rest between them, then pointed to the dock. "I've spent many hours on that dock."

Sage leaned into Cannon to soak up more of his body heat. "I could think of worse places to be stuck. If it wasn't so cold, it would be perfect."

"This feels kind of perfect."

He adjusted the blanket and pulled her closer. The arm of her chair dug into her side, but she didn't complain. For the first time since she arrived in Aspen Cove, she wasn't alone or lonely. It was an odd sensation to be so comfortable with a man who made her temper flare, and her insides turn soft. The most interesting thing was he made her feel something other than empty. She would take rage and passion over apathy any day.

They sat in companionable silence for minutes. Cannon turned toward her and tilted his head. A kiss was coming, and all her questions about his lips would be answered. She leaned in, relaxed her lips and inhaled. Just as the lids of her eyes fluttered closed, she felt him shift.

"I think they're done." He rolled to his feet, taking the blanket with him. "Let's get you inside and warmed up." He offered her a hand and pulled her to her feet. "I'll clean this up." With his arm at her back, he led her to the door.

Sage wasn't ready to say goodbye, but it was the smart choice. There was no point in starting something that wouldn't go anywhere. She wrapped her arms around him and hugged him tightly. "Thank you. This was probably the best night I've had in a while."

He held her close, and his lips touched the top of her head in a gentle kiss. "You need to get out more."

"I do. I really do."

"Tomorrow night, you should come to the bar." He stepped back. "It's karaoke night. Bring Otis."

"Okay." She nodded. It would be the first Saturday night where she wasn't pulling a shift or spending it curled on the couch, watching reruns.

"It's a date." He stepped away and started down the stairs.

"It is?" Did he mean a real date, or was he using it as a figure of speech?

"Just come to the bar." He disappeared into the night. She watched his outline as he picked up the glasses and bottles by the water and moved toward his cabin.

She giggled as she walked into the house. Suddenly, nothing bothered her. Not her nose. Not the newlyweds going at it like rabbits. Not the thought of being stuck here until the house sold.

A voice from deep down told her she could be happy here if she'd let herself. Flopping onto her bed, she grinned up at the ceiling, thinking of the magical effect that a long hug and light kiss from the right man could have. She wasn't sure if it was the wine talking or her hormones, but something was telling her to trust Cannon.

CHAPTER TWENTY-ONE

Sage barely peeled an eye open for Katie when she arrived at exactly seven thirty to deliver muffins. Apple and cinnamon filled the air the minute she walked inside.

Not wanting to wake her guests, she pulled her finger to her lips in a "be quiet" motion and led Katie into the kitchen, where a decent cup of coffee awaited them.

"What do I owe you?" she whispered, reaching for her purse she had tucked under the sink. Sage lived by big-city rules. She locked her doors at night and kept her purse hidden out of sight.

Katie shook her head. "You're not paying me. I'm here because of you, and a bunch of lunatics who keep leaving flour and produce on my doorstep."

"More?" Sage took a seat at the oak table and patted the chair next to her. "What came today?"

Katie slid a K-cup into the slot and pressed the brew button. "Bananas and walnuts."

Sage bounced up and down in her seat. "I love banana nut muffins." She took a twenty-dollar bill out of her purse and pushed it across the table. "Can I swing by in the morning and pick some up?"

Once she had her coffee, Katie took a seat next to Sage, but ignored the money and hummed at her first sip. "I'll deliver if you make me a cup of coffee. I need to get one of these machines for the bakery."

"Forget the Keurig. Go for an espresso machine."

"An espresso machine is the dream." She pointed to the pot on the counter. "For now, that's the reality."

Sage pushed the money closer to her friend. "This will get you closer to the dream."

Katie stared at the twenty as if warring with herself, but she must have known Sage would insist, so she picked it up and tucked it into the front pocket of her jeans.

"What about you? How are your first guests faring?"

Her cheeks heated. "Oh my God. They haven't stopped having sex. Even Otis climbed under the blanket around three in the morning to muffle the noise."

"Shut up. Really?" She stared out the window. "I can't remember a time when I had sex with a guy and wanted a repeat, nonetheless a marathon."

"That bad?" Sage thought back to her relationship with Todd. It's not that the sex was bad, but to call it *good* overstated his skill. There were certainly no *Oh Gods* or *Yeses*. Just sex. No foreplay. No cuddling. In hindsight, she realized that Todd took, and like her sister said, she always gave.

"Can't say it was good."

"You'll have to change that. What about the sheriff?" She waggled her brows. "He likes your muffins."

"And he's willing to pay for them, but he's not my type. First, he's too old. He's, like, forty. Second, I have a type."

Sage looked at Katie. Her hair was styled, and her makeup perfect. Her clothes were conservative, sweet, and expensive. She guessed her type to be trust-fund baby or banker.

"Not sure if you'll find the pretty boys here in Aspen Cove."

Katie took a sip of coffee and laughed so hard, it dripped from the corners of her mouth. She rushed for a napkin to clean up the mess running down her chin. "You are so far off the mark. I like mine damaged, dark, and brooding. The kind of man that looks like he'll murder you in your sleep, but in reality, he's got you wrapped in his arms for protection."

"I didn't take you for the caveman type." Sage snatched a muffin from the box. She brought it to her nose and smiled. She imagined Bea serving muffins on this table to her family.

"Cavemen are hair pullers." She ran her fingers through the perfect hot-ironed curls. "I'd kill a man who messed up my hair."

Sage laughed and remembered her sleeping guests. "You're like Cinderella without her dress, glass slippers, and fairy godmother."

"I'm pretty sure Bea was my fairy godmother. No-go on the slippers; imagine how awful those would have been? I had the dress at my cotillion. Not blue, but white, and it rivaled the beauty of any wedding dress out there."

"They still hold those?"

"Any southern girl worth her salt was drowned in etiquette and lace for that one day she'd be presented to society." Katie's southern accent grew stronger with each word.

"And I thought prom was a big deal."

"I did that, too, but I wore red. My mama nearly fainted and said wearing red was a sin."

"It's going to take me some time to figure you out." Sage stood and got plates from the cupboard.

"Does that mean you're going to stay?"

She shook her head. "I'm not quite there yet, but I'm not packing my bags today." She set the table for the newlyweds and took out the various breakfast options she'd purchased. She arranged the cereal and yogurt and fruit. While she worked, she caught Katie up about the bird and Cannon.

"I think you two would be cute together."

She ignored the comment because while she found Cannon

Bishop to be cute, he was cantankerous at the same time. That wasn't necessarily a good mix.

When the banging began, they looked toward the guest hallway. The newlyweds were awake.

"And so, it begins." Sage covered her face with her hands.

"On that note, I should go. Besides, the sheriff will be waiting at the bakery at eight."

"Do you think he's the one bringing the supplies?" She walked Katie to the door.

"I don't know. That's another mystery I'd like to solve."

Sage stood at the door and watched her friend drive away.

She dressed, picked up the shoebox, fed Otis, and retreated to the deck. She opened the lid carefully, looking in on the bird. It cowered in the corner until she filled its bowl with seeds and creamed worms. With the lid open, she set it on the handrail to catch some fresh air and sun. When it was strong enough, she hoped it would take flight.

Off to the left, a deer leaned down to the water to take a drink. He was a young buck with a small rack of antlers and the most beautiful sight Sage had ever seen. Otis growled, and she shushed him. The deer lifted its head but didn't bolt. He watched her for several seconds, then bent to drink more.

Otis got to his feet and wagged his tail.

"Good morning," Mr. Morello said.

"Here." Sage rose from the adirondack chair. "Have the deck to yourselves." She closed the lid on the bird and called Otis to follow her.

"No, it's okay, we're just grabbing a bite to eat and then taking a walk around the lake."

Sage looked past him to his wife. With all the action they had, it was a wonder she could move.

"We didn't keep you up, did we?" A blush covered the young woman's cheeks.

It took everything in Sage not to roll her eyes or make a sound. "No, Otis and I hung out with a friend, so we weren't around."

"Oh, good." She bit into one of the muffins and moaned. "These are amazing. Did you make them?"

"No, the bakery in town delivered them." The couple took over Sage's space on the deck when she moved into the house. "Have a good time on your walk."

As soon as they left the house, she entered their room to make their bed. As a nurse, she'd been around a lot of body fluids, but something about touching the sheets made her skin crawl. Instead of making the bed, she stripped it and tossed the sheets into the washer. She started a whites cycle with hot water and extra soap, then remade the bed with fresh linens before she raced to the bathroom and climbed into the shower to clean herself.

With everything back in order, she climbed under the covers of her bed for a long nap.

The headboard banging woke her. She'd slept long enough for the sun to set. Not wanting to endure multiple rounds of newlywed bliss, she dressed and took Otis to the bar.

ABOUT A DOZEN PEOPLE were inside when she arrived. She recognized a few from Bea's funeral. She walked her dog to the end of the bar, where she took the stool, and Otis curled up in a ball at her feet.

Cannon put a coaster in front of her. "Beer? Wine?"

Another glass of wine would make her stomach turn and her head ache. She drank too much last night, but carbonation called to her. "I'd love a beer."

The clank of pool balls grabbed her attention. A group of rough-looking men circled the table, and Sage considered Katie.

"Glad you made it. Get any sleep?" He lifted one brow.

"Some. I took a nap after they left."

Cannon set the dark beer in front of her. It didn't go unnoticed that he remembered what she drank the last time she sat on the same barstool. It seemed like a lifetime ago, but it hadn't even been a week. "Since you're here, I'll assume they're back at it." He slid a bowl of bar mix toward her.

"That's not the only reason I came. I know the bartender, and he pulls a wicked beer."

When Cannon smiled, he lit up the room. Sage understood why the girl at the liquor mart seemed disappointed. She'd probably seen that smile a time or two, and like peanut M&M's or Skittles, it was addictive. A few here and there were never enough.

He leaned over the bar, and Sage thought he'd touch her—or give her another brush of his lips against her hair. Instead, he looked down at her dog. "Hey, Otis, don't eat Mike, okay?" He shoved back and walked down to the other end of the bar, leaving her alone.

Sage shot off a quick text to Katie, telling her to come over and have a beer.

Five minutes later, Katie walked in and turned every head at the pool table. It seemed that opposites did attract.

"Oh my." She took the stool next to Sage. "There's quite a selection tonight."

The comment surprised her. "You've been here before?"

Katie lifted her shoulders. "I live across the street." She pointed to the man who looked like a criminal, minus the cuffs. "That's Dalton. You met him at the funeral. He's a cook at the diner."

"He looks right up your alley."

"Not really. He's a big teddy bear."

"He's *exactly* your type. Big, burly, and dangerous-looking." Sage sipped her beer.

"You'd think, but I'll know when I see the one, and he's not the one." Katie perused around the room. "That young one over there is Mark, and he's the deputy sheriff."

Sage remembered meeting most of the people in the bar except the men around the pool table.

"Those are Dalton's biker friends," Katie said as if knowing where Sage's mind went.

Someone dropped a coin into the jukebox, and a song began to play.

"Oh, I love this song." Katie pulled the mug from Sage's hand and dragged her to the one place in the room with space to move. "Dance with me."

"I don't really—"

"You do tonight."

She moved to the upbeat tempo, and Sage found herself getting lost in the moment. When she looked at the bar, she found Cannon staring at her. It wasn't the stare of a bar owner making sure his patrons were okay, but the look of an interested man, and a rush of heat flooded through her.

"You like him, don't you?" Katie followed Sage's eyes.

"He has his moments."

"Then what are you doing over here with me? Get going, you." Katie walked to the pool table and left Sage on her own.

Back at the bar, Otis no longer lay curled on the floor. Her heart beat fast in a panicked rhythm. "Otis." She bent over, looking under tables.

"He's okay, he's right here." Cannon pointed to the floor in front of him.

Being height-challenged, Sage climbed onto the bar to see. "How did that happen?" In the corner lay Otis, curled around Mike. The two slept perfectly as if they'd been raised together.

"They say opposites attract."

"If that's possible," she nodded toward the animals, "I'm bringing the bird here tomorrow." It was only a joke, but if Cannon's dark look was any indication, he didn't find her comment humorous.

"You should give Aspen Cove a try." Did she hear a hint of hope in his voice?

"It was a joke. I told you I'd stay until the bird healed."

"What happens after?"

Her gut twisted. She didn't have a plan. "I don't know. I'm taking it one day at a time."

"Fair enough." The shadow of disappointment disappeared. "Katie seems to be settling in okay."

She looked at the woman, who was crying into the sleeve of her sweater just a few days ago. Gone were the tears, and in their place, optimism and promise filled her bright blue eyes. In her hand was the microphone. It was karaoke night, and Katie was the entertainment.

"She makes a mean muffin," Sage said, thinking about the morning delivery. "Any idea of who's leaving supplies on her doorstep?"

"I imagine it could be anyone who received a pink envelope. Just because Bea died, doesn't mean her generosity did."

"So, the pink envelopes, they weren't necessarily for the people who received them?" she fished for answers.

"You tell me. Was your pink envelope for you?"

CHAPTER TWENTY-TWO

Sage returned home from the bar but didn't bother taking off her jacket. She walked in the front door, heard the newlyweds, and steered Otis to the kitchen. With pockets full of Milk-Bones and a thermos filled with coffee, she took her seat by the water.

Crisp air filled her lungs while the crickets sang. A mural of stars hung in the crystal, clear sky. Otis sat dutifully at her feet, not because he was well behaved, but because he loved treats. She hoped the couple would tire out early tonight. It was past nine, and she didn't want to spend another evening like the one before. Then again, last night was pleasant—more than pleasant, if she were honest with herself.

That was the problem, Sage, although honest with others, often told herself the biggest lies. Her relationship with Todd was a doozy. In hindsight, they were no more than roommates who had sex together. They shared an apartment, an occupation, and their bodies. She found him on the bulletin board at work, looking for a roomie, and everything happened rather quickly. She wanted it to be more, but she should have known it never would be. Todd looked after Todd, and Sage looked after Todd. It was a good deal for Todd.

When her pockets were empty, Otis trolled the beach for something else. He came back with a stick, and for the next half hour, they played fetch until he tired and collapsed at her feet.

She looked across the lake, who lived in the lit-up houses? Were they happy? Did they have full lives, or were they like her, still looking for that one thing that would change their existence?

Otis's deep, low growl stopped all thoughts about her past life and set her focus on this one. "What is it, boy?"

Low and halting, he snarled into the blackness of the night.

Sage hadn't thought much about dangerous wildlife. She'd seen birds and a rabbit or two scurry from bush to bush. There was the beautiful buck, but she hadn't considered anything menacing. How stupid could she get? She was in the mountains, and with that came predators like bears, mountain lions, and wolves.

Moving slowly, she reached for the thermos. It was as close to a weapon as she could get. Otis rose up on all threes, and Sage's heart exploded inside her chest. There was no way she'd be supper for a beast. Movement on her left had her brandishing the thermos like a bat and swinging into the darkness to connect with nothing.

Instead of a hungry bear or lion was the shadow of a man on Cannon's dock. His clothes flew through the air. Was that Ben? There was no time to speculate because the thin pale body disappeared with a splash into the freezing water. Then nothing. No paddling. No movement. Only silence.

Trained to react, she ran toward the end of the dock. With only a sliver of a moon, it was difficult to see anything. She scanned the surface for any disturbance and then saw the rise of a few bubbles. Without thinking, she kicked off her shoes and dove into the cold water. If it was Ben Bishop, and she could help him, he would not die tonight.

Frigid water wrapped around her, its iciness so intense, it burned. She searched, arms reaching through the dark to find the body. She couldn't get a full breath, but she dove below the murky surface anyway. The cold and lack of visibility made her task impossible. Up for air, she stilled and listened. Her muscles atrophied and lungs ached, but she didn't give up. To her left, a body broke the surface, coughing and sputtering for its next breath.

"I'm here." She reached him in three strokes. "Don't fight me, Ben. I'm not in the mood for you tonight." Her right arm wrapped around his chest. She used the lifeguard training Grandma Dotty had insisted on when she was a teen.

It took her five minutes to get him to shore, another two to get him pulled out of the water. She collapsed on her bottom and took the underwear-clad man into her arms.

"I couldn't do it," he cried. "I was so close to finally being with Carly."

On the muddy bank, she put her arms around Ben and listened while he cried. Despite the crisp air, it was warmer outside than it was in the water. Steam rose from their bodies.

Otis did his share by sidling up next to her, but within minutes she was shaking uncontrollably with her teeth chattering so much, her jaw hurt.

"Ben, I n-n-need to g-g-get you inside. You're g-g-going to g-g-get hypothermia."

He tried to shrug her off, but she held him tighter. "Just leave me here and let me die."

"I won't." She planted her heels into the mud and inched them back. "You need to help me."

"Just let me go." Ben curled into a ball and sobbed.

"I can't." She struggled out of her wet coat and wrapped it around him. It was only a matter of time before they'd both be in trouble. She thought about letting him go long enough to grab blankets but feared he'd enter the water again, and she'd never be able to save him twice.

Instead, she pulled Otis closer and soaked in the body heat he offered.

Despite Ben's dip in the lake, he smelled like a distillery. She rocked him back and forth while she listened to him cry about losing the love of his life.

It occurred to her that Aspen Cove was a town of sad people, and maybe that was why Bea thought she'd fit in. Deep sorrow was etched into every one of Sage's cells. It was bad enough to carry it around; she didn't want to be surrounded by it. No, that was another reason Sage couldn't stay. Monday, when she went to pay her debt to Doc, she'd ask him to put the property up for sale.

"What the hell?" Cannon raced to the spot where the water lapped at his father's bare feet.

"Thank G-god. I couldn't get him to m-move inside. I can't c-carry him." She looked down at Ben, who had passed out in her lap. "He's out, b-but he's f-f-freezing."

Cannon bent over and lifted his father like he weighed nothing, then looked at her. "Can you walk?"

"Yes." Every muscle in her body screamed *no*, but she pulled herself to standing, and she and Otis followed Cannon into his house.

He nodded toward a pellet stove. "Go stand in front of the stove, and I'll be right back."

She held her hands forward and soaked in the heat that rose from the cast-iron box. Bea's house had central heat and a fireplace. Cannon's used wood pellets. That's where the smell of burning wood came from each night. Mystery solved.

In-between shudders, she took in the house. Clean and tidy, it reminded her of the bed and breakfast. The furniture was old but sturdy. Bookshelves lined one wall. Interspersed with books were whittled wooden animals. She searched for photos, but there were none.

The room was warm, but not in the cozy family way, and she imagined everything that had reminded Ben of his wife was gone.

"Sorry about that." Cannon walked into the room with an arm full of dry clothes. "Put these on."

"I can go home and change." She inched closer to the stove, trying to get more warmth before she had to venture outside. Otis had found a chair he liked and was curled up and looking comfy. "Is your dad okay?"

Cannon laughed in an in-need-of-a-strait-jacket way. "No, he's not okay. Did he try to drown himself again?"

"Yes, I was sitting outside because ... well ... you know, and he took a dip in the lake." She stared at the clothes he'd set on the chair closest to her. "He needs help, Cannon. You can't ignore him."

He shook his head. "Get changed and meet me in the kitchen." He didn't wait for her to answer; instead, he walked away.

Water puddled on the wood floor at her feet. More cold than shy, she stripped off her clothes and tugged on the pair of sweatpants that would fit four of her. Thank God for drawstrings. She snugged the waist as tight as she could and rolled the legs up a foot. The soft cotton T-shirt reminded her of Cannon and their drive to Copper Creek—it smelled of pine and fresh air or possibly dryer sheets. She wasn't sure because her nose was only starting to thaw. She gathered her wet clothes and brought them into the kitchen to place in the sink.

At the table, Cannon sat with his head in his hands. There were two steaming cups of coffee in front of him.

The chair squeaked when she sat, and he lifted his head to look at her. "Are you getting warm?"

Wrapping her hands around the hot mug, she nodded. "Yes, I'll be fine." She tucked her cold feet under the chair and regretted rolling up the sweatpants. "Is your dad in warm clothes?"

"Yes, he's in bed, in dry clothes, and asleep. He's in better shape than you."

Giving up the battle, she bent over to unroll the sweat pants and cover her feet.

"Let me get you some socks." He stood, but she shook her head.

"No need, I'm okay."

He sat back down and patted his lap. "Then give me your feet."

It was a directive, not a suggestion, and Sage was too tired to argue. She scooted her chair closer and placed her nearly blue feet into his lap. Strong hands rubbed warmth into her toes. "Thank you. That feels so good."

"Thank you for being there for him, but it's a wasted effort." He lifted his hand from her feet and rubbed it across the neatly trimmed beard that framed his face.

"Helping those you love is never a waste." The clipped tone of her voice surprised her. Ben could be a pain, but she'd never consider him a waste.

Cannon continued to rub life back into her toes. "Have you ever loved someone who doesn't love you enough to stay?"

His question hit her like an ax to the stomach. Somewhere deep inside, she believed if her parents or grandmother had loved her enough, they would have fought harder to survive. It was a ridiculous expectation, but the child inside her was hard to convince.

She pulled her feet from his lap and lowered them to the ground. Instead of a puddle of water surrounding them, she now had a pool of fleece. "I've loved someone enough that I wanted them to stay."

His eyes latched on to hers. Did he see her pain? She saw his from the roll of his shoulders to the creases on his forehead. Moving her chair closer, she reached out to hold his hands.

"Tell me about your mother."

She expected him to shake his head and refuse. He had a tightened-down, buttoned-up persona, and she was certain he didn't talk much to anyone. Cannon wasn't the kind of man who tore open his wounds and let them bleed in public. Rather than silence himself, he lowered his head and spoke.

"She was perfect. Not because I'm her son, but because she was truly perfect. She was a school teacher in Copper Creek, who taught second grade. The day she died, Dad was supposed to do the liquor run, but he got sick. He'd been in bed with bronchitis, so Mom turned around after a full day of work and went back to town. My brother, Bowie, and his fiancée, Brandy, took the drive with her."

"Oh no, your dad feels responsible." There were two things that made her want to cry. The knowledge that Ben felt like it was his fault and the fact that the Brandy Cannon spoke of had to be Bea's daughter.

"Yes, but he's not the only one. Bowie wasn't well either, so he slept in the back seat. A spring storm arrived with a mixture of rain and snow that covered the ground. Mom hit a slick patch, and that was it. Her car went over the edge at the only place where the drop off went into the lake. Mom and Bea's daughter died, and Bowie was the only survivor. He tried to save them, but he couldn't."

She inched her chair closer and leaned and rested against his chest. "I'm so sorry. That was an awful tragedy. What happened to your brother?"

"I was living in Los Angeles, so I came home. We buried Brandy and my mother several days after the accident, and the next day, Bowie enlisted in the army. He hasn't been back in town since. My father was a mess, and I couldn't abandon him, so I had to stay."

His arm wrapped around her, and she left her chair to crawl into his lap. Was it to comfort him or herself? She couldn't say. "I'm so sorry for your loss."

His hands threaded through her now damp hair. "I lost everything that week. My mom died. My brother left. My father fell into a bottle of vodka."

She lifted her head from his chest. "Have you tried rehab?"

Every muscle froze beneath her. "You don't think I've tried everything? I'm holding on to the bar and the house by a thread. I've sold everything I can to pay for two stints in rehab. He comes home sober and goes back to the bottle within a couple of weeks." He cupped her face with his hands. "I know you mean well. You're an amazing woman, and I can see you have an endless supply of love and compassion, but me ... I can't afford to care anymore."

She pulled him toward her and whispered against his lips, "I'll care for both of us."

Her mouth brushed against his ever so slightly. It was a tentative kiss that quickly turned desperate. Mouth against mouth, tongue against tongue, body against body, they clung to each other. Sage needed to be needed, and she imagined Cannon needed to be loved.

CHAPTER TWENTY-THREE

Cannon never felt anything as comforting as the kiss Sage gave him. At first, he was surprised by the tenderness. Here she was, sitting in his lap, dressed in clothes he could wrap around her twice. She almost froze to death saving his father, and now she was saving him. Did she know how much her care and consideration meant to him?

He was like a love-starved man. Not because women didn't find him attractive, but because he never wanted to open his heart to any of them. There was too much risk in exposing his soul and letting himself be vulnerable. Giving another the power to hurt him was unwise.

When his hands threaded through her hair and he deepened the kiss, he fed the ache in his heart—the one that had chewed at his insides for years and hollowed him out. The longer the kiss lasted, the less empty he felt.

He soaked in the sense of being connected to something—to someone—to her. He took what she gave him and let it warm him through and through. Though her body was chilled to the touch, the heat of the kiss spread through him from limb to limb. He wanted this moment—a brief respite from his everyday existence—a second where he could kiss a woman and experience the bliss of it. He could take advantage of the closeness, but he wouldn't because the kiss was simply too small of a Band-Aid for the size of his wound.

Immersed in her, he wanted to stay lip to lip, chest to chest, tongue to tongue, forever. He wanted the kiss more than he'd like to admit. It was a perfect moment shared by two. His heart held on to the lie that she was his. The truth continued outside this bubble, and Sage would leave, and he'd be alone—again.

Pulling away from her was like fighting the force of a magnet. He wanted her since that first day he saw her on the sidewalk, but he couldn't expect her to be the panacea for all his problems. "I'm sorry. That shouldn't have happened." He hated the look on her face. The downturn of her pink lips and the question in her eyes.

She cupped his cheek. "Maybe not, but it did, and I don't regret the kiss. It was something we both needed."

"But I don't want this." He lifted her and set her in her chair. The hurt etched on her face made his stomach churn. Was he lying to himself or to her? Probably both. He wanted her badly but knew that if he opened his heart, she'd only leave and take it with her. He had so little left of himself that he couldn't afford to take the chance.

CHAPTER TWENTY-FOUR

Two days later, her knuckles hit the front door with the strength she didn't feel inside. It was a risk both to her person and her ego to stand on Cannon's front porch and wait. Normally not one to step out of her comfort zone, she looked at her car and considered bailing on her mission if her first try wasn't answered.

Who was she kidding? She couldn't quit because that kiss two nights ago changed everything. It made her realize life was less without the touch of another human. By keeping herself safe, she remained lonely, and she wanted more, but Cannon would never be able to offer her anything if the burdens in his life continued to shut him down.

When he said he didn't want this, he lied. Like her, he was protecting himself. She had felt his passion and his burgeoning want pressed against her body. The taste of desire dripped like honey from his lips while his heart pounded so hard it reverberated in her chest.

Cannon was just like her—a liar.

How many times had she deceived herself to make life palatable?

Damaged. Tortured. Those two words she used to describe the man who was as fabulous as he was frustrating.

Her grandma once told her not to judge a man until she'd walked a mile in his shoes. After seeing what Cannon went through on a daily basis, she felt the need to help.

Once he'd driven away this morning, she hurried over, hopeful she'd find Ben at home. She lifted her hand and knocked again, this time hard enough to bruise her knuckles. Moments later, there was a shuffle of feet beyond the door.

Small in stature, she didn't send a rush of fear through anyone. Most times, her mean face made people laugh. She was as scary as a guard dog in a tutu. Despite her less than intimidating appearance, she squared her shoulders and pulled herself as tall as her five-foot, two-inch frame would allow.

Dressed in navy-blue scrubs, she listened to the old man on the other side of the door cuss and complain about the noise.

Ben flung the door open and stood before her, looking like a homeless man in soiled jeans and a torn T-shirt.

"What do you want?" he snapped.

She breezed past him. "Good morning, Ben." A thread of fear raced down her spine. She no longer sported two black eyes, but she'd never forget what they felt like. The bruising was now a faint greenish yellow that she did her best to conceal. Too bad there wasn't something a frightened girl could apply to ease her anxiety or cover her fear.

"What are you doing?" He slammed the door and followed her into the kitchen.

"I'm here to pick you up." Her time in Aspen Cove hadn't been a complete waste. She learned the fine art of manipulation from Doc Parker. He'd helped her out, and she owed him, and now the same was true for Ben.

"Pick me up for what? I'm not going to rehab again."

She opened the cupboards to find a coffee cup. Her first challenge was to get him drinking coffee instead of vodka. "No rehab for you. You owe me."

"I owe you?" His breath floated through the air like a green cloud, the smell putrid and ripe. The last time something so foul touched her nostrils was when Lydia put her egg salad sandwich in a drawer instead of the refrigerator. It took Sage three days to find the offending odor. She couldn't be upset, though, because Lydia had pulled a thirty-hour shift.

The roiling in her gut forced her to breathe through her mouth. She popped a K-cup into the coffee maker and pressed brew. Leaning over the cup to smell the ground coffee beans, she inhaled deeply.

"Yes, sir. You owe me because I saved your life. The way I see it, you stole time from me with your antics. My time is valuable."

When the pot stopped spitting coffee into the cup, she passed it to Ben. "Drink." The tone she used was reminiscent of Cannon's when he told her to put her feet in his lap.

A victorious smile fought to break loose when he brought the cup to his mouth. He swallowed and shivered from his silver-gray hair to his bare feet.

"I didn't ask for your help."

Emboldened, she pulled out a chair and pointed to it, and to her surprise, he sat.

"No, you did not, but it doesn't matter to me. I spent yesterday calculating the value of my time and effort. A life saved is worth something, and you will pay me back." The reality was, she spent yesterday reliving the kiss and figuring out how to get more of them. She also sanitized the hell out of the newlyweds' room.

"What do you want from me?"

On top of the bowl of fruit was a banana that matched the hue of Ben's skin. She pulled back the peel and pressed it into his free hand. "Eat."

"If I eat this, you'll leave?" He lifted his bushy brows to where they nearly touched his shaggy bangs.

"You're not getting off that easy, mister. You broke my nose, and you hurt my feelings. Besides almost making me freeze to death, you've turned into a real pain in my keister. Many would turn their back on you, but not me." She laughed. "I'm told I have a savior complex, and you're my next project."

"Bullshit. I'm no one's project." He took a bite of the banana and drank more coffee.

She said a silent thank you to the universe. She'd been with Ben for ten minutes, and despite his bad breath and surly disposition, she was still in one piece. There was also the coffee and banana being consumed, and that was a victory in her book. "If I owe Doc an entire day for the half hour he spent fixing my nose, you owe me more. By my calculations, I'd say it's at least a few days of labor."

His jaw dropped, and she got a good look at his half-chewed breakfast. "I've got plans today."

"Yep, you do. Get in the shower, Ben, because we're leaving in fifteen minutes."

He shoved the rest of the banana into his mouth and downed the remaining coffee before he left her alone in the kitchen.

Ben's problem wasn't that he wanted to die, it was that he didn't have a reason to live. One would think that two sons were enough, but with some people, family didn't count.

Yesterday, while she licked her wounds after being rebuffed, she considered the needs of the town as it pertained to the individuals. Doc needed her help today. She owed him, so she'd help. Ben needed more help than anyone could offer, but he could help Katie, and maybe in helping her, he'd help himself.

When he walked back into the kitchen, he appeared a cleaner version of his drunken self. With shaking hands, he reached under the sink and grabbed a bottle of glass cleaner, except it wasn't a bottle of cleaner. Her first clue? It was clear. Her second—Ben twisted off the cap and took a drink.

"What are you doing?" She swiped the bottle from him and gave it a good sniff. "Really, Ben? In the cleaning supplies?"

He shrugged. "I can't do anything if my body shakes from detox."

Sage hadn't considered his alcoholism. A man didn't become sober overnight after years of inebriation. She paced back and forth while her eyes focused on the bottle. She needed to find a way to move him from stumbling drunk to regular drunk to not a drunk.

"How much can you drink and still function?"

Ben chuckled. "I always function."

"Geez, Ben, I need you to be able to follow directions. How many drinks do you need to keep the shakes away?"

"One an hour." His answer came too quick, to be honest.

"You'll get one every three." Sage grabbed the bottle from the counter and pushed past him. "Let's go. You're needed at the bakery, and I'm needed at the clinic."

Otis waited in the front seat, his tail waggling with exuberance when he saw her.

Once Ben was seated, she pulled her SUV out of the driveway and headed into town.

"Why's the mutt in the front, and I'm in the back?" Ben leaned between the seats to look at Otis.

"He's earned his place, and you haven't. Listen, Ben, I get that you're hurting, but let's put those emotions to work someplace more positive."

"Did Cannon put you up to this?"

She shook her head. "Absolutely not. This is about what you owe me. As for Cannon, you'll have to figure out how to repay him, and from what I've seen, it's a huge debt." She looked at him in the rearview mirror. There was no bow of his head or look of regret. The only sign he'd heard her was a grim thin line of his lips.

"I'm only here because you've got my stash held hostage, and I'm working to ransom it."

"The reason doesn't matter." At least Ben wasn't drowning himself inside a bottle today, or the lake for that matter.

Last night, she'd called Katie and asked for help. This whole give-and-take was an odd concept for Sage. She'd never been one to ask for anything, but there was a good lesson to be learned in the process. By asking others for help, she gave them purpose.

She pulled in front of the bakery and had fifteen minutes to get

Ben settled and get herself to the clinic.

The smell of muffins seeped through the crack in the door. The display case was filled with today's special. Sage closed her eyes and tried to figure out what it was. Spices and sweetness filled the air, but she couldn't begin to guess. There was no doubt the right ingredients had arrived just in time.

Ben opened the car door and stood in the street, looking ready to bolt.

"Let's go, Ben." She held up the bottle of vodka and shook it, and the liquid sloshed back and forth.

He grumbled something unintelligible but followed her into the shop. On the counter sat a tray of samples, and Sage plucked two from the plate. She popped one into her mouth and one into Ben's.

They both hummed in unison.

"What do you think?" Katie appeared from the back room, wiping her wet hands on her apron. She took in Ben and smiled.

He frowned.

Sage tried to see him through Katie's eyes. He was thin and had a sickly pallor to his skin. This wasn't a quick fix, but a long journey. At least he was showered and on two feet. She knew the measurement of success for Ben would have to be celebrated breath by shaky breath.

She ignored his scowl and looked at the tented card in the display case that read "Carrot Cake." "They're amazing." She stood aside. "This is Ben. Put him to work. You know the drill."

Sage looked at Ben. She tucked his drink of choice into her purse. "I'll be back at noon to dose you."

She hated to saddle Katie with him, but the woman's excitement at being able to help lessened the guilt.

What was it that she was told when she arrived in town? *Aspen Cove takes care of its own.* That seemed to apply to everyone but Ben. Wasn't it time someone took care of him?

She grabbed another muffin bite and walked out the door. Once she freed Otis, they walked across the street to pay her debt for caring for the bird. No good deed went unpunished.

CHAPTER TWENTY-FIVE

Two giggling boys ran past Sage. She caught one by the hoodie before he could knock over the cardboard Pepto Bismol display sign.

"Thank you." Louise Williams waddled from the back room to the boys, who both had mastered the repentant look with their downcast eyes and pouty lips.

"Go sit down." She pointed toward the clinic door where a row of seats lined the wall.

Disobedience looked like it was only a second away. The boys took in Otis, and Sage could tell they were warring with themselves. Did they mind their mother or rush to the dog?

Wanting to save Louise the trouble of a punishment, Sage said, "Go sit down, and I'll bring Otis over to say hello."

Light shined in their expressions as they ran off to the hallway that led to the exam room.

"Thanks, they're good boys, but they're a handful." She set her hands on her big belly. It was like a tabletop. Set a plate of spaghetti on it, and all Louise would have to do is scoop it into her mouth. She put her hand to her own stomach and wondered if she'd ever know the joys of motherhood.

"How far along are you?" Otis followed her to the hallway, where six eager Williamses sat like angels.

"I'm almost fully cooked. Another few weeks should do it." Louise walked past the kids and took the empty seat at the end.

Sage looked at each child as she passed. They were all brown haired and brown eyed. She could tell by the way most of them rocked and fidgeted in their seats, they were barely controlling themselves. "You've got quite a collection. I don't know how you do it." There were a lot of Williamses present, but they were all healthy looking and clean—well cared for.

Otis's tail thumped impatiently on the floor. He was ready for the attention of six little hooligans, but he knew better than to take off. Sage hadn't trained him in this way. Maybe it was his missing leg that tempered his reactions.

She knew little about how he'd lost it, except that he'd been hit by a car and abandoned by his family.

"Is it okay if I introduce Otis to the kids?" His tail's pace and power increased; a *thump thump thump* filled the air. Little bodies moved like unearthed worms in the chairs.

"They'd love to pet your dog."

Sage held up her hand, which was Otis's cue to lie down. He flopped in the center of the hallway and rolled to his back.

"Okay, one at a time." The kids sat in order from tallest to smallest. "We'll start with the little guy here." Sage pointed to the youngest Williams, who couldn't have been more than eighteen months or so. His barely bigger sister let him loose, and he toddled to the dog.

"That's David," Louise said. She went down the line of children as they each rose for their turn. There was Jill, Melissa, Thomas, Eric, and Brian. Otis was happy to be a recipient of their sticky hands and sloppy kisses. That was the wonderful thing about dogs. To them, love was love, and it didn't matter the package it came in.

"Are you going to dawdle all day or earn your keep?" a gruff voice came from behind.

Sage smiled, knowing that Doc Parker hid behind his grumpy-old-man persona, but was a big softie.

"I'm coming. I'm offering that warm, thoughtful part of medical care you must have forgotten years ago."

"No dogs in the clinic." His eyes narrowed in on Otis.

Louise piped in, "He's not a dog; he's the sitter."

Doc shook his head, and with spread fingers, he rubbed his eyebrows, making the white tufts stand up. "In that case, he can stay."

"You're up, Louise."

She struggled to stand, and Doc offered her a hand.

She turned to her children while Sage looked at Otis, and they both said, "Stay," at the same time.

Louise smiled. "Raising dogs and kids are similar."

Sage laughed. "It would seem." She glanced at Doc. "I can hold the fort down out here if you want."

"I'm not paying you to babysit."

"You're not paying me at all." She rose to her feet and followed him into the exam room.

"You owe *me* time, not her." He pivoted toward Louise. "If you want to hire Sage, do it on your time, not mine."

Not afraid of the Doc's salty demeanor, Louise fired back, "It's either a lack of coffee or sex?" The big woman looked at the mug in Doc's hand and laughed. "You need more sex."

Doc patted the exam table and helped her up. "You need less. Now let's see how this little girl is doing."

While Doc thumbed through her file, Sage asked her a few questions, then took her vitals and checked her ankles for swelling.

"You trying to take my job?" He handed her the patient file to record Louise's numbers.

Feeling comfortable enough to tease the old goat, she fired back, "You could always turn back to real estate." She pulled out the table and helped Louise lie down and realized how easy it was to work next to Doc Parker, even though he tried to pretend he was disagreeable and cantankerous.

"It's a good thing you decided to stay. Even if you wanted to sell, it could take years to offload that property."

"Really?" She was surprised because it was a lovely house on a lake.

"It takes a certain kind of person to live in a small town." He palpated his patient's stomach. "Hell, Bobby and Louise might populate Aspen Cove by themselves."

Sage was surprised when Louise reached up and cuffed Doc lightly on the side of the head.

"I left a message for a developer, but he never called back or stopped by," Sage said.

Doc ignored her. "Everything looks good, Louise. You could go anytime now." He talked to her like she was an active volcano ready to erupt. "Get the first kid ready for their shots." He helped her down while Sage wiped the table and prepared for the children.

Doc set out a tray of syringes.

"You know," he said, "it would be a crime to sell that property to a developer. They'd turn Aspen Cove into something it's not. Probably push the locals out to make room for hotels and tourist shit like Starbucks."

She tilted her head. It was something to think about. She didn't want people like Louise and Doc to have their lives turned upside down, but on the other hand, a Starbucks seemed reasonable.

Doc gave each of the Williams kids a shot. As soon as they opened their mouths to cry, he popped in a Life Saver and sent them out to have Otis lick the tears from their faces.

By the time they'd run through the family, it was lunchtime.

Sage walked over to the bakery with her bag in hand and Otis by her side. Before she could open the door, she found Cannon walking up the sidewalk. Last time he approached her in this location, he was coming at her like a runaway freight train. Today, he warmed her with a smile.

CHAPTER TWENTY-SIX

Cannon stepped out of his truck and saw Sage walking to the bakery. Like a bug to a light, he found himself heading in her direction. Stopping in front of her, he looked at her navy-blue scrubs. "The old coot was serious and put you to work." He leaned down and petted Otis, who was happy to give him a lick.

"It seems to be a thing in this town." She tugged him up from his crouch and threaded her arm through his. At the corner of the shop, they peeked through the window.

He didn't know what she wanted him to look at, but what he saw was his father pulling down the old wallpaper next to the display case. Dad's hands shook like he was suffering from withdrawal, but he pulled and tore at the stubborn striped paper without regard to his unsteady grip.

"What the hell?" Cannon's eyes grew big, and his mouth dropped open when he turned toward her.

She lifted her shoulders in an it's-not-a-big-deal gesture. "He owes me for saving him."

"And he agreed?" He walked her to the next shop, so they were out of sight. If she got his father out of the house and working, he didn't want to interrupt the progress.

A sly smile lifted her plump pink lips. Lips he wanted to kiss again but was too afraid where that might lead.

"He didn't have much choice. I walked over after you left this morning." She looked up at him with a look that squeezed his heart and groin.

"He could have ..." Cannon shuddered at the thought of his father hitting her again. He would never hit a woman intentionally, but the booze clouded his judgment. "I should have been there, just in case. That was risky."

She placed her hand on his chest, and his heart rate kicked into overdrive.

"Some risks are worth taking." She peeked around the brick pillar that divided the shops to watch his dad again. "Besides, you seemed to be avoiding me after that kiss."

"About that. It was ..." What did he tell her? It was the best kiss of his life? That he wanted to spend the rest of the day with her on his lap and his lips pressed to her delicious mouth?

"I get it. You don't like my kisses."

"That's bull, and you know it. You felt how much I liked your kisses." He tugged her back to stand in front of him. His hands came up to cup her cheeks. "I loved your kisses, but I think you can do better than me."

She laughed. "If you're talking about career aspirations, portfolios, and stuff like that, then I have done better than you. To be honest, better isn't always the best. Sometimes the value of a good kiss is priceless if it makes your heart sing." She walked her fingers up his chest until her index finger rested on his lower lip. "You, Cannon Bishop, make my heart sing." She let her hand fall and pushed against his chest. Before she turned to walk away, she said, "I have to dose your dad before his shakes take over."

He didn't let her take but one step before he spun her around and covered her mouth with his. Her lips were warm, her mouth hot, and getting hotter with each second they touched. She opened, and his tongue sought and found hers. It was over for him because no kiss had ever made *his* heart sing—until now.

Like teenagers, they made out for endless minutes, tucked into the alcove of the bait and tackle store. When Sage pulled away, they were breathless. "I really have to go, or your dad will be in a bad way. How about dinner tonight? My place, six o'clock. You bring the wine. I'll microwave something."

"Are you going to try to woo me with your culinary skills?"

"No, but I'll try not to kill you with my warming up skills. I'll woo you with my kisses." She turned around and strutted through the door of the bakery.

He stood on the sidewalk, smiling like a fool. It had been a long time since he felt light and carefree, but seeing his father doing something other than drink or sleep changed things. Or maybe it was the kiss. He loved and hated the idea that a kiss could have so much influence. Then he reminded himself it wasn't just any kiss. It was the right kiss.

CHAPTER TWENTY-SEVEN

Back at the clinic, Doc walked out of the back room with a half-eaten apple in his hand.

Sage's stomach was full of carrot cake muffins and coffee.

Old man Tucker was up front getting a bottle of Tums.

"You know, old man," Doc said. "If you stopped drinking all that moonshine you make, you wouldn't have an ulcer." Doc tossed his apple core into a nearby trash can and pulled a prescription pad from his pocket. He scribbled something on it before he handed the slip to Tucker.

"Without my 'shine, I'd be mean and crotchety like you, and I'd still have an ulcer. Got it from being married for fifty years to the same damn woman."

Tucker reminded Sage of a lumberjack with his soiled jeans, plaid shirt, and a beard that reached the center of his chest. He crammed the prescription into his pocket and snagged the bottle of Tums from the stand before he walked out.

"He didn't pay for that." She opened the door, ready to pursue.

"Let him be." Doc went to the sign and flipped the switch to off, killing the flashing red light. "Not all things require money."

"Don't tell me you make him come into the clinic and work." She glanced around for Otis, who had taken up a spot staring out the window.

"Nope, he's not an RN like you, but his skills are still important."

"You don't drink his moonshine, do you?"

"No, but I stay warm all year with the wood he chops and delivers. I've got a wood stove upstairs that has a big appetite." Doc walked to the rear of the store and leaned against the counter. "Sometimes, the barter system works better. Bobby Williams fixes my car. Maisey and her son feed me. Abby Garrett raises bees and keeps me in honey and soap. And you ... you have your tradable talents, too." He lowered his head for a second, then raised it with a big smile that pulled at the whiskers on his face. "It would seem that Cannon is bartering for kisses. What are you getting out of it?"

The heat of embarrassment rose to her cheeks. "Were you spying on me?"

Doc dismissed her with a wave of his hand. "Nope, you were on a deserted sidewalk in the middle of town. Hard to miss you sucking face with that boy."

"I'm not bartering anything for kisses." She bristled at the thought of trading something for Cannon's kisses. "Those kisses are free."

"Best kind. Now tell me what you need so I can barter for more clinic hours."

"I still owe you for the bird."

"True. I'll see you Wednesday. By the way, how is the bird?"

"I think its wing is getting better." She fed it that morning and allowed it fresh air. For a moment, she thought it would fly away. It ruffled its feathers and even hopped up to the edge of the shoebox but ultimately settled back into the soft towel. "You sold yourself short. Veterinarian is another cap you could wear."

"Don't be spreading rumors. I don't want the Dawsons calling me to foal their horses. The last thing I need is to have my arm elbow-deep in a horse's ass."

"If you're birthing their horses, you'd be doing it wrong. Baby horses don't come out of their mom's ass." Sage picked up a few candy bars and set them on the counter. "Since I'm staying a bit longer than expected, can you tell me where to transfer my prescription?" She was almost out of her birth control pills, and if things got any hotter with Cannon, she'd need a refill.

"What do you need?" He bagged up her treats and slid them across the counter.

Once again, her cheeks heated. "None of your business."

He opened a drawer under the register and pulled out a box of birth control pills. "By your blush, I imagine it's something like this. Any of these your brand?"

She didn't know how he'd deduced birth control from a blush. "You're impossible." She rummaged through the packages. "Where do you get these?"

"They send me samples every month."

She found the exact type she took and held them up. "Maybe you should be giving these to Louise."

Doc snatched them from her hand and put them into the bag. "Why do you think I get all these samples? I've been trying to get her to take them off my hands for years, but she says she'll have babies until Bobby's peter falls off or her uterus drops to the ground."

"Looks like you're right. The Williamses might populate Aspen Cove on their own."

He raised his bushy brows. "Of course, you could have a few pups and give Louise a run for her money."

"On that note, I'm going home." She walked out with a laugh on her lips and a warm spot in her heart for Doc Parker and a certain sexy bartender who was showing up that night for frozen lasagna and kisses.

"I'VE GOT to go in a minute because he's going to be here soon," Sage told her sister.

"Now that you're dating someone, does that mean you're staying?"

Sage didn't know what her budding relationship with Cannon meant. As for staying, she hadn't decided one way or the other.

"We're not dating, and I'm not committing to anything at this point. I'm keeping my options open." She had been in town for a week, and a lot had happened, but she wasn't ready to sever her ties to Denver. "Any calls from human resources?"

"No. There aren't any positions open except your old one."

Sage released a sigh. "All right. I guess I'll hang around here for a while longer." Three days ago, staying in Aspen Cove felt like a sentence handed down for a crime, but with Doc and Katie and Cannon, it had turned into something different. "You keep telling me to stay. Is that because you don't want me to come back?" There was a tiny part of Sage that wondered if her sister wanted the space between them that Aspen Cove provided.

"No. You can come back tomorrow if you want, but I don't think what you're looking for is in the basement of my house."

Sage centered the flower arrangement she'd taken from the newlyweds' room on the kitchen table. "How do you know what I'm looking for if I don't?"

Lydia let go of a growl that Sage was positive came with an eye roll. "It's what you've always been looking for—a purpose."

Some things people said passed right through without another thought, but Lydia's words resonated with her. She always wanted to be wanted. Needed to be needed. Loved to be loved.

A soft knock sounded at the door. "Got to go."

"Love you, sis. Have fun."

Sage looked at herself in the mirror by the door. Only a faint yellow bruise remained under her right eye; the left was completely healed. She pinched her cheeks to give them a little color.

She agonized over what to wear. A dress seemed like she was trying too hard. Sweatpants yelled, "Not trying at all." She settled on a pair of khaki pants and a pink sweater.

When the second knock came, she opened the door, and in front of her stood Cannon holding a bottle of wine and wearing a smile.

"I didn't think you were going to answer."

She stepped back and let him in.

Otis lifted his head from his chair to see who was there and went back to his nap.

"I was on the phone with my sister."

"How is she?" He handed her the bottle of wine.

Sage wasn't sure what to do. She had been out of the dating game for years. Did she rise up on tiptoes to kiss him? Did she press her body into his for a hug? She opted for neither and led him into the kitchen, where the microwave heated their dinner.

"Busy as usual." She set the bottle on the table and handed the corkscrew to him. "Can you open it?"

He went to work on the cork while she removed their dinner from the microwave.

"Does she miss you?"

That was a good question. There was no doubt that Lydia missed her, but she wasn't selfish that way. They'd taken care of each other since they were kids. Lydia had Sage's interests at heart, and for some reason, she felt like Sage's best interests were in Aspen Cove.

"Yes, but she wants me to stay."

The cork popped from the bottle, and Cannon set it and the bottle on the table. "She does?" Surprise suffused his tone.

"She says I sound happy, and maybe I've found my purpose." She put the plastic container of pasta on the table.

"Have you?"

She rose onto her toes and tilted her head back. "I don't know. Kiss me again, and I'll decide."

"That's a lot of pressure," he took a step forward. "A lot riding on the quality of one kiss."

She gripped the collar of his button-down shirt and tugged him to her. "Give it your best shot."

His lips touched hers with tenderness at first. It was a gentle kiss where their lips brushed back and forth. When one of his hands weaved through her curls and the other pressed against her back, she moaned into his mouth, and the kiss deepened.

Moments later, their bodies shifted, and he lifted her to sit on the counter. Up there, their height difference diminished. She thought about her sister and the quickie with Adam she'd described in the kitchen in Denver. At the time it didn't sound appealing, but with Cannon pressed between her thighs, his hands wrapped around her back and his lips fused to hers, she had to reconsider the value of a counter and a handsome man.

It had been a long time since she explored a body in passion. Her fingers ran from the waistband of his pants up the rivers and valleys of his abs and chest before they reached around to touch the expanse of his back and finally came to rest on the curve of his firm ass.

His hand followed a similar path with her, skimming her stomach and floating along the edge of her breasts until he wrapped his arms around her and pulled her to his chest.

They broke apart to breathe.

"What is it about you?" He stepped back and licked his lips.

She watched the path of his tongue as it circled his mouth. One look into his eyes showed that the color had changed. The blue in them was gone, and a deep green took over. It was a lustful, greedy look that screamed for more.

She hopped off the counter and stalked toward him. "What is it about *you*?"

Neither of them answered the question; only dove together for another kiss.

When his stomach growled, she pulled away. "Time to feed you something other than my mouth."

They sat down in side-by-side chairs, looking out at the lake.

"I'd give up food for your kisses," he said in a voice too small to match the hulking man he was.

"I'll feed you now and then kiss you more." Her voice was larger than her tiny frame portrayed.

Somewhere between microwave lasagna and wine and kisses, they found each other.

After dinner, they took the last of the wine to the chairs by the lake and watched Otis frolic in the water.

"Does Mike live at the bar?"

"Yes, he likes it there. I brought him home a few times, but he wouldn't stop meowing at the door."

"He likes his home." She looked up and down the shoreline. "Who are our neighbors?"

Cannon pulled her seat closer to his and pointed to the house on the other side of his. "My family owned the two houses next to mine, but I had to sell them for Dad. The one closest to me is now Dalton's. The one on the other side of him was purchased by a broker for his client. I have no idea who it is because no one has ever shown up."

"Interesting." She turned her head to the house that sat about three hundred yards to her left. "And that one?"

"That belongs to a seasonal family. They show up in May and leave before the first snow. Their last name is Bergh. He's a hockey coach for some big team, and she's a trophy wife. Nice enough people. Next to them is Frank Arden, who's a lawyer that works in Silver Springs."

She had looked at a map of the area after she was introduced to Copper Creek. Silver Springs was over an hour away.

"That's a long commute." She leaned her head on his shoulder and watched the sun disappear into the lake.

"It's a family home. The older Ardens passed within a few years of each other. Frank and his sister Sara inherited the house. She went off to school to become a veterinarian. Last I heard, she was living in Tulsa. Frank stayed in town and makes the drive. The commute isn't bad once you get used to it."

"I can't imagine." Sage never cared for commuting. Her drive home from the hospital in the morning was always a nightmare. The I-25 in rush hour was not her idea of fun.

Cannon lifted her from her chair and placed her in his lap. "Last week, I couldn't imagine you sitting in my lap. Days ago, I would have never thought I'd kiss you. And this morning, I would have never anticipated seeing my dad work in the bakery. But then you came to Aspen Cove and brought something with you."

She leaned her head against his chest. "I brought a three-legged dog and a bad attitude."

"Yes, you brought those things, but you also brought hope, and, in my experience, hope can be dangerous. Then again, maybe Bea knew what she was doing."

CHAPTER TWENTY-EIGHT

It had been a week of kisses, shared meals, and a mostly sober Ben. Sage settled into her life in Aspen Cove. She had no plan—just a goal of making it through each day and ending it with a smile and a grade-A Cannon Bishop kiss. He knew how to make her toes curl with a touch of his lips.

Her sister had all but given up asking about her plans to return to Denver. The conversations were now focused on Lydia's boyfriend, Adam, and how he spent his life at the hospital. Lydia's twelve-hour shifts made it seem impossible for her to be lonely, but she sounded like a castaway on a deserted island.

Sage tried to support her and downplay the loneliness by saying, "I know he's taking on more work, but that puts him in a good position to be influential when you're finished with your residency and looking for a permanent job."

Lydia groaned. "I'll need a job because my savings are on the low end."

Residents weren't paid a full salary, and for the last three years, Lydia made the equivalent of a coffee shop manager.

As an RN, Sage made $20,000 more a year than her sister, but there was less room for pay increases and advancement. Lydia's salary would increase exponentially with experience and a full-time position.

"I've got money, I can help." Sage was on her last week of paid vacation, but saving was second nature to her, and there was no one more deserving to share her nest egg with than Lydia.

"Are you still working for birth control pills?"

To say it was a mistake to tell Lydia that Sage had traded shifts at the clinic for birth control was an understatement because her sister would never let her live it down.

"It's different here. Besides, I'm not in need of anything."

"Liar," she teased. "You need to get Cannon between the sheets."

Another mistake was to talk to Lydia about her sex life—or lack thereof.

"It's only been two weeks."

"He's nine days past Cosmo's three-date requirement."

"He's cautious, and I respect that." Remembering back to that day at the liquor mart and that girl Mel didn't give Sage the impression that Cannon used caution with regularity. What made Sage different? "If I'm giving this place a try, I have to take my time and make smart decisions. He does too because it's not like there's an abundance of single men or women living here. We have to be picky and prudent."

"I can't imagine living there." In the background, the hospital intercom paged someone. "I've got to go. I love you."

"Love you, too." Sage looked over the rail at Otis, who chased a bird into the water. It reminded her that she needed to bring her winged creature out on the deck for its daily dose of fresh air.

When she returned from her room to the rail, she opened the box. The bandage had fallen off days ago. The bird hopped to the edge like it did every day. It spread its wings and flapped. Each day, it grew stronger from exercise, and then it would sink back into the fresh towel Sage had folded at the bottom of the box.

Today, it flapped and stopped, then flapped and stopped. Sage leaned on the handrail that held the cardboard container. The bird hopped to the edge closest to her and squawked like it was trying to get her attention. She took her eyes off Otis and focused on the demanding bird.

"What do you want, you little troublemaker?" She looked down at the critter that had bridged the gap between Cannon and her.

It squawked again. With its wings spread, it flapped with force and took flight. The journey was one of joy and sorrow for Sage. She had grown accustomed to feeding it and caring for it had become one of her daily pleasures.

She used the bird as an excuse to stay in town, but it was probably time to be honest with herself. She overstayed her welcome in Denver, and the moment had come for her to spread her wings and fly. Bea made sure she landed safely in the little town. She was happy in Aspen Cove.

She watched the tiny thing until it became a dot on the horizon.

Sage thought about Cannon, Katie, and Ben, her three best reasons to stay in Aspen Cove now that the bird had healed.

Cannon was at the bar doing inventory for his Friday liquor run, and Katie was probably elbow-deep in muffin batter and supervising Ben, who, despite having paid back his debt, showed up to help her each morning.

Down to three drinks a day, his shakes had stopped, and his skin had a healthy pink glow. He was still far too skinny, but Ben was like Rome and couldn't be built in a day.

"Let's go, Otis." The dog looked up at her like a child. "I've got a lunch date with Katie."

He trotted up to the deck and shook himself off. Water flew from his fur in every direction, giving Sage an unexpected shower.

"Thanks a lot, buddy." She pulled the towel she kept handy from the deck chair and gave him a good rubdown. "You're staying here today."

As long as he had a comfy chair and a bowl of kibble, Otis couldn't care less where he stayed.

She got him situated and left for Maisey's Diner and her first local dining experience.

Five minutes later, she walked into the little eatery. It wasn't the fifties experience she expected with records on the wall and Elvis posters everywhere. Nope, Maisey's was a James Dean adventure. Highly shined motorcycles were perched like trophies on pedestals between the booths. Hubcaps and handlebars decked the walls. On the soffit above the counter was a James Dean quote that read, "Dream as if you'll live forever, live as if you'll die today."

Blonde hair drew her attention to the center booth on the right. Katie raised her hand high in the air and waved. It wasn't like Sage could miss her; she was one of two people in the place, and the other diner was a frail bald man.

Sage tucked herself into the booth across from her friend. "Why haven't I been here before?"

"Because they're hardly ever open." Katie glanced around. "Dalton says it's off-season, but next week they open full-time."

"Nights, too?" There would be another option besides her microwave.

"Nope. The nights are for pool and beer."

That seemed to be the way of it. It was as if there was an unwritten rule that the local businesses didn't encroach on each other. Maisey's didn't sell muffins or other bake goods except for pie, and B's Bakery sold everything but pie. Bishop's Brewhouse didn't sell food, while Maisey's didn't sell alcohol. The Corner Store sold food and soda, but they didn't sell pharmacy-related items. Doc's didn't sell food unless you counted candy. Everyone had their little corner of the world here, and they worked in harmony, except for old man Tucker. He bootlegged, which probably ate up some of Cannon's profits.

The bell above the door rang, and in walked the devil himself. Cannon looked absolutely delicious in his jeans and black T-shirt. All he needed to do was grease back his hair and straddle a motorcycle, and he'd fit right in. Behind him, to her surprise, was Ben.

"Oh, wow." Katie leaned forward so she could watch them around the edge of the booth.

"Wow is right." If Sage thought Cannon was cautious with her, he was more so with his father. The two men hadn't talked much because Cannon kept a safe distance. Close enough to step in if needed, but far enough away that if Ben erupted into proverbial flames, Cannon wouldn't get burned. The fact that they were dining together was a big deal.

The men sat across from each other. Ben stared at the menu as if it was the first time he'd seen it. Cannon looked Sage and Katie's way and smiled before he rose from his seat and walked over to where they sat.

"Dad said you were here." He bent over and brushed a light kiss across Sage's lips. "I thought I'd feed him."

Katie flipped her hair over her shoulder. "I feed him."

He looked at her. "I know you do, but today is more than that."

Sage wrapped her arms around his waist and hugged. "I'm glad you're here with him." She wanted to tell him she was proud, but it seemed a stupid thing to say. She didn't have the history he had with Ben, and proud wasn't a strong enough word. It was one thing to lose a parent because they died, another to lose a parent because they walked around like they were dead. Her situation was far easier to swallow.

"Come to the bar tonight?" His eyes were soft and bluer than green today. She'd learned over the days she'd spent with him that green was the color of passion for him. Blue meant something else. Generally, his eyes took on that icy look when he pulled away.

"Sure. I'll be there." He gave her another peck on the lips and walked away.

Dressed in a frilly apron and a bouffant updo, Maisey approached their table. "Hello, girls, what's it going to be?"

Although Sage had never been in the diner, she recognized Maisey from the funeral. The scuttlebutt around town was that the blue-plate special was the best thing to order.

"Blue plate for me," she said, then looked over at Ben and Cannon and wondered if they'd order the same. She would have loved to invite them to join her, but they needed this time to reconnect.

"Same for me," Katie said.

Maisey moved on to Cannon and Ben's table.

Out of the kitchen came Dalton, who walked to Sage and Katie's booth.

Katie jumped up and gave him a friendly hug. There was nothing intimate about the gesture. It was the kind of hug a person gave a friend or relative. "I don't think you've formally met Sage."

He looked at Sage with a scowl that could slice her in half. Dalton was central casting for *Sons of Anarchy*, all the way from the skull-and-crossbones bandana to his black boots. In between were ink and muscle and attitude.

"Nice to meet you, Sage." His voice was rough and low. "You get the special?"

They both nodded, and he grunted and walked away.

"Not long on words."

Katie laughed. "No, but don't let him scare you because he's a really nice guy."

Sage looked right to see him stop at Cannon's booth. All three men turned her way.

She moved into the corner of the red vinyl bench. "He looks like a murderer."

"He is," Katie said as if that wasn't an odd thing to say. She liked the bad boys, but a murderer? "He's on parole."

"No way." Sage leaned forward to glance at the man who was as big as an oak tree and as mean-looking as a rabid dog.

Katie's blonde locks floated over her shoulders with the nod of her head. "No, seriously, he's only been out of prison for a month or so."

Sage was speechless. She'd been living in a town with a paroled murderer for weeks. Shouldn't there be a neighborhood watch letter that informed people of the dangers in town? Living two doors down from the man could easily make her his next victim. "Oh my God, and I had started to like this place."

Katie's trophy smile turned into a thin line of disappointment. "Unless you're beating up women, you have nothing to worry about."

"What?" Sage's head was still wrapped around the word murderer.

Katie rearranged her silverware and then leaned into the center of the table. "He came out of a bar one night and saw a man beating up a woman and stepped in to help. The two men fought, and Dalton knocked him out, but the other guy never got up."

"Wouldn't that be self-defense?"

"No, not in this case. Dalton was angry to see a woman abused, and he stepped into a fight that didn't involve him. It was considered an act of passion. The guy hit the ground dead."

"How do you know all this?"

Her pageant smile was back. "I own a bakery where people sit, eat muffins, and chat."

"Geez. I need to get out more. The only stuff I hear is from people complaining about skin conditions, sore throats, and hemorrhoids. I don't get the good stuff working for Doc." Like Ben at the bakery, Sage had shown up for clinic days to help Doc because it gave her a purpose and made her feel like a member of the community.

"You need to bring a book and sit in the corner of the bakery for a day. It's amazing what you can learn. This town is like a soap opera."

"I'm missing everything. If I plan to stick around, I need more information."

"So, you're staying?" She said it loud enough for everyone in the place to hear, and Cannon turned and stared.

"I'm not committing to anything permanent, but I don't have plans to leave."

Katie squealed with delight. "I'm so happy."

When Sage looked at Cannon, he looked happy, too.

CHAPTER TWENTY-NINE

Cannon watched the door since he opened the bar at six. His regulars trickled in, but he was looking for one person—Sage. She'd become an important part of his life over the last week because she gave him a reason to smile.

Doc walked in and sat at the bar. He held up his finger for his first beer. "How are things in the heart department, son?"

Cannon pulled a lager and set it on a coaster. "I'm not talking about my love life with you."

Doc lifted his beer to his lips and took a long, lazy drink. When he set the mug down, the foam stuck to his whiskers. "You've got a love life now? That's good to know. Don't screw it up like the last time."

Cannon knew he was referring to Mel. "That was different."

Doc's brow lifted. Not a day went by that Cannon didn't want to reach into his drawer for the scissors and trim off the winged brows that shot skyward from the old man's forehead.

"She's a girl, and you like her, so what makes it different?"

"Mel was nice enough, but Sage is special." When he was with her, every emotion was intensified.

"Special, huh? I once had a special girl."

Cannon leaned against the counter, waiting for him to go on. He knew how this worked. He would get unsolicited advice. Doc wouldn't come out and say what he wanted to say. He'd wrap it in a story.

"I met her for the first time on my family's farm when she tried to steal my prize hog." Doc chuckled and closed his eyes, obviously reliving the memory.

"She stole your pig?" Cannon knew the girl he talked about was Phyllis, Doc's wife of over forty years.

"No, son, she stole my heart. I gave her the pig because her family was hungry." He pulled the bowl of bar mix forward and picked out the spicy peanuts he loved. "I knew then that I'd do anything for that girl, so I butchered the animal and took it to her house."

"What did she say?"

"Nothing, I didn't see her that day. I met up with her ornery-as-snot father and told him I wanted to court his daughter."

"And?" Cannon took Doc's half-empty beer and filled it up.

"He took my gift and told me he'd think about it." Doc still wore his wedding ring, even though Phyllis had passed several years ago. "I went to her house every Friday with offerings that ranged from freshly baked bread to a butchered chicken. My family wasn't rich, but we ate, and we had extra. Six weeks later, I showed up, and her father was waiting on the porch. His shotgun leaned against the door, and Phyllis stood by his side. She was the prettiest thing I ever saw and dressed in her Sunday best." He sipped his beer. "It was a blue and white polka-dotted dress that reached past her knees. She had on white bobby socks and shiny black shoes."

Cannon leaned toward him completely enthralled by the story. "And ...?"

"It was the start of forever. Her father let me walk her to the end of the driveway and back, and that was our first date. He sat on the porch with his shotgun in his lap and watched."

"No kiss?"

"No, we didn't move along as fast as you youngsters do nowadays. In a way, I think it's better to wait. You get to know a person's heart before their body. One can satisfy you for life, the other for minutes. Anyway, by our fourth walk down the driveway, her father had moved into the house. I knew he was watching, and my only move to touch her was to wipe the dust off her shiny shoes when we returned. Two months later, he didn't bother to chaperone. A month after that, she was able to take a drive with me. Two months past that, I walked her down the aisle of a little church in Gold Gulch."

"Was that the first time you kissed her?"

"Hell no, I kissed her nonstop from the minute we got out of shotgun range. That's my point. You know they're special when all you get is a kiss, and it's enough for now. Are Sage's kisses enough?"

Cannon smiled. "For now."

The door opened, and like Doc said, Cannon's forever started. It was a daily thing for him. His days began with her smile and ended with her kiss.

Dressed in pink, she was as pretty as he could remember. She took a seat at the end stool, the one he thought of as hers. He poured her favorite beer and went to greet her with a kiss.

The doc threw a five on the table and stood.

"You want to play for that beer?" Cannon asked.

The old man shook his head. "You got better things to do with your time, son. I'll be next door with my shotgun." He laughed all the way out the door.

"What was that about?" Sage looked at him with a question quirking her lips.

"I think he likes you, and he's warning me to treat you right."

When she smiled, the whole room warmed. "I think he wants to keep me around for free labor."

"You work for free?" This town worked differently than most. If not for the people, he would have given up long ago. It was Bea who kept him glued together because she never gave up, and she didn't allow him to either.

"Not really, I work for peanut butter cups and Skittles." She smiled over her mug of beer. "I'm cheap, but I'm not easy."

Cannon went to the only other customer in the bar and settled his tab. When the man walked out, he closed and locked the door.

Sage looked up at the clock that hung over the bar. "You closing early?"

He approached her and spun the barstool around, so she faced him. He stood between her legs with just a piece of pink material keeping them apart. "I realized today that I've been an awful boyfriend." He watched her face for any hint of discomfort at his chosen word but didn't see anything but affection. He was an exclusive kind of man and didn't want to share what he considered his, especially Sage. "I've never actually asked you on a date."

Her fingers trailed the buttons of his shirt until they sat at the waist of his pants. "You want to be my boyfriend and date?"

He couldn't remember a time when he blushed, but the heat rose to his cheeks, and all he knew was, he wanted her. Not in the same way as Mel because from Sage, he wanted more, and he'd wait for as long as it took to get it.

"Let's just say I want more and want to *be* more." He leaned in and gave her a sweet kiss before he led her to the empty spot where people often danced. He put a coin in the jukebox and selected D-47, one of his mother's favorite tunes by Etta James. As "At Last" played, he pulled her into his arms. It was a bittersweet moment as he reflected on a past where his mother and father danced in the same spot to the same song and looked to the future for the first time in a long time. He towered over the girl who was the size of a grade-schooler. His body was bigger in every way, but somehow her curves filled all his hollows, and it was perfect. She was perfect. The moment was perfect—at last.

CHAPTER THIRTY

On Friday morning, Sage kissed Cannon goodbye. He was off to make the liquor run, and although he invited her to join him, she'd made a personal commitment to garden and get moved into the other wing of the house.

She infrequently ventured into Bea's quarters because it made her sad. Like somehow, by taking over her space, she would erase her memory.

While she tugged at the weeds sprouting from the ground, she was surprised to find her favorite flower growing. With care, she cleaned around the lilac bush.

The heavily scented flowers reminded her of happy days, cotton candy, Ferris wheels, and her mom, who had a vase of the flowers on the table all summer long. They were nostalgic and romantic blooms of hope.

An hour later, she went into the house because she couldn't put her next task off forever. She opened the door that led to Bea's space. It smelled like lemon wax and the comforting scent of books and leather. She pulled a plastic bin behind her to the first room, Bea's bedroom, where she expected to find a closet full of clothes. Instead, she found an empty walk-in. Sage pulled open the drawers of the dressers and found the same. The only thing they contained was floral paper that lined the bottom and smelled like lavender.

Her first instinct was to think someone had robbed Bea, but she knew better. The woman had planned for everything, including setting this room up for its next occupant.

She walked into the den, where the pictures of Bea's life held a place of honor on the table. She picked up the only picture of Bea and held it to her chest. "Why me, Bea?"

In the silence, she heard the memory of Bea's voice say, *"Aspen Cove needed you."*

There wasn't much to do except move her stuff to the room, so she unpacked her car for the first time since she arrived.

Once her clothes were neatly hung in the closet and placed in the scented drawers, she curled up in the den with Otis by her feet.

She'd added pictures to the table by interspersing photos of her family with Bea's. It felt right to meld the two families together.

Comfy in the old leather chair, she opened a cozy mystery and got lost in the book until a pounding at the door pulled her away.

Cannon stood on her doorstep, but his usual smile was gone. In its place was agitation. The Cannon she kissed for hours each night was absent, and back was the predator she met on the sidewalk.

"Have you seen my father?" His voice was hard and clipped.

There was no brush of his lips. No sly smile. No hug.

Her protective mechanisms slid into place, and she crossed her arms and stepped back. "Have you checked the bakery?" She wanted to reach out and touch him, but did she dare? Any perceived snub could set their relationship back, and things were moving slowly as it was. Not because Sage didn't want more, but because Cannon seemed content to hold her and hug her and kiss her and hadn't pushed for more.

She had two choices. Let this moment come between them or bridge the gap she felt growing. She stepped forward and reached up to touch his cheek, letting her fingers slide over the perfectly trimmed hair that was both rough and soft at the same time. "Come inside."

He leaned into her caress, which was a good sign. "He's not at the bakery. Katie said he left at ten and never came back."

She thought that through. "He doesn't work for her in the true sense." Sure, Katie set up credits around town for Ben to get what he needed, because giving an alcoholic cash was not a wise choice. "Maybe he's taking a break. Did you check the house?"

"I did."

She led him to the couch and sat beside him, snuggling into the soft cotton of his shirt. She loved the pine and fresh air and all man smell of him.

"If he's not here, then I know where to find him. I had hoped you put him to work, but if he's not at the bakery or here or at home, he's either at Tucker's or the cemetery."

Deep inside, she knew he was right. It was a shame because Ben had done so well. It had been almost two weeks since he'd cut back his drinking. He was never fully sober, but he wasn't raging drunk either.

"I'll come with you."

He pulled her into his lap and hugged her tight. "I love that you want to, but if he's fallen off the wagon, he's not safe."

She pressed her lips to his and felt his tense muscles relax. "If it's not safe for me, then it's not safe for you. You should call the sheriff."

He cupped her face and looked at her with raw emotions. Love and sadness and disappointment pooled in the depths of his eyes. "He doesn't need to deal with my domestic issues."

"It's his job." She fluttered kisses across his face. She watched the men over the last week mend the break in their relationship and hoped Ben didn't do something that would fracture it beyond repair. Maybe it was best to let the sheriff step in and preserve what they had.

"Dad is my responsibility."

Sage couldn't argue with that. She'd go to any lengths to help

Lydia. Hell, she went to great lengths to help her grandmother by putting herself in the worst possible job to spend extra minutes with her, and now she was unemployed.

"Go get him." She pressed her lips lightly against his and whispered, "I'll be here for you when you get home." She deepened the kiss, hoping it would give him the strength for what was to come.

An hour later, gravel crunched under tires, and she rushed to the door to see a combative Ben returned to his home. There was yelling and doors slamming, but at least this time, Cannon wasn't bleeding. He gripped his father's arms and forced him up the porch steps and into the house.

Sage waited for as long as she could before she ventured next door and knocked lightly. If Cannon didn't answer, she'd go back home, but the door opened, and he stepped aside.

"He's passed out in bed." Defeated was the only way to describe his voice. "I knew it wasn't going to last. He's good for a week or two, and then it's back to a binge that can last a week, a month, a year."

She stepped inside and shut the door behind her. "I'm sorry, Cannon. I thought I could help." She leaned into his big body and rested her head on his chest.

He hung his head so it touched the top of hers. "I was furious when you tried, and then something amazing happened. There was a moment when I had a glimpse of my old man— the one who loved us and raised us, so I can't be angry with that, or with you. I'm frustrated at myself for letting hope slide into my heart."

She felt him swallow hard. Cannon didn't appear the emotional type, but maybe she had that wrong about him, too. Maybe his feelings were tucked behind that fortress that protected his heart.

"Don't give up hope. For people like us who have lost so much, it's all we have, so don't let him take that away."

He picked her up, and she wrapped her legs around his waist. "How lucky am I that you have bad taste in men?" He brought her to the couch, and when he sat, she was left straddling his lap.

Despite the somber situation, she giggled. "I'd say you're pretty damn lucky."

"You're right about that. Looks like we have the night together. What do you want to microwave?"

She was thrilled to spend the evening with him, but he couldn't afford to close up business for another night. "What about the bar?"

His forehead furrowed when he turned toward the hallway that led to where his father slept. "I can't leave him alone, so I'll have to take the hit."

"Otis and I will stay with him. If he's passed out, he'll be out for hours."

"You'd do that for me?" He looked at her like she'd offered him something with real value.

"I'd do anything for you."

His eyes turned greener. "Be careful what you offer."

"I said *anything*, Cannon."

He left her with a sexy, heated look in his eyes.

Otis curled up next to her while she read Bea's book. The sun had set, and Ben had been asleep for hours. It was when she heard the retching that she went in search of the sound and found Ben folded over the toilet, losing the contents of his stomach.

Vomit was nothing in her book. It came with her job. When there wasn't anything left for him to expel, she sat him down on the closed seat and cleaned him up. She gave him two painkillers and a glass of water and put him back to bed.

How long would Ben mourn his wife? How long would he abuse his son? The former made her sympathetic, and the latter made her furious.

She sat at the edge of his bed and tucked the blankets up to his chin.

"I'm going to give you some Sage advice, Ben." He opened his eyes and closed them again, but she figured he was listening. "You're really screwing this up. The way you feel about your wife dying is the way your son feels about you, but it's worse because Carly couldn't

169

help leaving you. On the other hand, you have a choice." She stood and looked down on him. "You're one selfish bastard, Ben, and you can do better." She leaned over and gave him a kiss on his clammy forehead.

He opened his eyes. "I'll try."

CHAPTER THIRTY-ONE

Cannon entered the house as quietly as possible. It was after midnight, and he didn't want to startle Sage if she'd fallen asleep.

Otis lifted his head from his bed on the floor and wagged his tail. He was a terrible watchdog but a good companion to Sage. He wondered how many tears his fur had soaked up and how many stories his floppy ears had heard.

Mike was often his sounding board. His one-eyed cat laid patiently on the bar and listened until the treats ran out. He was Cannon's closest confidant until the little redhead sleeping on his couch came to town.

The glow of the lamp bathed her in warm light. Her pale skin, her red hair, and the freckles across the bridge of her nose, which looked like oil on a canvas. He sat on the edge of the coffee table and stared at her for endless minutes, thinking about how beautiful she was when she slept.

"Anything," she said earlier, and he wondered if that was true. He wanted more and needed more, but more was a dangerous concept. He wasn't a taker because to take more meant he had to give

more. To give anything less than everything to her wouldn't be enough, but could he give her all of him?

All he had left was his heart. Could he trust her with it? Part of him screamed yes. That might have been the part throbbing between his legs. Part of him said no because to love was to hurt. The problem was, with Sage, to not love her was to hurt worse.

He slid his hands under her body and lifted her to his chest. Tonight, he'd risk everything. Tonight, he would give her his heart if she'd take it.

"You're back." She turned and nuzzled into his chest. She always smelled him like his scent brought her comfort.

He tightened his hold. "I missed you." The entire night, he thought about her and what her presence in Aspen Cove meant to him. He wasn't sure what Bea had in mind when she gave Sage her property, but he was grateful it was her. Deep inside, the most logical part of his brain knew it would always be her.

He stood in the middle of his living room, arms full, but thoughts uncertain. Emotions and logic warred within him. "Where do you want me to take you?"

She tilted her head back and stared up at him with those eyes that seemed to speak to his soul. "What are my options?"

"I can take you home and put you to bed with a kiss, or ... I can take you to my bed and make you mine."

Her expression was unreadable, except for the tiny upturn of her sweet pink lips. "I'll take option two." She wrapped her arms around his neck and hung on tightly. Did she fear he'd change his mind? There was no way.

"Will Otis be okay out here?"

Her body shifted as she looked down at the dog. "He'll be fine."

With her cradled against him, Cannon moved toward his room— to his bed where no woman had ever slept before. That was an important fact he wanted to share with her. "You're the first."

Laughter made her shake in his arms. "I'm fairly confident that's not the truth. I saw the way Mel looked at you."

In his attempt to be honest, he'd misled her. "No, I'm not talking about sexual experiences. I'm talking about you being the first woman to be in my bed."

"Oh," she whispered. "I thought ..." She shook her head. "Never mind."

At the far end of the hall, he kicked open the door and walked into the dark room. A sliver of moonlight peeked through the blinds like a beacon softly guiding them to the bed.

"Can we have a night that's just you and me? I don't want Mel or my father in this bed. All I want is you—only you." Cannon gently laid her on his bedspread. He'd seen many a negligee and plenty of naked, willing women in his lifetime, but he'd never seen anything as sexy as Sage dressed in blue jeans and a T-shirt. Fully clothed, she was far more enticing than any woman he'd been with.

"Just you and me," she replied.

Maybe Doc was right; maybe the time they spent getting to know each other was the payoff. They'd stripped each other every night in conversation, but not one piece of clothing hit the floor. Now they were in this place where they would share their bodies where the goal wasn't the climax. Oh, they'd get there for sure, but what he wanted was far more than sex.

"Stay here." He walked out of the room.

He was halfway down the hallway when he heard her say, "As if I'd leave."

That was the one thing he feared the most, which was eventually everyone would leave him. Even his dad, though physically present, had checked out of his life years ago.

He put up barriers to protect himself from the pain of abandonment, but he could no longer keep Sage out when he wanted so badly to let her in.

He came back to the room with an open bottle of wine and two glasses.

She'd turned on the bedside lamp and sat up against the headboard.

"I thought you might like some wine."

She tugged at one of her corkscrew curls until he was certain she'd pull it from her head. Was she nervous? He'd seen her be many things, from happy to concerned, but never nervous. "Don't be nervous because this is going to be perfect." He poured a glass of wine and handed it to her. After he filled his glass, he sat on the edge of the bed and raised it in a toast. "Here's to being together."

They tapped glasses and drank. "If you're looking for perfect, I'm afraid I might fall short."

It was his turn to laugh. "Are you making height jokes?"

She regarded him for the longest time and then giggled. She regarded him for the longest time and then giggled. "No, although in hindsight, that is funny." There was a soft lilt to her voice that was almost hypnotic.

He set their wine glasses down and cupped her cheek before tilting her face toward him to make sure he had her full attention. "No one else is in this room but you and me. Let go of what others have done to make you feel less than you are. You are everything to me." His chest tightened, and in that moment, his life changed. The minute their bodies connected, he'd no longer be alone, and yet if she left, he'd be more alone than he'd ever been before.

It started with a kiss to her forehead, then her nose, and her mouth. He lay down next to her. His hands roamed over her clothes, but he needed more. To touch the denim of her jeans was not truly touching her.

"I need to see you—to touch you." Permission was what he sought when he gripped the hem of her shirt. He waited until her curls bounced with a nod.

She lifted her body from the bed as he pulled the shirt free to reveal pale pink skin and a simple white bra. It wasn't the type to seduce. Instead, it was practical but perfect. He didn't need lace; he just needed her.

Propped on an elbow beside her, he traced his calloused fingers around the edge of her bra, his hands shaking like a teenager getting his first feel.

She reached behind her back and set the fabric free. It fell to the side of her body, exposing handfuls of softness with tight pink buds.

When she reached for his hands and pressed them to her breasts, his heart halted a beat, while hers raced under his palms.

"It looks like it's my time to say, don't be nervous," she told him.

While his fingertips traced her skin, he memorized every nuance, from the tiny mole above her right breast to the scar below her rib cage.

"What's this from?" He rubbed it with the pad of his thumb over and over again.

"Fell off my bike when I was little." Her breath hitched when his fingers skimmed her taut nipples.

"The fall couldn't have been too great, given your height."

"Haha, height jokes?" She reached up and slugged him in the chest.

"Ouch," he said in mock pain. For a little thing, she packed quite a punch. "Now you'll have to kiss it."

"Gladly." It took her no time to divest him of his shirt. Next to go was her pants. While he kicked out of his boots, she exposed herself completely to him.

"Oh holy hell. You're stunning." She may have been small, but she had all the right curves. The one he liked the best was the curve of her smile when he told her she was beautiful.

Once again, he went back to exploring. Not an inch of her skin was overlooked. Her chest heaved, and her body blushed under his touch.

By her heavy breaths, he could tell she was on the edge, even though he hadn't gone deeper than a touch or a kiss. This had been a journey to map the landscape, and she was a damn sight to explore.

"Not fair." She sat up and pulled at the waistband of his jeans. "I want to see you, too. Touch you. Taste you."

God almighty, if those words didn't make him ache. He'd never been so turned on—so hard, but his needs be damned. He'd see to hers first.

"Soon." He leaned into her and let his tongue explore where his fingers had been. She moved beneath him as if she were on fire, the way her body responded to his lips, his touch, his tongue. At the first taste of her sweetness, she came undone.

Cannon had never seen or felt such a response. She'd unraveled because of him.

Her fingers threaded through his hair and held him in place until the last shudder left her body.

"More. I want more."

He repeated her words from earlier. "I'll give you anything—anything you want."

With nimble fingers, she unbuttoned his jeans. He stood up and let them fall to the floor. He wasn't much for underwear, so there was nothing to cover his arousal.

"Oh." She'd said that word many times before, but not while looking at him naked.

"Are you surprised?"

She shook her head. "No, I'm just—"

"Afraid?"

"No, I'm—"

He puffed out his chest and pulled a condom from his wallet. "Impressed."

"No, dammit. I was going to say I'm ready. I want this."

Gloved, Cannon was all set to be loved. "Sage, look at me." He waited until her eyes rose from his rod to his face. "This isn't about sex. It's about so much more because it's the beginning of everything."

In her eyes, he saw a mirror of his feelings. She seemed scared and vulnerable and broken like him. But at the same time, she was willing to let him be the glue to put her back together.

"Yes, I want everything." She rose up to kiss him, and when he pressed inside her, everything dark became light. He gave her his body and his heart.

CHAPTER THIRTY-TWO

Sage sucked in a breath. Stretched to her limits, she was full of him, but it was more than their bodies joining. Like liquid, he seeped into the holes of her heart and soul, sealing all the fissures and making her complete.

Never had a man looked at her the way he did with eyes full of love and compassion and kissed her with lips that left heat long after they were gone. His hands held her gently, but firmly enough to let her know he was there and had her.

No one had seen to her needs before their own—not purposefully anyway.

His movements were slow and deep. Every stroke, every touch, every kiss was a promise of completeness. If this was everything, she wanted more. Nothing different. Just more.

"Oh God." Her hips lifted to meet each thrust.

Her fingertips skimmed the hard edges of his body. She reveled in the ridges and ravines of his muscles. His skin remained bronzed, despite the lack of sun from a long, cold winter. She loved the way his eyes turned emerald green when passion filled him. Eyes that stared down at her now. In their depths, past the hint of blue and green and speckles of gold circling the black, was love.

Her lungs seized as the impact of what she saw and felt became known. Cannon Bishop loved her.

Although it would be so easy to lie to herself, she couldn't. What she felt for him was profound. What started as animosity had turned to love.

She cautioned herself because she gave her heart too easily. Was this love she was feeling for him, or was he another project like the goldfish, the butterfly, the bird? Was he the man who could fill her world with happiness or another who would take everything and leave her in despair?

As he moved, she held her hand to his heart and felt it beating, its steady rhythm a reminder he had taken nothing from her that she hadn't given freely. She'd opened her heart to love him, and if that turned to hurt, so be it. To have loved him for a second was better than not to have loved him at all.

"You with me, sweetheart?" He pressed his lips to hers. The fog of her thoughts cleared. It was just them, and no one else.

"I'm with you, always."

She lifted her knees and wrapped her legs around him, pulling him closer—deeper. Mouths met. Tongues sparred. Hands roamed. All the while, their eyes never lost sight of each other.

The buildup was slow and delicious. Each time she didn't think she could rise any further, he took her a step higher. What started as a tingling in her core burst like an explosion around him with his name rushing from her lips.

She gripped his hips tightly so he'd stall his motion and feel her quiver. He plunged forward once more and stilled. "Geezus, Sage." Strung tight with tension, he fell over the edge with her, then collapsed half on and half off her body.

Entwined with each other, they fought for calm.

Her hand slid up and down his back, feeling bumps rise under her fingertips. "I'd give anything to hear your thoughts," she said.

The low rumble of laughter vibrated against her skin. "Are you sure about that?"

She pushed him off her and rolled onto her side to face him. "What are you thinking?" Even though she would have loved for him to say something like, "I'm thinking about how much I love you." It was too soon. The thirty-year-old cynic knew it wouldn't happen, but her inner sixteen-year-old romantic wanted it anyway. "Tell me," she pressed.

He pulled her close to his body, where she could feel his steely hardness probe her thigh. "I think we need to do that again."

"Seriously?" She had no idea a man could be ready again so fast, but then again, it became apparent that Cannon wasn't an average man.

He pulled off the spent condom and wrapped it in a nearby tissue. "Only when you're ready."

She curled into his open arms. "Anything for you."

"Be careful what you promise." He reached for his wallet, where another foil packet waited.

She took it from his hand. "Be careful what you ask for."

In spite of all the words of caution, she rolled on the condom and straddled him. She was a giver, not a taker. She'd accepted everything he offered and intended to give more than she took.

When she settled her body onto his length, she watched his eyes roll back. Never had she seen the look of bliss until then. Pure, unadulterated satisfaction shone in the softness of his expression, beat in the rhythm of his heart, and hummed in the deep timbre of his voice.

She paced herself so they climaxed together, and although it was the end of this moment, although it was the end of this moment, it felt like it was the beginning of their future.

THE RICH AROMA of coffee filled the air. Sage rolled over,

reaching for the body that had enveloped her all night. It was no longer naked or under the blankets. She opened her eyes one at a time to take in the sight of a shirtless Cannon sitting in bed beside her, propped up against the headboard. In one hand he had a cup of coffee, in the other a newspaper.

She rolled over and laid her head on his bare stomach while her hands rubbed the soft cotton of his sweatpants.

"You awake?" He set the paper down and ran his free hand through her hair. She wanted to groan because she knew what her hair looked like on a good day. There was no telling what the mop on her head was like after a naughty night.

"Barely." She pulled herself up to sit beside him. Her head rested on his arm. "Are you going to share that coffee?"

"It'll cost you a kiss." He tipped it to her lips. Something about a cup of fresh brew made her blood pump, or maybe it was the sexy man who had rocked her world all night. Or ... maybe it was both. She swished the coffee in her mouth and swallowed. With a tilt of her head, she sought out his lips, and that was the start of their morning.

In all honesty, she was game to stay in bed and feast on Cannon all day. Under the sheets, it was only them. There were no stresses of the world. No drunken father. No noisy honeymooners. It was just them. But by noon, both of their stomachs were louder than their sounds of satisfaction, and to keep up with the activity that brought them so much pleasure would require sustenance.

"I've got Pop-Tarts at my place."

"Let's shower, and I'll cook." He stood. Before she could roll out of bed herself, he had her wrapped in his arms.

"You cook?" All she could think about was how she'd hit the lottery. He was a man who had mad bedroom skills, *and* he cooked.

"My mother insisted on it." He set her on the cold bathroom counter while he turned on the shower. "She sat Bowie and me down when we were teenagers." He pulled two towels out from under the sink and placed them next to her.

"Was this the birds and bees talk?"

"Yes, but it was more. She said if we had a woman in our lives, it should be because we wanted a partner, not because we wanted a hot meal or clean clothes."

"I wish I could have met her."

A soft smile framed his face. "I wish you could have, too. She would have liked you."

Although Sage would never meet Cannon's mom, it meant a lot that he gave the seal of approval on her behalf.

"Did you check on your dad?" They had left the cocoon of Cannon's bed, where nothing but them existed. Back in the real world, she had to consider others, and Ben's well-being was a huge consideration.

"I did. He's not here."

Her heart raced. "Oh no."

Cannon brought his hands to her lips. "He's okay." The steam from the shower floated around them. He dropped his sweatpants, lifted her from the counter, and they entered the warmth of the soothing water.

"Good." There were so many questions she had, but she leaned back and let the water wash them away. Cannon would share what he wanted. One thing she'd realized about him was that if she waited long enough, he'd give her everything.

"I got up when I heard him, and I made him coffee. Even set a bottle of vodka on the table."

Sage picked up the bar of soap and ran it over his body. He leaned against the wall and closed his eyes.

"What did he do?"

"He measured a shot, downed it, and drank the coffee." He pushed off the wall and towered over her. "You know what else he did?"

Sage searched Cannon for injury and tried to analyze his expression for internal pain. There was nothing but a smile. "No idea."

"He apologized, and then he asked me for a ride to the bakery. Told me he had painting to do."

Sage dropped the bar of soap. "No kidding."

"How is it you show up here and turn everything upside down, and yet it all feels right? Your presence, unwelcome at first, has become my saving grace. You came when I needed you the most and saved me." He covered her mouth with his and showed his gratitude with an earth-moving kiss.

"I didn't save you." She hated the word *save* or anything to do with it. Saving someone was impossible. She recognized the truth of that now. "All I did was come into town and stir things up. Sometimes that's all it takes."

"Call it what you want. I know what you did."

It sounded like she had a master plan, but she didn't. "All I did was care."

"That was enough."

CHAPTER THIRTY-THREE

For the next two weeks, Sage didn't sleep alone. Ben was back on track and doing his best to stay that way. The bakery had lost its dinginess and flourished under a new coat of paint and the kindness of strangers who were fast becoming friends.

The secret deliveries slowed down to where Katie found items on her doorstep less frequently, but she no longer needed the handouts. What started as a dozen muffins a day turned into two, then five, then ten dozen. And although her earnings wouldn't make her wealthy, it was quite a lot for a town the size of Aspen Cove since the property was paid for, and the only overhead was utilities, taxes, and supplies. Katie was in good shape.

The bed and breakfast turned around a few guests, too. Nothing to write home about, but spring brought with it, fishermen and hikers. Thankfully, there were no honeymooners to speak of. The biggest risk now was her guests being disturbed by the noises she and Cannon created.

"So, you made all these beds?" Sage ran her hand over the wood of the big king-size frame in Bea's room—the bed they'd shared for weeks. Her fingers rested on the inlaid seashell. "Why didn't you say anything?"

He pulled the bedspread over the pillows and tucked it with the precision of a hotel housekeeper.

"I didn't think about it because it's part of my old life." He swiped the change from the nightstand and put it in his pocket.

"Did you love it?" Over time, Cannon had opened up about his life and his experiences. They talked about past relationships, past hurts and future wants, but never did he say he was a furniture maker.

"I saw things in the wood that no one else could. I took items I found and made them treasures."

"You should do it again." She sat on the bed and pulled on her white loafers. It was Wednesday, and Doc needed her help at the clinic. "Don't give up something so important to you."

He rounded the bed and stood in front of her. "I found something more important. I found you."

Sage gave him a passing kiss. "Maybe you should thank your father for that introduction."

Cannon winced. Even after all the weeks of love and affection, he continued to apologize for that day.

"Let's not replace alcoholism with an inflated ego."

Ben had gone from three drinks a day to two, and now he was down to one. It wasn't because he needed it, but somehow it comforted him.

"I'll stop by the bar after work." She kissed him and ran out of the house as Otis watched her from the door. He liked going to Doc's, but he liked being with Cannon and Mike more. Sage couldn't remember the last time he'd snuggled his stuffed bunny. Why settle for fake when Mike purred and licked Otis's fur?

When she arrived at the clinic, Doc was brewing a cup of coffee. She'd convinced him to get rid of the old drip maker and buy a Keurig. If she was volunteering her time, the least he could do was provide a decent cup of coffee. He never missed a chance to tell her that she ate her wages in peanut butter cups.

The bell above the door rang, and in stumbled Zachariah Tucker cradling his right arm. The smell the charred flesh reached her before he did. It was a smell she'd never forget. Even though her parents' coffins were closed, the acrid smell sat under the scent of roses and lilies covering the casket. To her, it was the scent of death.

She rushed him to the exam room. Filling a basin with ice and water, she submerged the wound into the frigid mix. The old man yelled and screamed until Doc walked in.

"All that screaming will not take the pain away." Doc donned a pair of gloves.

The only sign that this was more than Doc could handle was the lift of his brows. "Good job, Sage."

She reacted instinctually. The problem with burns was that they continued to burn at a sub-dermal level. Ice was the only way to neutralize the heat.

Doc picked up Zachariah's arm, and the flesh fell off in jagged pieces.

"I can't help you here. You need a burn center."

At the mention of a burn center, Zachariah became angry. He picked up the metal ice basin and hit Doc across the head, leaving a deep, bleeding gash on his forehead. Doc stumbled back and slid down the wall to the floor, where he sat in a puddle of cold water and ice cubes.

"What the hell do you think you're doing?" Sage yelled.

Zachariah lunged forward and headed to the door.

"Sit yourself back down, now!" The power of her voice surprised her. She stalked toward the grizzled old man, and fear flashed across his features as he shuffled back and sat on the table. "Don't you move."

She opened a package of gauze and pressed the bundle to Doc's bloody head. He attempted to get up but slipped on the ice and water.

"Stay." She held up her finger like she did with Otis.

Once Zachariah's arm was back on ice, she picked up the phone to call for a Copper Creek ambulance. The old man argued, but she silenced him with a look.

"You want to get up and walk out of here? That's fine, but let me tell you what will happen." She pulled a chair over to Doc and helped him into it while blood oozed through the gauze. She faced the old bootlegger and continued. "I know your type. You'll go home, coat the burn in butter, wrap it in a towel, and secure it with duct tape. It will fester. Next, you'll be at the emergency room for an amputation." She pressed a damp cloth to Doc's pale forehead.

"Mr. Tucker, your bootlegging has hurt many in this town, including Ben Bishop, and now you. If you want to live longer, I suggest you switch careers."

Doc gripped the chair one-handed and tried to stand.

"I told you to sit down!" Sage glared at her boss.

"Last time I looked, I was the doctor."

Sage had it with these two stubborn men. "You two are impossible." She slammed the drawer that held the sterile gauze and walked toward the door. "Suit yourself. If you want to bleed all over the clinic, go ahead."

"You're acting like a bossy nurse," Doc said.

She narrowed her eyes and shook her head. "I was a bossy nurse."

Behind the grimace of pain, he smiled. "You still are and will always be a nurse because it's in your blood, bossy or not."

Zachariah groaned. "She's a mean, bossy nurse."

"Shut up," Doc and Sage said together.

The old man pressed his arm deeper into the bin.

"My ice is melting."

She ignored his complaint. Minutes ago, he was ready to walk out the door, and now he wanted to argue about ice levels? As long as cubes were floating on the surface, he was fine, so she turned her attention to Doc.

"What do you need?"

He pulled a hand mirror from a nearby drawer and peeled the gauze from his head to inspect the wound. "I need suturing supplies." He staunched the flow of blood and leaned back into the chair.

"You're going to stitch yourself up?"

"No, you are."

"I can't legally suture your wound. I could lose my license." While she argued, she gathered supplies.

"I won't turn you in. Now get to it." He rose and took a seat next to Zachariah. "Old man, all I have to say is you better heal fast because this will cost you a lot of firewood. I'll expect mine by the end of the summer." He turned toward Sage, who gloved up. "When would you like yours?"

While she shook her head, the Doc nodded his. "Everything has a consequence. This old man knows that. You mix grain alcohol with fire, and you get burned. If you get burned and need help, you have to pay. Our payment is firewood, and I think a cord for each of us will be fine."

Zachariah grumbled but nodded.

Sage dabbed at Doc's wound with antiseptic.

He growled. "That hurts like a son of a bitch."

"Maybe you should numb yourself up. I can't stitch you if you cry like one of the Williams kids when I pierce your skin."

"When did you get so cantankerous?"

"Born that way." Sage pressed the needle into his forehead. His pink skin blanched white, but she continued to stitch the gash until it closed. Once the gut was snipped, she dabbed on antibiotic ointment and handed him a mirror.

"You may have missed your calling. You'd make a fine doctor." He looked at his injury the same way Sage looked at art—with appreciation.

"One in the family is enough. My sister is an ER doctor in Denver."

"Is that right?"

188

In the distance, Sage heard the ambulance and looked to both men. "Both of you stay put."

Once Zachariah was on his way to Copper Creek, and she helped Doc upstairs to his apartment, she cleaned up the exam room, canceled the day's appointments, and turned off the blinking red sign before she left for the day.

She considered a stop at the bar but decided to go home instead.

When she arrived, a woman with her face buried in her hands sat on the steps. She lifted her head, and Sage sucked in a breath. To say she was bruised was an understatement. The woman looked like she'd been mugged—twice.

"Are you okay?" Sage knelt before her.

"Do you have a room I can rent?" Her voice was small and desperate.

Sage looked around to make sure there was no immediate danger. "Come in, let me help you."

"Thank you."

She led the woman into the kitchen, where she pulled out a chair. "Have a seat. I'm a nurse. Let me clean you up."

There was nothing better than a cup of tea when life got stressful. It was that or a bottle of wine, and since Cannon and Sage had finished the wine last night, she made tea.

Sage picked up the phone. "I'll call the sheriff."

"No," the woman cried. "Please. No." Tears ran past her black and blue eyes and over her swollen cheek.

"Okay. Okay. How about some ice?"

She nodded. Her shaking hands brought the cup of hot tea to her lips. "I need a day or two."

"Have you been here before?"

She nodded.

"A lot?"

She nodded.

"What's your name?"

The woman's eyes grew wide, and she shook her head.

"Okay, well, my name is Sage. Will you tell me who did this to you?"

She shook her head.

It broke Sage's heart that she couldn't offer anything more than a safe place and an ice pack. But then again, she'd learned a lot about people lately. Healing couldn't start until the problem was acknowledged.

"You deserve better." Sage pulled a bottle of ibuprofen from the cupboard and set it on the table. Sage's black eye had hurt like the dickens, and this woman was in worse shape. She dabbed antibiotic cream on the worst parts and stepped back. There was nothing she could do until the woman acknowledged the problem. "Help yourself to anything you need." She pointed to the private wing of the house. The place where she and Cannon fell into each other's arms each night. "I'm down that hallway if you need something." Sage walked away but stopped and turned toward the battered woman. "My boyfriend will be home later. His name is Cannon. He'll cause you no harm."

CHAPTER THIRTY-FOUR

The next morning, Sage hid behind a table in the bakery while Ben crouched behind another on the opposite side. "Do you see anyone?" she asked him.

"No. You?" His voice was strong and healthy. Ben was on top of his sobriety, and she couldn't have been prouder. Too bad Cannon remained guarded, although, she couldn't blame him. He had years of disappointment to work through.

Katie walked out of the back room, drying her hands on her apron. Today, she added cookies to the menu. They were simple snickerdoodles, but the smell of cinnamon filled the air, making them seem like so much more than a cookie.

"I'm telling you, they're ghosts. I've been watching all week to see who drops off supplies. The minute I turn my back, something shows up." The timer rang, and Katie pulled a tray of perfectly round, golden-brown cookies from the oven.

Ben abandoned his post to get the first taste. He'd become an integral part of Katie's success. Not only had he cleaned, but *handy* was his middle name—or should have been. A week ago, there was a plumbing leak, and Ben fixed it. Two days ago, she found ants, and now they were gone.

Today, leaning against the freshly painted wall was a bulletin board waiting to be hung. The top of it read "The Wishing Wall." One half was a section for wishes, the other for wishes granted.

Sage walked away from the window and pointed to the board. "Tell me about the Wishing Wall."

Katie placed two trays of hot cookies on a cooling rack and closed the oven door. She picked up a spatula and scooped a hot cookie from the silver tray, plopping it on a napkin and handing it to an impatient Ben, who stood in front of the display case tapping the tip of his shoe on the clean checkerboard tile.

The floor wasn't the only thing that had been spruced up. Ben looked good dressed in blue slacks and a button-down shirt. His hair had been trimmed, and his scraggly facial hair shaved away to reveal a smooth complexion and ruddy cheeks. It was hard to believe this was the same man who, only weeks ago, lay passed out on her deck.

Katie poured coffees and plated up a few cookies and walked around to one of the tables.

The tables and chairs were still in need of repair, but with the pace she was moving through the needed fixes in the bakery, Sage was certain Katie would have everything in good shape in no time.

Sage sat across from Katie at the table nearest the window. It was a good perch from where to watch the day pass. Ben had devoured his cookie and was back at work, hanging the bulletin board. He'd all but forgotten about his job as private eye.

"First things first," Sage said. "Tell me about the Wishing Wall."

Katie lifted her shoulders. "I thought it would be a nice touch—a tribute to Bea." She said Bea's name in a way that almost sounded like the word *bay*. "A place where people could post their wants and needs and dreams. A place where others could see them and help fulfill them."

How was it that this woman had come from such a place of need weeks ago and was already in a position to help others?

"That's amazing." Sage broke off a corner of a cookie and popped it into her mouth. It nearly melted against her tongue. "So good. I'll take a dozen of these when you make them again."

Katie bounced in her chair with giddy excitement. "Really, you like them?"

By the time her friend had finished her sentence, Sage had devoured the entire cookie. "I've never tasted better."

"I'm baking more this afternoon, and I'll make you a batch."

"That'll be perfect. I have someone at the bed and breakfast, and I'd like to brighten her day." Sage thought of the woman staying in one of her rooms. "She showed up yesterday, black and blue, and won't let me call the sheriff. I'm afraid for her."

Katie's hand lifted to cover her mouth. "Oh no. Should you tell him anyway?"

Sage shook her head. "I have a feeling she doesn't have anyone to confide in, and I don't want to push her away by making her not trust me."

"I'd never stay with a man who hit me." Katie doctored up her coffee with cream and sugar and took a sip.

Ben tapped a few nails into the wall beside them.

"I've only been hit by one man." Sage turned toward Ben. "He packed quite a wallop. Isn't that right, Ben?"

He picked up the bulletin board and hung it from the nails. "You know I'm sorry about that. I thought you were Cannon. I've apologized at least a dozen times." He wore the repentant look well.

"I'm just giving you a hard time, Ben," Sage said. "I realize it was my dumb luck, but there's never a reason for violence. I'm just glad you're back to your sweet self, or at least, that's what I hear."

"Who's telling you I'm sweet?" He reached over the women and snagged the last cookie from the tray. "I need this cookie to keep me sweet."

Katie grinned. "I told her you were sweet. Now, will you be really sweet and get the ingredients together for another batch of cookies?"

Ben smiled warmly at Katie and walked to the storage room.

"Speaking of Cannon," Katie said. "How are you two doing?"

Did the heat Sage felt rise to her cheeks give her away? "He's hot. I'm ... I'm—"

"You're in love." Katie put her hand on top of Sage's. "It shows in your smile and the way you light up around him."

Sage leaned into the center of the table. "I can't be in love with him. It hasn't been long enough for me to fall in love." Sage had argued with herself for weeks about love and the possibility.

"Did you love Bea?"

"Yes, but that's different. Our relationship was different. I wasn't sleeping with Bea."

What started as a giggle swelled into laughter. "Exactly. You knew Bea less intimately, and for just over a month, but you loved her. You share everything with Cannon, so how could you not love him?"

It was hard to fight her logic. She shared every minute she could with Cannon. When they weren't in bed making love, they were holding hands walking around the lake, or eating meals together with Ben like they were a family. She'd come to depend on him and couldn't imagine her life without him. Was that love?

She had no real gauge from which to judge. Todd had been her longest-running relationship, and it turned out to be a friend-with-benefits arrangement. Too bad she hadn't realized that before her heart got broken.

"I have to be cautious. I wound easily." At least she was honest with herself these days.

Sage picked up her coffee and sipped while she watched Louise Williams struggle to get out of her car. She waddled to the back door and opened it.

"I swear, she's ready to pop any second." Katie took one last look out the window at Louise before she picked up the tray. "I'll get those cookies started." She looked over her shoulder to the back room. "If I leave Ben too long, he eats all my chocolate chips. I think vodka may be a cheaper addiction."

Sage turned from the window to frown at her friend's comment. Katie dropped the tray and bolted toward the door. When Sage looked out the window, she saw Louise was on the ground, sitting in a puddle of water.

"Go get Doc," Sage told Katie as she ran past her. She dropped to her knees in front of the pregnant woman. By the pained look on her face, it was obvious Louise was in labor.

"I thought I had some time to make the delivery."

Sage kneeled behind Louise's back, offering her support. She reached for the woman's wrist and took her pulse. "Your pulse is elevated, but not too much of a concern. How long have you been in labor?"

Louise's face twisted with discomfort. She let out a few *hoo hoo hoos* before she took a deep breath.

"Don't you push," Sage said. "How long?"

"A few hours. The last one took ten hours of labor, so I thought I was okay." She stiffened and started to pant again. When the contraction eased, she said, "I don't want to have this baby in the middle of the street."

"Not happening," Doc's voice rose over the clank of the gurney he and Katie pushed in front of them. "I told you to take it easy. Where's Bobby?" Doc put the brakes on the gurney, and he helped Sage get Louise onto the bed before the next pain ripped through her.

"He's at the shop. Hoo hoo hoo hoo," she breathed.

Doc turned to Katie. "Ben in the back of the bakery?" She nodded. "Send him down the street to get Bobby. Tell him his daughter is on her way, and he's got about five minutes before she arrives."

Katie took off like a bullet shot from a pistol.

"Five minutes?" Sage said. "How do you know?"

Doc unlocked the gurney and started to push the grunting woman toward the clinic.

"Louise is quick once her water breaks. Usually takes ten minutes

195

or so. I'm thinking she's been here with you for about five." He nodded toward the door. "We'll be lucky to get her into the room."

Sage held the door open while Doc pushed the gurney through.

Louise rose up on the bed, her face pinched and red.

"Not yet, Louise."

"I can't wait," she screamed.

They rushed her down the hallway and into the examination room. Doc threw a pair of gloves at Sage and snapped a pair on himself. She went to the sink to wash up, but the minute Doc pushed Louise's dress out of the way and pulled her underwear off, a crown of black hair told Sage she didn't have time to do much.

"It's time," Doc called.

Sage's training kicked into gear. She'd assisted in the delivery of hundreds of babies when she worked in labor and delivery. She offered words of encouragement and coached in the breathing process.

She fished through the cabinets for the supplies they needed to bring a baby into the world. Bulb suction. Clamps. Sterilized scissors. Sutures. Warm blankets. She gloved up just in time to play catch.

On the next contraction, Louise pushed, and that head of black hair turned into a beautiful baby. Sage had missed the miracle of life. To bring a baby into the world was a completely different feeling than holding the hand of someone leaving it. Both were heartfelt, and both were important, but Sage would take this over death any day.

Doc laid the screaming pink bundle on Louise's sheet-covered chest. While he clamped and cut the cord, Sage wiped down the baby, spoke to Louise and told her how well she had done, and how beautiful her daughter was.

In the hallway, there was a rumble of mixed voices, Katie, Ben, and Bobby. But the loudest voice was Bobby's, calling out for his wife. When he burst through the door, Sage watched the big, tough-looking man fall to his knees and cry.

Doc wrapped up the little girl and handed her to her father.

Bobby looked at the baby as if he'd seen heaven. Then he leaned over and kissed his wife.

Sage's heart squeezed at the scene unfolding before her. Would she ever have a child or a man who looked at her like she hung the moon? She thought about Cannon and realized she wanted this exact scene with him. Not now, but someday.

"What were you thinking?" he asked his wife. His voice was soft but questioning.

Louise turned a loving smile to her husband. "I had to fulfill Bea's wish. She wanted me to deliver pecans and brown sugar to the bakery today."

At that, Sage laughed. "Was that a pink letter wish?"

The Williamses turned to her like they just noticed she was there. They both nodded. "We were the last delivery."

"That was quite a delivery," Sage said. "What are you going to call this little girl?"

Doc had pulled a scale from the cupboard. He took the little bundle and unwrapped her. "At eight pounds, five ounces, she isn't that little."

Louise looked at her husband. There was a silent message exchanged between the two. He nodded, and she smiled. "Her name is Beatrice Olivia Williams."

"God help us," Doc said.

An hour later, after everyone had gone, an ambulance from Copper Creek picked up Louise and little Bea. Mother and daughter looked healthy, but Doc thought a night of observation in a proper hospital would be wise.

Sage returned home to find fifty dollars on the table, and the battered woman gone. In the basket that caught the mail was an envelope from the developer she'd called the day she arrived in town.

Inside was a letter, thanking her for her interest in selling the property. They weren't interested in the house but would like to discuss purchasing the land.

Sage walked into the kitchen and put the letter in the catchall drawer. Tomorrow, she'd contact the company and tell them she wasn't interested in their offer. Without a doubt, she knew Bea would never sell this house to a developer. No amount of money could replace what Aspen Cove had given her. There wasn't a price for hope or love or community.

She had to keep the bed and breakfast open to offer shelter to battered women, a place for the fishermen arriving this week, and for noisy newlyweds.

CHAPTER THIRTY-FIVE

Cannon tiptoed down the hallway to Sage's room and sat on the edge of her bed. Tucked under the covers, she looked so small and vulnerable. A bare shoulder peeked out of the blankets where soft pale skin picked up the moonlight shining on her through the blinds. Wild red hair fanned across the pillow. Pink lips puckered as if waiting for a kiss.

There was nothing he'd rather do than strip down and slide between the sheets with her, but he couldn't. Tomorrow was the anniversary of his mother's death, and although his father was doing well, he didn't want to leave him alone in case he had a setback. And yet, he couldn't go to sleep without one last look at Sage.

Weeks ago, Doc said there would be a change in Aspen Cove, but Cannon didn't dare hope that a woman would change everything about his life. Make it different. Make it better. She arrived and disrupted his status quo, making him realize it had been status woe.

He'd moved along day-to-day. His pattern had been to hang on and make it to the next breath. He didn't plan for the future because he lived minute by minute. He couldn't afford to risk the disappointment of thinking about tomorrow, but Sage turned his world around.

The woman lying in front of him made him look forward to the next day and next week and next year. He saw a future beyond his exhale.

Caring for Sage put him at risk. That was the scariest revelation of all, because like it or hate it, he was exactly like his father, minus the alcoholism.

When it came to love, his dad was all in. He loved Cannon's mom without reservation. Ben Bishop's entire life had been consumed by that love, and when she died, so did he. He had become the walking dead.

Since then, Cannon held back. He didn't want to risk everything by allowing someone to become the center of his universe, and yet, here was Sage. She wheedled her way into his life, and then his heart.

He warred with himself. Wake her and make love to her, or let her sleep? With her working a shift at Doc's in the morning, he wouldn't be selfish and wake her up, but he wanted her to know how important she'd become to him. So instead of leaning over and kissing those beautiful lips, burying his face in her hair, or sliding his body next to hers, he rose from the edge of the bed with the words "I love you" a breath away from being said out loud.

After tomorrow, he'd tell her the truth. He'd let her know the depth of his feelings. How hard it was for him to trust that she wasn't going to leave him when everyone he loved did. For now, he'd find a piece of paper and let her know he'd been there, and he missed her.

Cannon stepped over Otis, who lay on his back with his feet pointed to the ceiling.

In the kitchen, he flipped the light switch and opened what Sage called her catchall drawer. It was the place she hid the stuff she wasn't ready to deal with. It was also the place she kept pens and paper.

On top was a page with the logo of the development company he loathed. His throat tightened, and his heart skipped a beat, then raced to catch up. It was none of his business, but it didn't stop him from reading the note.

Dear Ms. Nichols,

Thank you for reaching out to us about your interest in selling the property at 1 Lake Circle, Aspen Cove, Colorado. We are interested in making a deal.

We have no use for the actual structure, but we can offer a fair price for the land. Please contact us at your earliest convenience so we can proceed.

Sincerely,

Stephen Tobler

Property Development Manager

Sterling Group

Cannon ground his teeth until he was sure the enamel would crack. All the progress he'd made tearing his barriers down was for naught. The fortress he had erected before Sage arrived slid back into place. Steel beam reinforcements resurrected around his heart.

He shoved the letter into the drawer and walked out of her house. On his way home, he screamed internally at himself. He should have known better. The heart couldn't be trusted, and neither could Sage. Then again, she never told him she'd stay. She only made him feel it was permanent by the way she invested herself in those around her. Hers was the worst kind of betrayal because there was no warning. It was like when his mom drove off the cliff. There was no way to prepare for the mess she would leave behind.

There would be so many people hurt when Sage left. She'd taken an interest in his father and he looked to her for support and encouragement and a kick in the pants when needed. Doc counted on her during clinic days. Hell, she helped deliver Louise's baby that morning. Katie was her friend and confidant. Then there was him. He'd let her in. He'd fallen in love with her and considered a future with her, but now there was nothing. She'd robbed him of everything. It was one thing to live in ignorance; it was another to have had a taste of heaven and then be shoved into hell.

Cannon walked into his house and looked in on his father, who was asleep in bed. He entered his bedroom and opened the safe to pull out a bottle of wine. Tonight, he would drink. Tomorrow, he would mourn the loss of his mother and Sage.

CHAPTER THIRTY-SIX

A loud crack of thunder woke Sage from a sound sleep as rain pelted the roof and windows. The smell of pine and dampness filled the air. At the next boom of thunder, Otis barked at the air around him.

"It's okay, it's just a storm. It'll pass."

She ran her hand over the smooth bedspread where Cannon normally slept. It had been weeks since that side of the bed had been empty, and having half the bed pristine didn't feel right or natural. She liked the way Cannon wrapped his body around hers every night and how she never got cold despite the way he kicked off the covers.

She missed not waking up to a cup of coffee next to the bed. It was his gift to her each morning, and she liked that almost as much as his morning kisses—almost.

Although he'd stayed with his father last night, his absence was profoundly felt. She made the offer to stay at his house, but he wasn't sure what the day would bring and said it would be safer for all involved if he stayed home and she stayed at her place.

She understood his apprehension. Although Ben had been sober for weeks, all it took was one thing to set him back. If there was a catalyst to worry about, it would be the anniversary of the death of his wife, Carly.

Sage slid out of bed and into her slippers. She walked Otis to the back door, where he made quick business of emptying his bladder. Otis wasn't fond of the rain.

While her cup of coffee brewed, she called Cannon. The phone rang four times, then went to voice mail.

"Hey, it's me. I miss you. Let me know if you need anything." She almost told him she loved him, but that should be said in person the first time.

She walked to the front door and peeked outside to see if his truck was in the driveway, but it wasn't.

She had no idea where he had gone but hoped everything was okay. Thinking he'd taken Ben to work because of the heavy rain, she showered, dressed in scrubs for her shift at Doc's, and drove to B's Bakery. The big black truck was nowhere in sight.

She raced through the rain into the bakery, where she took in a breath of comfort that came by way of sugar, butter, flour, and fruit. It was eight o'clock, and the muffins were ready. Thursday was cranberry-orange day. She wasn't sure which day she liked the best. It was a tie between banana-nut-muffin day and today. Then there was raspberry-muffin day. She liked those too. Who was she kidding? She simply liked muffins, and it didn't matter what flavor.

"Be right there," Katie called from the back room.

"Take your time. It's just me." Sage walked over to the Wishing Wall. It had been up one day, and there was already a wish posted. She opened the folded page thumbtacked to the corkboard, and her heart fell into her stomach. The wish was from Ben.

Please make the pain go away. Help me have the courage to move on to the next phase of my life.

Ben

She heard many speak this way. People often begged for release into the next life when the pain of cancer or liver disease racked a body. Was that what Ben wished for?

"Sad, huh?" Katie stood behind the counter and poured two cups of coffee. She walked to the other side of the display case and handed Sage a cup. They stared at the lone note stuck to the board.

"You don't think he's going to kill himself, do you?"

By Katie's shocked expression, she obviously didn't consider the possibility. "I never thought about it." She tapped the note with a soft touch, opening it up to expose the wish. "I assumed he was asking everyone to help him move on. As in be supportive. That kind of thing."

Sage went to the table and sat. She put her coffee down and pulled her phone from her purse. Once again, she dialed Cannon, but he didn't answer. This time she didn't leave a message but followed the call with a text.

Is your dad okay?

Katie left and came back with muffins. "He was sad yesterday, but he talked about today like he planned to be here. We laughed at how Louise nearly had her baby on the street because she was so intent on delivering the baking supplies."

Sage picked up the muffin and peeled off the paper baking cup. "At least that mystery is solved. I wondered what all of those pink envelopes were for. It was Bea's way of giving even after she was gone. Too bad she couldn't fix things for Ben."

"You don't really think—" Katie looked up at the note and shook her head. "I'll kill him myself for even considering it. What did Cannon say?"

Sage looked down at the blank screen of her phone. "Nothing. He isn't answering my calls or texts."

"That can't be good." Katie stared out the window.

"I'm not going to jump to conclusions just yet," Sage replied.

"No, I mean *that* can't be good." Katie pointed to the sheriff's car parked in front of Doc's with its lights flashing, but the siren was off. Sheriff Cooper bolted from his cruiser and ran into the clinic. "Something's up."

Sage dropped her muffin, grabbed her purse, and sprinted

through the rain across the street. When she got to the door, Doc was on his way out—black bag in hand and a grim expression on his face.

"Is it Ben?" she asked, trying to keep up with both men.

"Yes," said the sheriff.

"I'm coming." She opened the back of the squad car, only to have Sheriff Cooper shut it.

"Cannon doesn't want you there," he said.

"What?" His words were like a hammer to her heart. "What do you mean?"

The sheriff didn't elaborate, just climbed inside the car with Doc and drove away, leaving Sage standing in the street.

There was no way she'd be left out in the rain, so she ran to her SUV and drove in the direction the sheriff had. When she reached the flashing lights, she was at the cemetery. By the time she got to the plot of land where everyone was standing, she was drenched, and the thin cotton of her scrubs clung to her body. Her teeth chattered, and her insides quivered.

None of that mattered, because all she could see was Cannon cradling his father's body. A trail of blood trickled from Ben's forehead. He finally did it. He killed himself. But as soon as Doc pressed a packet of gauze to Ben's head, he let out a torrent of foul words that would make a hooker blush.

"You'll need stitches." Doc looked over his shoulder to Sage. "She can help." He touched the healing wound on his own forehead. "She's good at them."

Cannon looked at her. "Nope, she doesn't have time for us because she's got other stuff on her plate."

She moved toward the man she'd come to love. "What the hell are you talking about?" The eyes that just yesterday morning looked at her with love and affection no longer held that sparkle of life. Gone was the warmth of the green, and in its place was ice-cold blue.

"Let's get him up," Doc said. He moved to the side while Cannon and Sheriff Cooper helped Ben to his feet. Ben groaned and tried to pull away, but the men wouldn't let him loose.

"I'm not dead," Ben grumbled. "I slipped on a wet gravestone and fell." He looked back at Carly's grave. "I'm pretty sure she's done with my moping and reached out from the heavens to trip me."

As the men walked Ben down the grassy slope, Doc and Sage followed.

"She was always a patient woman, but do you really think it took her nearly a decade to set you straight?" Doc opened the back door of the sheriff's car and helped Ben inside. He looked at Sage. "Meet me at the clinic because I could use your help."

Sage nodded and stood in the parking lot to watch everyone but Cannon drive away. What was she supposed to think? Had the situation shaken him so much?

"Cannon," she started to walk toward him. "What's going on?" Her entire body shivered, but she wasn't sure if it was the cold or something else. A feeling of dread washed over her.

"Now's not the time, Sage. I don't have the energy or desire to deal with you right now." He took a step toward her, then turned back to his truck.

She was certain he'd climb inside and drive away. Instead, he said, "Dammit," and rushed toward her. He removed his jacket and wrapped it around her shoulders.

She leaned into him. "What's going on here?"

He cocked his head. "Apparently, nothing worth your effort." He turned away and stalked back to his truck, jumped inside, and drove off.

She was left in the middle of the cemetery, soaked to the bone, and confused as hell.

CHAPTER THIRTY-SEVEN

Cannon knew he needed to gain distance from Sage because his heart would never survive the hit of her leaving if he didn't. Torn between begging her to stay and running away, he hit the steering wheel. Pain shot up his arm, but it was a welcome relief to the stabbing hurt in his heart. One, he'd feel for a few seconds, the other, a lifetime.

He drove into town and pulled into the parking spot in front of the clinic. There was no one to turn to even though he needed someone to talk to. For the first time in years, he wanted to cry. Instead, he pulled out his phone and called Bowie.

Whether he'd pick up was anyone's guess. It wasn't only the anniversary of their mom's death, but the anniversary of Brandy's as well, but if their dad could work his way past it, so could his brother.

On the fourth ring, he answered. "He alive?" It was the way Bowie answered all his calls from Cannon, which weren't many since he spent most of his time deployed.

"Yep, where are you?" The last time he talked to him, he was in Afghanistan in a hospital bed, recovering from injuries sustained from a bombing.

"I'm close."

That answer shocked the hell out of him because Bowie did his best not to set foot in Colorado.

"What does close mean?"

"I was gonna call you tomorrow. It's not a good day, Cannon."

Something inside him snapped. "Don't talk to me about good days. I haven't had one in years. I get that you lost your girl, but I lost too. I lost you and Mom and Dad." He didn't tell him that he'd also lost his girl. What was the point? "I've been here picking up the pieces ever since, and I'm tired. Now, where the hell are you?"

Sage pulled her SUV next to Cannon's truck and got out. She stared at him for a minute, and by the look she gave him, he thought she'd come over, but she pulled his jacket up to her nose and took a deep breath. Then she took it off and laid it on the hood of his truck before she turned away and walked inside the clinic.

"I'm at Fort Carson," Bowie said drawing his attention back to the call.

"You're where?" He couldn't believe his ears. Fort Carson was a few hours away. It was a military post Bowie had avoided his whole enlistment. In fact, when Bowie signed up, he drove to Oklahoma to swear in. "You need to come home."

He might not beg Sage to stay, but he'd press his brother to return. "That's kind of the plan for now. I'm here to process out. Not because I want to, but the army decided I was no longer fit to fight, and I'm out of options."

Cannon didn't know what to say. Bowie had never been honest about his injuries. With all the deployments, he'd been hurt plenty, and Cannon guessed his brother ran into the fights hoping not to make it out. Like his father, the two men had been shattered when they lost the women they loved. That's why Cannon had to let Sage go.

"You okay?" Cannon asked.

There was a long moment of silence. "I will be." Bowie cleared his throat. "Is Dad passed out on her grave again?"

"No, man. I have so much to tell you, but you should know, Dad's sober. He fell today, and when I found him, I thought he was dead, but he wasn't. He was mad. Right now, he's at Doc's getting stitched up, but he's okay. And another thing, he's working at B's Bakery."

"The old girl put him to work?" There was a hint of nostalgia in Bowie's voice.

It had been way too long since they touched base. "Bea died over a month ago. She gave the bakery to a woman named Katie, and the bed and breakfast to a woman named Sage. Dad's been helping Katie, and Sage has been helping Dad." *And me.*

"Oh man, I'm so sorry about Bea. I had no idea."

"It's hard to stay informed when you don't stay connected." He didn't want to bust his brother's balls, but it was time he was honest. "You're coming home just in time to run the bait and tackle shop. When will you get here?"

"I'm working myself up to it. Could be a week or two or three."

He knew his brother would have a tough time coming back to Aspen Cove. Memories of Brandy waited around every corner. "I'll be here for you."

"You always were."

CHAPTER THIRTY-EIGHT

Once Doc stitched Ben's head, he walked out with the sheriff and left Sage to bandage him up. "You had Katie and me worried." She peeled off the backing and lined up the jumbo Band-Aid to cover the wound.

Ben smiled. "Did you think I was gonna do myself in?" He reached up and touched his forehead. "I'd choose something more effective and less painful."

"You want something for the pain?" Sage gathered up the bloody gauze and paper and tossed it into the nearby biohazard bag.

He shook his head. "I've been numb for years. I think it's about time I feel something, even if it's only a headache. The way I see it, it's payback for all the headaches I gave others—especially Cannon. How will I ever make it up to him?"

"Just be present. All he wants is to have the people he loves around." She offered him one of Doc's Life Savers, but Ben declined. "Speaking of Cannon, he seems a bit off today. I know it's *the* day, but he isn't himself, and I'm worried."

Ben laid a hand on her shoulder. "He's lost a lot on this day already. It was a blow to him to find out you were leaving."

Sage staggered back. "Leaving? Where did he get the idea I was leaving?" She replayed recent conversations in her mind and couldn't come up with one where she gave Cannon the impression she was going anywhere. "I'm not leaving."

Ben narrowed his eyes. "While we waited for Doc, he said he found a letter from some development agent who offered you a buyout for Bea's property."

"That's what this is about?" She turned and stomped to the door, then called over her shoulder, "Stick around, Ben, because there's going to be another head bashing, and Cannon might need your assistance."

She marched outside to where he sat in his truck and pulled on the door handle, not expecting it to open. Cannon had barricaded himself from her all day, so why not lock the door? When it opened, she stumbled back and fell to her bottom on the wet ground.

He hopped out to help her up. "Geez, Sage. What the hell is your problem?"

With his hands on her shoulders, he lifted her to a standing position, and she poked him in the chest. "You. You're my problem."

"Not for long."

The rain fell around them. "Are you going somewhere? Because I'm not, and I don't know where you got some foolish idea that I was."

"I found the letter."

"So, you found a letter from a company that wanted to buy the property. They leave stuff all over town. I even saw one of their cards tucked into the door of the bar one day. Are you selling?"

"No." She pushed against his chest until he fell against the truck, pinned between the cold, wet metal and her body.

"Exactly." She reached to the side of him and pulled his jacket from the seat. At least he'd brought it in from where she left it on the hood. "It's freezing." She pulled the damp coat over her shoulders and shivered.

"Climb into the truck before you freeze to death," he said.

She wasn't stupid, only cold, so she slid to the passenger's side while Cannon took his seat behind the wheel and closed the door. The windows fogged immediately. "I wouldn't be near freezing if you hadn't ignored my calls and message. This could have been talked out."

"I was angry."

Sage shook with fury. "You haven't seen angry."

He scooted closer and reached for her, but she pressed her back to the door. "Oh no, you don't. You don't get to break up with me, and then think you can make it better because you offer me shelter from the storm."

"I was hurt."

"I am hurt, Cannon, because you thought I'd keep something that big from you. I called that guy the day I arrived. Remember that day? The day I thought you were an asshole. Now I'm thinking that maybe my first impression was right."

"Come on, Sage. I was confused. Hell, I'm *still* confused." He pointed to her and back to him. "This thing between us. It's been more of a storm than the one outside. You struck me like lightning. You washed over me like rain. You rattled me to the core like thunder. I'm afraid of losing everything."

"You could have asked or said something. And to think I was going to tell you I loved you." She lowered her eyes. "My grandmother always said, 'No risk, no reward,' and she was right. If you can't risk your heart, Cannon, then I can't reward you with my love."

She opened the passenger-side door and walked back into the storm, leaving him to contemplate her words.

Back at the bakery, she plopped herself in the nearest chair and laid her head on the table. When Katie came to the front of the display case, Sage was fully committed to an ugly cry.

"Oh, sweetie." Katie knelt beside her and wrapped her arms around her shoulder. "You need a cookie?"

Laughter bubbled inside Sage. She was certain she looked like a crazed woman. "I need more than a cookie. This might be one of the worst days I've had in years."

"Hold that thought." Katie dashed into the back room. The echo of footsteps on the stairs meant she'd gone to her apartment. A few minutes later, she came back winded and in her hand was a light pink envelope. *Give to Sage on her darkest day* was written across the front in Bea's distinctive handwriting. She took the seat across from her and handed over the envelope. "I figure if this is the worst day you've had in years, it qualifies as a dark day." She stood. "While you open your letter, I'll get the cookies."

The last time Sage received a pink envelope, it changed her life. What would this contain? She ran her finger under the flap to reveal a single handwritten page.

Dearest Sage,

If you're reading this, you've come to a turning point in your life. I have no idea what that might be, but I'll offer you my solution. Many call it a list of pros and cons. I simply call it one hundred reasons. Whatever you're debating, write it down. Come up with one hundred reasons to move forward. If you can't come up with a solid list, then feel free to quit or move in another direction.

If you're still confused, look around you. The people of Aspen Cove are never too busy to lend a hand, an ear, or an opinion.

With love and affection,

Bea

The smell of the baked goods arrived before Katie, who delivered a plate of heart-shaped sugar cookies.

"If the letter didn't help, these will."

Sage set the letter down and picked up a cookie. "It's Bea's way of reminding me to consider the positives and not make decisions without thought." She took a bite and hummed. "These are a positive."

"Tell me what's happening."

Once she'd swallowed the cookie, Sage explained everything.

When Sage was finished, Katie lifted her eyes skyward. "Is that all?"

"All? Are you kidding? How do we build a relationship when we can't communicate? Cannon is so afraid of a broken heart, he refuses to use his."

"I've seen Cannon look at you. Girl, he already gave you his heart. What will you do with it?"

"I thought he loved me too, but he's never said the words."

"Have you said them to him?" Katie reached over the table and tugged her damp curls. "You yourself just figured it out. He's a man, and they're slower."

"You really think he loves me?"

Katie handed her another cookie. "Eat up. You must be weak because your brain isn't working. He wouldn't have been so upset at the thought of losing you if he didn't care. You make a difference in his life."

Sage nibbled around and around the cookie until she reached the center. Maybe she'd reached Cannon's heart the same way. She chipped away at the edges until she made her way inside. The way he kissed her and held her spoke volumes. In the back of her mind, she could hear her mom telling her that actions spoke louder than words. Maybe the words weren't important.

"He really loves me." Sage said it with awe in her voice. "I make a difference, and in the end, that's enough for me."

Katie looked down at the pink paper. "You need a pen?" She didn't wait for an answer and pulled one from her pocket.

Sage didn't need a hundred reasons. She only needed one. The best reason was Cannon because she loved him one hundred times over.

On the page, she wrote his name, hugged Katie, and left. She needed to talk to him about a property. Not the kind that sat on the lake, but the real estate in his heart.

CHAPTER THIRTY-NINE

Cannon sat on the deck of his house with his head in his hands, and a pink piece of paper in his lap. It was a letter from Bea, and all it said was:

Cannon,

It's time to live your life.

Love you,

Bea

She always knew what to say. Even in death, she had uncanny timing. He'd stopped by the bar to pick up the letter that said *Open on a dark day*. No day could be darker than the day he lost the woman he loved. He'd been an ass when he thought he'd lost Sage.

He picked up the bottle of wine and brought it to his lips. Staring at the water, his thoughts were consumed by a little redhead who had made him love again.

"I know you're not good at sharing words, but what about wine?" Her voice startled him.

The bottle fell from his hand and landed at his boots, spilling through the gaps of the wooden deck. Scrambling, he saved what wine he could, and handed it to Sage. "I don't know what to say to you." Where did he start? "I'll start with I'm sorry, but after that, I'm lost. There are so many words you should hear, and I don't know where to begin."

She leaned against the rail and took a drink.

No longer dressed in wet scrubs, she was bundled up in a sweater and jeans. Cannon was happy she was dry and warm.

The storm had passed, and the sky was clear. Warmth rushed through him that could have been the wine, but he wanted to believe it was their connection. One he hoped they still had.

"You'll have to figure it out because this is your chance to tell me how you feel."

"Do I have a limit on words?"

"This isn't a game show, Cannon. This is life, where people who care about each other communicate."

He rose from the chair and reached for her. He turned her around and gave her his seat. Once he had her in his place, he dropped to his knees in front of her. The pink page from Bea broke free and took flight on the breeze toward the lake.

Sage lifted herself up. "Should we get that?"

He pressed her back into the seat. "It's not nearly as important as you. You want to know how I feel?" He lowered his hands to her thighs. Touching her gave him strength. "I love you, Sage. I sat at the edge of your bed last night, watching you and wanting you. I know I'm not worthy of you because I have nothing to offer, but I'll give you anything I have just to spend another minute in your presence."

She lifted her hands to his head and ran her fingers through his hair. "You have plenty to offer. I'm not interested in money or things. All I want is your love and to make my home in your heart."

"My heart is yours." He leaned forward, stopping before their lips touched. "Can I kiss you?"

She lunged forward, knocking him over and falling on top of his body. The wine bottle rolled from her hand and disappeared off the edge of the deck. "I wish you would."

It was a kiss to beat all kisses. Everything they never said was put into it. He felt her love and gave her his, but she broke away too soon.

"Something wrong?" His heart raced.

"Yes, I need something else."

"What's that?" He would give her anything she asked for as long as it wasn't space.

"You—in bed—in me."

Thank God. Cannon scooped her up and took her home.

With every touch, every kiss, every stroke, he told her he loved her.

The next morning, he put coffee and a note on the nightstand, then sat waiting for her to wake. The note had the nine most wonderful words in the universe written neatly across the paper. *You are mine. I am yours. We are love.*

When she opened her eyes and read it, she pulled it to her chest. "Yes, we are."

CHAPTER FORTY

Sage and Otis walked down Main Street. What once looked like an abandoned town had become home.

Who would have thought a speck of land in the middle of nowhere could offer her everything a girl needed? The call she made to HR this morning telling them she wouldn't be returning was so easy.

Aspen Cove didn't have a Target, a Starbucks, or a movie theater. There was no Dunkin' Donuts, Taco Bell, or shopping mall. There was Cannon, and he made up for all the shortcomings.

As she walked, she caught the smell of chocolate floating on the air. Her pace picked up because who didn't like chocolate? Even Otis seemed eager to close the gap between him and the bakery, but that was because Katie had a bucket of treats she kept inside for him. There was one thing Otis liked more than belly rubs, and that was Milk-Bones.

"Wait up," came a familiar, sexy voice from behind. Cannon jogged to catch up to her.

Sage tilted her head in confusion. "I thought you were meeting up with Bowie?"

His shoulders sagged. "He canceled again."

Sage stopped and pulled him in for a hug. She knew how important it was to both Cannon and Ben that Bowie come home, but this was his third cancellation, and she was certain he was losing hope.

"He'll come home when he's ready. He needs time to figure things out," Cannon said.

Sage couldn't imagine coming back to the place where he'd lost it all. "I know, but I'm sure you miss your brother."

He set his head on top of hers and hugged her back.

Sage thought about how quickly a life could change. It had changed in a matter of seconds for Cannon, Ben, and Bowie. For her, it took a little longer, but the outcome was better. She found love. Things had been easy between them since that day on the deck. Everything had fallen into place like someone had planned it with precision. She looked to the sky and said a silent prayer to Bea because, without her gift of hope and love and faith, Sage would still be walking the lonely halls of some hospital in her squeaky white loafers.

"I can't get your brother to come home, but I can offer an alternative." She gave him what she hoped was a sex-kitten smile. "How about we grab a muffin and go back to our home—back to our bed? We've got the house to ourselves. No guests are arriving until later."

Cannon had all but moved in with her. Little by little, she found his clothes hanging in the closet and his toothbrush on the counter in the bathroom. His socks shared space with hers. She liked the way he decorated her life with happiness and love.

"Sweetheart, you make it sound like spending time with you comes in second place."

"Not at all. Get me a muffin, and I'll show you how first-rate I can be."

She laughed when Cannon rushed into the bakery ahead of her.

Katie was boxing up a four-pack when Sage and Otis made it inside. "Treat?" Katie called out. Though Otis couldn't rise up on one leg, it didn't stop him from trying. His back end whipped around like a wrecking ball, overturning everything in its path. By the time Katie laid down a handful of Milk-Bones, three chairs were down.

"It doesn't take much to make him happy," Cannon handed Katie a twenty to pay for the muffins while Sage righted the chairs.

Katie looked down at the dog lying at Sage's feet. "He's male. You guys are easy to please," she said.

Sage and Cannon walked out hand in hand. She had muffins, a loyal pet, and a sexy boyfriend. Life didn't get better than that. Their hands swung back and forth between them as they headed home.

Sage looked up at him. "When I moved to Aspen Cove, there were three things I knew for certain, but I was more wrong than I was right."

"You? Wrong?" Cannon pulled a warm muffin from the box and offered her the first bite. "No way."

She choked on her bite of muffin. "I know. Unbelievable, right? But it's true." She gave him an exaggerated roll of her eyes. "Seriously, I have 'Sage' observations." She air-quoted her name for effect.

"First, death can't be escaped, but neither can life. It should be lived with love and passion, and you."

"I agree." He leaned over and gave her a soft kiss on the lips.

"Second, hell isn't a cold day in Denver, but heaven is living in Aspen Cove wrapped in your arms."

"You trying to make me blush?" he asked.

They neared the end of Main Street and made a slight left toward the bed and breakfast.

"Last." She stood at the doorstep. "Mr. Right is definitely Mr. Right Now, who will also be Mr. Right tomorrow and the next day after that until forever."

He turned the handle and held the door open. Otis walked in first and made his way to his chair.

"As happy as I am to be your Mr. Right Now, I'm even happier to be your forever. I love you, Sage Nichols, with every cell in my body."

Although the sheriff's friends were arriving in a few hours, Sage knew there was enough time to reaffirm that love, because today there was one thing she knew for certain. The rest of her life started now.

A SNEAK PEEK AT ONE HUNDRED HEARTBEATS

There were three things Katie Middleton knew with absolute certainty:

Hope appeared in a pink envelope.

Prince charming rode a Harley.

Some secrets were better left unspoken.

She relaxed at her favorite table in the bakery—the one directly under the Wishing Wall—and checked items off her bucket list. Not the list most people had with dreams like climbing Mount Kilimanjaro, running a marathon, or writing a book. Katie's list had the simple things she had never done, like flying a kite, rowing a boat, and baking a muffin.

Her life had been full of wishes for as long as she could remember, most of which had never materialized, so when she got a pink envelope with a deed to a bakery inside, she packed up her stuff and moved from Dallas, Texas, to Aspen Cove, Colorado.

It came as a shock to her family and friends when she disappeared without a word to a location she hadn't shared. She refused to allow anyone else control over her life. Illness had been her jailer—her parents her parole officers. She scribbled the word *independence* at the bottom of her list. Katie knew her happiness would come from within herself. Family was great. Friends were fabulous. But to feel truly independent, she needed to be the helper, not the helped. Wasn't it ironic that the most generous help she had received came from a stranger? It was a gift that allowed her to bury her past and become her future.

"Why me, Bea?" Her voice echoed off the walls of the empty bakery. It was a question she'd asked herself countless times over the last seven weeks. Why would a woman whom she'd never met give her a bakery in a town she'd never been to?

She flipped to the back of her journal, where a piece of worn pink stationery sat tucked close to the binding. The tri-folded paper had been opened and closed hundreds of times. She'd read every line, looking for clues. There was a list of one hundred reasons Bea gave the bakery to Katie, but not one made sense.

You have a good heart, it began, but how did she know? That might have been the biggest clue because it sat at the number one position, but it didn't lead Katie to anything conclusive. *You're a good person* was the second entry. Although Katie tried to give more than she took, she didn't consider herself any more deserving than the next. She'd logged hundreds of volunteer hours in the pediatric cardiac unit in Dallas, but it never felt like work, and she didn't do it for any reason other than to bring a smile to those around her. Was that what Bea meant when she wrote reason number one?

Katie scrolled down the list.

Joyful to be around

Pretty smile

Resilient

"How do you know?" she said in a voice filled with question.

Part of her glowed under the positive accolades. The other part couldn't grasp how this woman knew her. Had Bea stalked her or had her followed? For what purpose? That was the million-dollar question.

She looked around the bakery. It wasn't a million-dollar property, but it was something special. Where the pinstriped wallpaper once hung, there was a fresh coat of paint the exact color of soft butter. On the walls were pictures of the muffins she had baked. Photos of the seven daily specials hung in a row.

Behind the counter was the new coffeepot she'd purchased. It wasn't the espresso machine her friend Sage had suggested, but it was better than the percolator that once sat spitting and sputtering on the Formica surface.

No, this place wasn't worth a million dollars. It was worth more because it changed Katie's life.

In the end, it didn't matter why the older woman had given her the gift. All that mattered was what Katie did with it.

She tucked the pink page into her notebook and flipped back to her bucket list of things she wanted to do and wrote things that came to mind.

Ride a roller coaster

Meet a celebrity

Cut down my own Christmas tree

Fall in love

Her number one priority was never to overlook an opportunity to try something new.

While Katie continued to jot down notes, she saw a flash of red out of the corner of her eye. Her friend Sage had hopped out of her SUV near Bishop's Brewhouse and headed her way.

The bell above the bakery door rang as Sage skipped inside. From her bright smile to her rosy cheeks, she glowed from her happy life with Cannon. Katie couldn't believe only seven weeks ago Sage had a black eye and an unquenchable desire to flee Aspen Cove, but no one knew better than she did that life could turn on a dime. Good could become bad and awful could become amazing in the time it took to take a breath.

"What's up?" Katie rose from her seat to give Sage a hug. At five foot six, she appeared a giant compared to her friend, who was pint-size.

"Sheriff Cooper's friends are back at the bed and breakfast tomorrow, and the last time they were around, they ate everything but the furniture. Can I take what you have, or do you want to make me two dozen muffins?"

"I'll make them fresh and bring them to the bar tonight." Katie looked at what she had left in the display case. There were just over two dozen muffins remaining. She'd have to whip up another batch for the afternoon crowd anyway. "Is Cannon's brother still coming home tonight?"

"It's still a go, as far as I know." Sage plucked a sample off the tray that sat on the glass counter and popped it into her mouth.

"That's great. I hope he follows through this time." Cannon had been expecting his brother Bowie for the last two weeks. Bowie had told him twice he was on his way and then canceled the day he was due to arrive.

Katie imagined how difficult it would be to come back to the town where both his mother and fiancée died. According to Doc Parker, it had been almost a decade. Wasn't it time to bury the past like Katie did when she left Dallas?

Sage's bright green eyes lit up. "Hey, I know cakes aren't your thing . . . yet, but maybe you can bake a welcome-home cake for Bowie."

When Katie showed up in Aspen Cove, she barely knew how to boil water. Now she made the best muffins in town. They were the only muffins in town, but still . . .

"I've never made a cake."

Sage cocked her head to the side. "Never? Not even from a mix out of a box?"

"I had a sheltered life. Ovens were hot and dangerous."

From the age of thirteen on, Katie had been sickly. Her mother stuck to her like lint on fabric, hovering over her like an aseptic balloon, warding off everything that could set Katie back or place her in danger.

"Unbelievable. Even *I've* made a cake. Although I'm most famous for my reheating skills."

"*Famous* isn't exactly the word I'd reach for. That makes it sound pleasant. *Notorious* is more like it."

Sage laughed as she rounded the corner to get herself a cup of coffee. Katie had a rule with her friends. If she'd served them a cup at least once, then they were family and could help themselves. However, if a stranger walked behind the display case, she would have nudged them out with a rolling pin. She'd consider a baking pan to the side of the head if they caused her trouble.

"We can't all be Betty Crocker," Sage said.

She followed her friend to the other side of the counter and prepped her new coffee maker for a cup of decaf. Sage liked her coffee laced with electricity whereas, Katie chose the heart-healthy option of decaffeinated.

Sage looked at the coffee dripping into the cup. "I don't know why you bother drinking that. It's just dirty water." She lifted her own octane-filled cup to her lips.

"It makes me feel grown-up without hurting my organs." Katie placed her hand on her chest. Under the cotton, she could feel the raised scar tissue from her surgery.

"I'm a nurse, and I don't take care of myself as well as you do."

"You have to take care of the body you've got." Katie had told no one her medical history. She'd kept it a secret. She didn't want people hovering over her. For once, she wanted to live her life like everyone else. Her anonymity in Aspen Cove had given that to her. What no one knew couldn't hurt her or influence how they perceived her.

"What about the cake? Are you up for the challenge?"

Katie looked over the counter at her journal sitting open on the table. This instance fit the bill as a new opportunity. How hard could making a cake from scratch be? "I'll do it. What flavor?"

"Let's keep it simple. White cake and white frosting."

"You want frosting, too?" she teased.

Sage shook her head. Katie had seen that incredulous look before on Sage's face. It was the one that screamed, *You're kidding right?* "Without frosting, cake is just flavored bread."

"Fine, frosting, too." She pulled her cup from the maker and took a sip. "What are Ben and Cannon doing today?"

The two women leaned against the counter and looked out the window. What once was a ghost town had new life. It experienced rebirth every year in May, when the tourists and fishermen showed up. The once whitewashed windows of the closed bookstore across the street were cleaned and now sparkled under the afternoon sun. It turned out that from May to October the women of Aspen Cove brought their wares to town to sell to the visitors. They offered everything from soy candles to beeswax soap.

"They're at the cemetery. The new grave marker for Bea's family is being set up today. Bowie will go there to say goodbye to Brandy, so Cannon wanted it to be perfect."

Katie had been to the gravesite that had a temporary marker that contained only the names Bill, Bea, and Brandy. It broke her heart that this little town had lost so much.

"At least Bowie's not coming home to a drunk father," Katie said. Ben had sobered up and stepped back into the role of father and friend. "He's been a lifesaver here. Without him, I'd be working seven days a week." Katie had kept him busy at the bakery. She'd taught him how to make the weekend muffins, which gave her much needed time off.

"That's a blessing, for sure." Sage snatched another muffin bite from the sample plate. "I'm not sure how Bowie will acclimate to being back in town. He never wanted to return. He's been tight-lipped about what happened to him in Afghanistan, but he was medically retired from the army, so it can't be good. It's one thing to come back home because he wants to. Another if he's back because he has no choice."

"That's so sad, an injury added to a broken heart." Katie imagined both would require recovery time, but she never considered it would take so long to adjust. "You'd think all those years would be plenty of time to get past the grief and move on. Ben eventually did, so I hope his son can, too."

Katie had no earthly idea how long it took to get over losing the love of her life. She'd never been in love, but she'd added it to her bucket list.

Sage drank the rest of her coffee and tossed the paper cup in the nearby garbage can. "Who knows how long that takes? Everyone works at a different pace."

"Speaking of pace." Katie needed time to figure out how to make a cake. She looked at the muffins in the case. With Ben gone, she was on her own. "You know what? If I'm going to make that cake, I better get to it." She opened the display case and boxed up the remaining muffins. "On second thought, why don't you take these? I think I'll close up early so I can do justice to Bowie's welcome-home cake." The least she could do was provide something sweet for a man no doubt filled with bitterness.

Sage gave her a sideways glance. "Are you sure? I've never known you to close early."

"You've known me for seven weeks."

"I think I've got a good handle on you."

What Katie wanted to say was, "You don't know me at all," but she didn't because that would open an entirely different dialogue. She wasn't ready to give up her secrets.

"Sometimes I don't think I know myself." She knew who she wanted to be, but there was a part of her that was a mystery. A part of her that had belonged to another—her heart. Donors were kept anonymous, so Katie had been in the dark. Records were sealed. She'd thought Bea's daughter's heart might sit in her chest, but the timeline didn't fit. Katie's second chance came years after Brandy's death.

Sage picked up the bakery box and gave Katie a one-armed hug. "The party starts at seven. Everyone will be there."

As soon as Sage left, Katie locked the doors and turned out the lights. There was only one thing left to do. She'd make the best cake she could for Bowie by adding a dash of courage, a pinch of resilience, and the love and compassion she had in her borrowed heart.

Chapter 2

At thirty-four years old, Bowie Bishop didn't think he'd ever come back to live at home. It was never his plan to return to Aspen Cove, but then again, he didn't expect to get shot again while in Afghanistan. When those bullets hit his femur and shattered the bone, everything changed.

He sat at the end of the dock and let his legs hang over the side. The soles of his boots skimmed the water, creating ripples that danced across the smooth surface.

He'd forgotten how high the lake could get after the snow melted; not exactly forgot, but banished it from his memory. He looked across the water to where the tree line split—it was the only place where the side of the mountain dropped off into the lake. He hated that patch of road. In fact, he hated just about everything.

At night in his dreams, he still saw her. Eyes the color of amber, chestnut hair, and a laugh that could warm even the coldest heart. Brandy was his everything, and when he lost her, he knew he'd never be happy again.

The familiar sound of a can popping open and the hiss of carbonation escaping meant he wasn't alone with his thoughts any longer.

"I thought you might like one before we go to the bar." Cannon sat down next to him and handed over the beer.

"I don't feel much like celebrating my return. I think I'll stay here."

"No can do, bro. You've got a lot of people looking forward to seeing you. If you don't show up, they'll come here. There's no way to avoid it."

Bowie lifted the can to his lips and took several big gulps. It would take a lot more than a beer to get him through the night.

"Why did you tell them I was coming back?" This trip wasn't a social visit. It was a place to land until the VA assessed his disability rating, and then he was gone.

"Because seeing you back in town would be like seeing a ghost."

Cannon had described it accurately. He'd been a ghost. Most of him died when Brandy did. "I don't want the attention."

"Fine, show up, stay a while. Paste on a fake smile. Then come back here and hide in the house until tomorrow morning, when you get up to run the bait and tackle shop. I've been taking it all on by myself for years. You're back, so you can help."

Bowie never knew his brother to be so stern, but then he figured years of dealing with a drunk had taken the softness out of him. He'd always felt bad he'd left his brother to pick up the pieces, but Bowie couldn't bear to spend another second in the town that reminded him of his loss.

"I'm not staying. Besides, Dad looks like he's got a handle on things. He can run the bait and tackle store." Cannon had told Bowie how bad his father had gotten, but to look at him now, he couldn't believe it. His brother wasn't one to exaggerate, but Ben looked fine.

"No, he's helping Katie at the bakery. It's the place he found his sobriety. It's best if things don't change too drastically for him."

Cannon picked up a few pebbles from the dock and tossed them into the water. Rings formed around the disturbance and spread out wide. That's how life was. One thing created a ripple, and an entire life changed.

"Change isn't good for Dad, but it's okay if I'm propelled into a nightmare?"

He pushed the boot of his good leg beneath the surface of the water and kicked forward, sending a splash outward. Ten feet in front of him, a fish leaped from the water to catch a bug.

"It's not my intent to pick at your wounds, but I want a life, too. I gave up everything. My life. My career. I gave it all up to come back here and try to save what we had. When will it be my turn to have something?" He emptied his beer and crushed the can in his fist. "Sage entered my life and changed everything. I'm in love with her, but I need time with her. I won't get that if I'm running two businesses and watching out after Dad."

Cannon was right. Bowie had bailed on his brother, but at the time he had nothing left to give. As he sat on the deck and looked around, he worried that he had less now than he did then.

"I'm not staying," he repeated.

"I hear you. Just remember, I stepped up when you couldn't. I'm asking you to step up while you're here. I'm rarely selfish, but dammit Bowie, you owe me."

That was another fact he couldn't deny. He owed Cannon. He'd given up his dream job to come home and be responsible for the family. He was only twenty-four years old when everything went to hell. Too old to be a kid, but too young to be a full-fledged adult.

"You're right. I owe you more than I could ever repay." He turned to his left and took a good, long look at his brother. He'd grown into a man while Bowie was gone.

They'd been close as kids but drifted apart when Bowie fell in love with Brandy. He'd spent all of his time with her. It was the hardest part about losing her. He didn't know how to live without her. He'd made a promise to himself the day they buried her. He'd never allow another woman to enter his heart.

"I'm not asking for blood. I'm only asking you to stay around for a bit. I've missed my brother." Cannon reached over with one arm and bro-hugged him.

"Let's take it a day at a time. Now tell me about this girl of yours."

Footsteps sounded behind them. They turned to see who approached.

Cannon's stoic expression softened, and a smile took over his face. "How about you meet her?" He stood and walked halfway down the dock to meet the tiny redhead. He picked her up and twirled her around. The only piece of Bowie's heart that remained squeezed so hard it was almost painful. He watched the two kiss.

It wasn't that Bowie hadn't had female companionship since Brandy died. He'd seen plenty of action, but he was always clear about where those relationships would go. You couldn't fill up a leaky vessel. Bowie was like a boat full of holes. He was a sinking ship and refused to take anyone else down with him.

He struggled to his feet and limped his way down the dock to meet Sage.

She stood in front of him and rose up onto her toes to kiss him on the cheek. It was an odd greeting from a complete stranger, but he liked her forwardness.

"Finally, I get to meet the infamous Bowie."

He looked town at the runt in front of him. "*Infamous*, huh?"

She smiled, and Bowie could see why his brother had fallen so hard. With a smile like that, it was like the sun radiated from her pores.

"Oh yes. I've heard everything from how you terrorized him as a kid to how you protected him at school."

Cannon looked at her and shook his head. "Sweetheart, that was bedroom talk and should have stayed in the bedroom."

Sage rolled her eyes. "That would mean we couldn't talk about anything. You work so much, I only get to talk to you in bed."

Cannon looked at his brother with a see-I-told-you-so look.

Although Bowie knew he'd never fall in love again, there wasn't any reason Cannon shouldn't. Someone in their family deserved to be happy.

"Let's see if we can change that. I'll be around for a bit so Cannon will have more time to spend outside the bedroom."

"Dude, I don't want to reduce my bedroom time; I only want to increase my other time. Who knows, I might want to spend that time in the bedroom, too."

Sage wound up and punched Cannon in the chest. "I'm not invisible here. Don't be talking about our bedroom activities to your brother."

It was hard not to laugh. Here was a woman who on her tallest day reached Cannon's neck, and yet she was in control. God, he missed those days.

"Although due to your height, you're easy to overlook, but now that I've seen you punch, you're hard to ignore." Bowie threw his arm around Sage and began the walk to the house. "One thing you should know, none of the Bishops kiss and tell. Your nocturnal secrets are safe. Nothing else is sacred, though, so give me some dirt on my brother. It's been a long time."

Sage told him about Cannon's one-eyed cat. She laughed at the fact that such a tough man could have such a soft spot for a special-needs pet, but she had no place to talk because when they walked into the house, lying at Ben's feet was her three-legged dog named Otis.

"Aren't you the pot calling the kettle black?"

While Bowie walked over to his Dad, Sage and Cannon disappeared into the kitchen, saying something about microwaving dinner.

"Hey, Pops. You're looking good." Dad had a nice scar on his forehead from where he fell at the cemetery.

"I'm alive, so that's a start." Ben pivoted on the old leather couch to face him. "I was wondering when you'd come in to say hello."

"You could have come outside."

Ben looked down at the beer in Bowie's hand. "I try to stay far away from alcohol."

"Shit, Dad. I'm sorry. I wasn't thinking." Bowie rocked forward to stand, but his dad pulled him back down.

"It's my problem, not yours. I can't expect the world to change because I have an issue with something. I'm learning."

Bowie took his beer and reached over the arm of the chair to put it out of sight. "You're right, but I don't have to flaunt your weakness in front of your face."

Ben did something unexpected. He leaned in and pulled his son against his body and hugged him tightly. "I'm glad you're here. I hope you'll stay a while."

His plans were short-term, but before he could tell his dad, Cannon and Sage called them for dinner.

Just like the old days, Bowie sat in his place at the family dinner table. While they ate microwaved stroganoff, Cannon and Ben filled him in on all the things that had happened over the years.

Louise Smith had married Bobby Williams, and they recently had their seventh kid. Doc still ran the clinic, although he was older than dirt. Dalton had done time for killing someone. The town finally got a sheriff, named Aiden Cooper, and Mark Bancroft was the deputy. Zachariah Thomas lit himself on fire when one of his stills blew up. While some things had changed, others remained the same. He'd missed having a place where he belonged. He'd missed his family. As much as he hated to admit it, Aspen Cove, no matter where he ended up, would always be home.

Chapter 3

Would anyone notice how lopsided the cake was? Katie tried to compensate for the error in baking with extra frosting. Whereas one half the cake had a mere quarter-inch layer of frosting, the other side had over an inch.

Even after watching a dozen YouTube videos and an episode of *Cake Boss*, it looked like an amateur baked it. In reality, that was exactly what happened. Her saving grace was that it tasted good, and hopefully everyone could look past the imperfections and enjoy the cake.

If the party started at seven, then Katie would wait until ten after to show up. That would give enough time for everyone to say hello to Bowie, or she hoped.

The only reason she was going, she told herself, was because Sage asked her, but in truth she was curious about the man who had left town almost a decade ago and never returned.

In some ways, they were alike. She'd packed up and left Dallas. Although her departure happened abruptly, she had considered it for years.

There were lots of reasons people ran away, but it always came down to either running *from* something or running *to* something. In her case, she was racing to have an authentic life. One she couldn't have in Dallas.

She looked at the clock. It was time to go. Dressed in blue jeans and a flowered thermal shirt, she entered the chill of the May night and walked across the street to Bishop's Brewhouse. She'd never seen the bar so full except for the day they buried Bea. It seemed like the town came out for deaths and births. Bowie coming back to town was a rebirth.

Katie knew his presence was important to Ben. She could only imagine what it meant to Cannon as well. With the sheet cake in her hands, she twisted and turned her body through the crowd until she was at the bar.

Sage stood behind the taps, pulling a pitcher of beer. "You came."

"Did you think I wouldn't? From the sound of the chitchat around town, this man coming home is like the second coming of Christ—a miracle." She set the cake on the worn wooden surface and looked around at the crowd. "I'm a true believer in miracles." Katie never put much faith in anything until the day her heart went bad. From that point on, faith was all she had.

"The cake looks amazing." Sage took it and put it on the back counter. "Was it hard?"

Hard was a matter of perspective. It was hard to get the courage to try something new, easy to do it once she decided. Hard to take the reality that it wasn't perfect, but easy to hide her mistake. "Not hard at all," she said with a roll of her eyes. "I imagine it's like anything you do the first time—scary but worth it."

She looked to the end of the bar toward the man everyone crowded around. Baking the cake wasn't as hard as what Bowie experienced. Even though she didn't know him, the telltale signs of stress were written on his handsome face. Hard eyes. Creased brow. The strained twitch from a fake smile. Katie knew all too well the look of being present for everyone else when all you wanted to do was be alone. *Poor Bowie.*

"You want to meet him?"

Sage poured her second pitcher of beer. She looked comfortable behind the bar. Katie was a bit envious that Sage had settled into Aspen Cove so easily, especially when she was the one who didn't want to stay. All this time, Katie had wanted to stay. She'd found lots of things in Aspen Cove she'd been searching for. She'd found friends. A sense of belonging. A purpose. The one thing that remained elusive was love. It was unlikely she'd find it here, where most men were seasonal visitors, and the ones who weren't were like brothers or a father. Besides, finding love wasn't her first priority. Finding independence was.

"I'll wait. He looks swamped."

She looked back at Bowie, who talked to Cannon. All she could see was his profile. Strong nose. Chiseled jaw. Tan skin. Brown hair. What looked like light eyes. Even sitting on a bar stool, he was taller than most men who stood around him. His fake smile was heart-warming. She could imagine his real smile would be heart-stopping.

She climbed onto the barstool at the opposite end of the room.

"I'm sure he is." Sage delivered the pitcher to Bowie and Cannon and came back to stand near Katie. "He didn't want to come."

Katie watched the man smile and chat with the town folk. It reminded her of all the visitors she got in the hospital. She'd smile and nod and make nice conversation, but all she wanted was to be alone.

"It's got to be overwhelming."

The crowd split, giving her a chance to get a look at the rest of him. When Sage had said he was medically retired from the army, Katie thought maybe he'd lost a limb, but he appeared fully intact.

A tight olive-colored T-shirt stretched across his chest, leaving little for her active imagination. His biceps bulged, stretching the band of cotton to its limit. Her eyes followed the line of his body. He was half on and half off the stool. One leg stretched out, as if ready to bolt at the first opportunity. His jeans, though worn, looked like they were custom made for his body. He was perfect all the way from his short hair to his black boots. The only thing missing was a Harley. He had that bad-boy look about him. She'd considered him almost too perfect, but then he'd turned his head toward her and her heart skipped a beat. A jagged scar ran from his temple to his chin, bisecting his cheek along the way.

Magazine men weren't her thing. Men who sought perfection in themselves often sought it in others, and Katie was far from perfect. She'd learned long ago that the true test of a man was in how he lived with his flaws. Bowie's scar was the sexiest thing about him. He wore it like a badge of honor. She was intrigued to find out how he got it.

"Can I have a soda?" Katie would have loved to imbibe with the rest, but she rarely drank. Given her health condition, it wasn't recommended.

Sage poured her a soda. "Let's give your cake to Bowie."

"You give it to him. I'm happy here."

Sage gave her a growl. "Suit yourself. He's much sweeter than he looks. Then again, wasn't it you who told me you like them to look like murderers?"

Sage picked up the cake and brought it over to Bowie. She said something that made the entire group look Katie's way. She gave them all a weak smile and a wave but stayed put.

Katie liked sitting in the corner, taking everything in. Rarely had she had the opportunity to be an observer. A girl could learn a lot about the people of Aspen Cove if she watched long enough. For example, it was obvious which men in town had grown up with Bowie. Bobby Williams, and Dalton Black had that easy look about them. The one that said, "I've got your back." They talked and laughed like they hadn't been separated a day.

The men who hung back, like Sheriff Aiden Cooper and resident lawyer Frank Arden, were taking it all in, just like Katie. Sitting back and observing. In the corner was a group that included Zachariah Thomas and Tilden Cool, who lived up in the mountains and made moonshine. The only reason for their appearance was the free beer.

Then there were the women. Abby the beekeeper was a bit old for Bowie, but it didn't stop her from hanging on to his every word.

Poppy Dawson showed the most interest in Bowie. Katie couldn't blame her. Living with her parents at twenty-eight was no fun. Katie figured marriage was Poppy's easiest way out of the house. Her five sisters lined the walls like wallflowers with names like Rose, Lily, Daisy, and Violet. Their only brother, Basil, hung back and drank beer with the sheriff.

Sage waved Katie over. It was a battle lost if Katie thought she'd get away without an introduction. That was, until her phone rang. She knew who it was. Only a few people had her new cell phone number, and 90 percent of them were in the bar, so when she pulled her phone from her pocket, it was no surprise it was her mother.

She pressed answer. "Hey, Mama. Hold on, okay?" Her mom continued to talk, but Katie pulled the phone away from her ear. She looked at Sage and pointed to her phone, mouthed the word "Mom" and disappeared out the door to take the call. People were overflowing onto the sidewalk, so she rounded the building and walked to the back of the bar.

"Are you there?" her mother asked.

"Yes, I told you to hold on. I had to get somewhere more quiet so I could hear you."

"It sounds like a party."

"It's a welcome-home party for a friend's brother." Katie counted to five because it wouldn't take longer than that to get to the next question.

She only got to the count of three when her mom asked, "Where are you?"

"You know I'm not telling. You have the ability to get in touch with me."

"About that, why did you change your phone? Daddy and I were happy to pay for your service."

Katie inhaled deeply and let it out slowly. She'd always considered herself a patient person, but Mama could try a saint on Sunday. "You were happy to pay for my phone when you could track it. I'm a grown woman, Mama. What's the point in living if I don't have a life?"

This was where her mama would spring a tear. "We only want what's best for you."

Katie heard people behind her, like someone had opened a door to the bar, but the sound muted right away, so she ignored it and replied to her mother, "You want what's safest, but safest isn't always what's best. I had to run away from you and Daddy just to breathe. Mama, I love you, but I can't live if I can't breathe."

"And I can't breathe not knowing you're okay."

There was no one to see her roll her eyes, but she did it anyway. She stood there staring at the woods behind the bar and rolled them in every direction she could. "You're talking to me. I'm okay. In fact, I'm finer than frog hair split seven ways."

"Are you taking your medicine?"

"Yes, ma'am. I'm eating healthy. I'm making friends. I even baked a cake today for the party. I'm happy for the first time in a long time. Please be happy for me." Katie heard a sound behind her and turned to find Bowie tucked into the shadows of the building. He lifted his beer like he was toasting her. She nodded back. "I've got to go. Please trust me to know what's right for me, okay?"

Her mother's exhale was a sign of surrender. Katie would have loved to tell her parents where she'd run off to, but the minute she did, they would be on her doorstep, ready to drag her back. She would eventually tell them, but on her terms.

"I love you, sweetheart. I trust you. It's just that I'm as lonely as a pine tree in a parking lot." Katie grew up on southernisms, but her mother never ceased to come up with a new one regularly.

"I'll call soon," she told her. She dialed them at least once a week. There was no sense in making them worry, but there was also no sense in talking to them daily. If she did, she might as well move back to Dallas.

"Come home soon," her mother replied.

That didn't deserve a response because if Katie said anything but

I will, the conversation would go full circle back to the beginning. "Love you, and tell Daddy I love him, too." She waited to hear *I love you, too,* before she hung up.

Katie walked over to where Bowie stood in the shadow of the overhang. His back leaned against the brick building. One leg anchored to the ground, the other knee bent with the sole of his boot against the wall. The moon glinted off his skin, making it look almost gold and godlike.

"Welcome home, Bowie." She pressed her hand in his direction for a shake. "I'm Katie Middleton."

He smiled.

Help me, Jesus, she said in her head. She was right, there was a difference between his forced smile and the one that came naturally. This smile came from his eyes instead of his lips.

"Nice to meet you, duchess." His hand was so large, it wrapped around hers when he shook it. He had hardworking hands. They weren't soft and fleshy like the account managers at the insurance office where she used to work. No, Bowie's hands were calloused and manly and warm and strong.

"Duchess, huh? I can live with that." She liked that he didn't call her "princess" the way everyone else did. He was the first person to call her "duchess." "I'm sure you're trying to get peace and quiet, so I'll let you be." She turned to walk away, but he stopped her with a question.

"You made the cake?"

"I did." She laughed, remembering the condition of the kitchen when she finished. She swore there was more flour on the floor than in the cake. "If it was terrible, just tell me you're a diabetic and couldn't have any. That way, I won't feel awful."

"I liked it . . . a lot. How did you know I liked extra frosting?"

"I'm intuitive or . . . I made a lopsided cake and straightened it out with the sweet stuff. You choose."

He gifted her with another smile. "I'll go with intuitive." He offered her his beer. "You want a drink?"

Katie didn't want to appear rude. "Thank you." She took the mug from his hand. It was no longer frosted, but the beer remained cold. She lifted it to her mouth and let the suds touch her upper lip.

"Has Aspen Cove been good to you?" His eyes left her and stared out into the blackness of the night. Up in the mountains, the minute the sun set it turned dark. Tonight, the moon was only a sliver and offered no light.

"I love it here. The people are good. It was a true blessing to come here."

"I hear Bea gave you the bakery." He reached for his beer and took a long swallow. "What's your connection to Bea?"

A moment of awkwardness hung in the air between them. They didn't know each other, but they had something in common. They both had a connection to Bea. Only Katie's was still a mystery.

"My inner sleuth is still trying to figure it out."

"You will. The one thing I've always known about Bea was she did nothing without a solid reason."

Katie laughed. "She gave me a list of a hundred, but none of them makes sense. The only thing I can think of is she found out I did a lot of volunteer hours at a children's hospital."

Bowie kicked off the wall. "That would make sense. Bea loved kids, and she was always quick to reward good behavior." He turned and headed to the bar's back door. "I suppose I should attend my welcome home party. Are you coming, duchess?"

Katie noticed a slight limp to his walk but ignored it. They entered the bar, where the crowd had diminished. All who were left fell under the categories of close friends and relatives. It made Katie sad that Bowie's father, Ben, had to stay away, but she gave him credit for knowing his limitations.

"Everything all right with your mom?" Sage asked as Katie took the bar stool beside her.

"She's still hovering like a true helicopter parent, but hey, she loves me."

"Can't fault her for that." Sage looked down the bar, where the men had congregated. They each had a plate of cake in their hands. Bowie was on his second piece. "Bowie seems to like it. I saw you two walk inside together. Did you get a chance to meet?"

"Briefly. He seems really nice."

"He is nice. I'd love it if you two hit it off. Wouldn't that be awesome?"

So awesome, but the timing is all wrong. She needed to establish herself first. In the five minutes they'd talked, Katie got a feel for Bowie. She'd always known that when she met *the one*, she'd know it, and something inside her told her he was it. It was more than his looks. His wounds attracted her. She knew what it felt like to hurt—to watch her life slip away from her and get a second chance to embrace it. Maybe that's what Aspen Cove would be for Bowie. Maybe coming home was his second chance.

"Still on for fishing tomorrow?" When Sage said the word *fishing*, she turned up her nose like she could already smell their catch.

"Yes."

Katie bounced with excitement in her seat. Fishing was on her bucket list, and after tomorrow she'd be able to cross it off. If she were lucky, she'd get *rowing a boat* completed soon, too. She looked at Bowie and wondered if he had a list. If so, would his include falling in love like hers did?

Available exclusively at Amazon.com

ABOUT THE AUTHOR

International bestselling author of more than thirty novels, Kelly Collins writes with the intention of keeping the love alive. Always a romantic, she blends real-life events with her vivid imagination to create characters and stories that lovers of contemporary romance, new adult, and romantic suspense will return to again and again.

Kelly lives in Colorado at the base of the Rocky Mountains with her husband of twenty-seven years, their two dogs, and a bird that hates her. She has three amazing children, whom she loves to pieces.

For More Information
www.authorkellycollins.com
kelly@authorkellycollins.com

Made in the USA
Middletown, DE
25 November 2020